VOLK

D. WERKMEISTER

PRAISE FOR VOLK

'Volk is a refreshing mash-up of a police procedural, spy novel, and shapeshifter story. Whenever I thought I knew what was coming next, the narrative took a delightful left turn. I devoured the book over two days and was sorry when I reached the end as I wanted more. A delightful mixture of fantasy and reality-based police procedure with engaging characters.

Who knew an author could make me root for a werewolf?'

Bradley Harper MD
COL (Ret) US Army
Fellow, Royal Scottish Society of the Arts
Author, 2019 Edgar's Finalist *A Knife in the Fog*
http://WWW.BHarperAuthor.Com

VOLK by D. Werkmeister is a riveting tale of revenge and self-discovery. With a clever mixture of paranormal and real life evil, Werkmeister delivers a rousing novel that is sure to keep you fascinated and will leave you wanting more. This page turner will keep you guessing the true nature of all the characters, most surprisingly, the antagonists. With just the right amount of mystery and suspense, Werkmeister has a compelling hit and is a must read.

D. M. Bourgeois
Author of Slipping Into Darkness, Misguided Revenge and Edge of Reality.

"A thrilling detective story with a sprinkling of werewolves—who could ask for more, really?" *Kirkus Reviews*

2023 Winner of the Killer Nashville International Writers Conference Claymore Award for Best Supernatural

Acknowledgements

I would like to recognize my editor, Lilith Fondulas. Thank you for your diligent dedication to this project.

Dedicated to my family, Amy, Catherine, and Sarah. I could not have written this without your support. Thank you.

"Hell is empty and all the devils
are here" – William Shakespere,
The Tempest

PROLOGUE
SIBERIA, 1994

THE LOCAL VILLAGERS HAD been searching for mammoth fossils in the thawing tundra when they found a large stone mound. Since the scale of such a structure in this location was unusual, they notified the regional government office, which instructed them not to disturb it. A scientific team of archeologists and biologists gathered in Moscow and set out for the site. A sense of excitement buzzed among them, particularly from a young genetic biologist, Peter Lavroski. New to the field, he was enjoying the thrill of discovery.

After several days of travel, the team arrived at the site. The structure appeared to be a burial mound of sorts, and it was quite large, measuring 3 meters above the ground and 20 meters across. Whoever built this had put in a tremendous amount of work. Typically, in this region, stone mounds were not used for burials.

The team set up camp and carefully began to excavate the site. Though they took full advantage of the long summer hours of daylight, it was midweek before they discovered the chamber. The room was 3 meters below the ground, completely covered by large stones. The team leader, Nikita, shone his flashlight into the space. Immediately, the group saw what appeared to be a massive wolf carcass lying on the frozen ground, perfectly preserved in the permafrost. The stone walls and floor of the chamber showed deep scratch marks, leading the scientists to believe that the creature had been alive when it was entombed. Carved into one of the walls was a crucifix, surrounded by what appeared to be older pagan symbols. A decaying bible rested on the frozen ground nearby.

The biologists immediately took the lead in investigating the carcass. The specimen was larger than any wolf they had ever seen and appeared to be in remarkable condition. The team packaged it in an airtight container with dry ice and drove it to the nearest freezer lab for closer examination. It was during this examination that a most curious item was discovered.

Around the neck of the creature was what looked like a 17th- or 18th-century necklace with a locket. The back of the locket was inscribed "With love to my dearest Anastasia." Inside, darkened by moisture and mold, appeared to be a painting of a man and a young girl.

Peter watched as the lead biologist began to excise a tissue sample from the creature. An audible gasp was heard from the group as the scalpel penetrated the flesh—and the muscle twitched.

In the commotion of the discovery, no one noticed Peter slip out.

Hesitant, but eager to please his new boss, he placed a call. "Konstantin, this is Peter Lavroski. I believe there is something out here that you may be interested in."

PART I

CHAPTER 1

PHILADELPHIA, PENNSYLVANIA, 2017

THE PREY IS NEARBY. There's no shortage of choices, but the one I have selected is close. I can feel the excitement start to build. My eyes have dilated in the dying light, and I can see the deserted neighborhood with crystal clarity. Row houses line the street, lights glittering in half of them. The rest are abandoned, their doors and windows barricaded by graffiti-covered plywood. A stray cat pads toward an alley a block away. Silhouetted by the lone streetlight at the end of the block, she pauses in the road and looks my way. Though she can't see me, she knows I am here. I can hear her hiss, and I watch as she darts out of sight. She is safe for now; I'm hunting larger game tonight. I am ravenous. The ache in my stomach sharpens my focus. I have starved myself for the day in anticipation of tonight's meal.

As I crouch in the shadow of what was once an auto repair shop, I can hear distant voices from one of the only corner stores still open. Two men converse about the price of cigarettes and Wild Turkey. The tone suddenly turns sharp, and one of the men orders the other to give him the money from the register, threatening to shoot if he doesn't move faster. I hear a metallic thump and a hollow, wet smack. I watch as the robber walks out of the store, past where the cat crossed, the cheap screen door creaking as it opens and then slams back into place. The man moves away from me, feet shuffling along the sidewalk. His pace is uneven, and he has a slight limp. He glances over his shoulder as he walks. I can hear him mutter to himself about only getting $80. I watch as he takes something out of a brown paper bag and tosses the bag into the street, which is already littered with urban detritus. The glass bottle he raises to his lips catches the light and flashes briefly as he takes a drink.

My senses are electric. I can pick up scents from the entire neighborhood. Windows are open tonight as people try to catch some breeze and cool their stifling apartments. Someone is cooking Italian food. The sweet fragrance of herbs and tomatoes hangs in the air and mixes with other, less pleasant, odors. But I am focused on him. I can smell him—his sweat, his breath, and the detergent he washed his clothes in last week. Within a few seconds, I can smell the tang of the cheap whiskey he has opened.

Slowly, I emerge from the shadows and begin to follow the man, 200 meters ahead of me. I know the transformation will happen soon. My heart is starting to pound.

I was frightened the first time it happened. Now it doesn't take very long, and I am no longer afraid. I relish it. The rush of strength and raw power is intoxicating.

I have closed the distance with the man, and my excitement builds as the change begins. I can smell his blood now, coursing through his arteries. I cover the last length with a few strides, huffing as I finish the change. I have timed my attack so that we are at the entrance to an alley. At the last moment, he hears my approach and starts to turn. I am on him in an instant. I bite into the back of his neck and crush his vertebrae, severing his spinal cord. There is no fight, no struggle—no sound save for the crack of bone. I drag him to the shadows of the alley as his heartbeat grows fainter. The prey's aura of violence is delicious. I will feast tonight.

FBI Field Office, Philadelphia

Terri Watson pulled into her parking spot in the basement of the federal building at 9:15 a.m. Her morning routine had been thrown off when she opened the refrigerator and realized she was out of milk. Her scramble for a backup breakfast plan left her running late. Not that anyone was tracking her arrival time, but she had a self-imposed schedule and tried to keep it. Some days she even succeeded.

As she made her way through the squad's cubicle maze, the aroma of fresh hot pretzels mixed with spicy brown mustard reminded her it was Friday. It was a Philadelphia FBI tradition to bring fresh pretzels in the office on Fridays. Some people ate them plain, which was fine, but with a nice mustard, the Philly Danish, as they were affectionately called, really shined. Like many things in Philadelphia, they seemed a little odd, but she had grown to appreciate them and the city that bore them.

Snagging a pretzel while they were still hot was tempting, but she had more pressing issues at the moment. Her blonde hair bun started to come loose while she shrugged her left shoulder to keep her bag strap in place while holding two cups of coffee. She just barely managed to make her cubicle as the bag slipped from her 5 '9" frame and plopped on her desk with a loud thud.

Even before she sat down, she noticed the FedEx package on her desk and her pulse quickened: maybe it contained the SWIFT records she had been waiting for? Most agents didn't care to pore through miles of financial records for hours on end, hoping to find a kernel of evidence, but Terri enjoyed the hunt. Finding hints in transactions that might lead to more hints and then clues and then eventually to evidence was her kind of thing. Some agents liked to kick in doors. Others liked working undercover. She liked records. There was something satisfying about it because she knew the evidence was right there, in black and white. It might be concealed behind a smokescreen, but if she could decipher the trail, she could get to the prize. In this case, the prize was a Swiss money launderer living in a Philadelphia suburb.

Her partner, Marc Peterson, a Philadelphia police detective and FBI task force officer or TFO, called out at the sound of her bag hitting the desk, "Yo Ter, I put a package on your desk from the mailroom. If it's what I think it is, Merry Christmas and Happy Birthday. I know I won't see ya for a few days."

"Thanks! Hey I brought you something too, cup of joe over here. "

Marc came around the divider wall as Terri was greedily tearing into the package. She paused long enough to take a sip of her coffee, perfect. The woman at Dunkin Donuts knew her order by heart, double cream with a shot of vanilla syrup. Running late or not, Terri needed her coffee in the morning. Presented with the prospect of some fresh records to review, Terri completely forgot about the pretzels.

Marc didn't share her love of financial reports, though he could appreciate the work involved and truly enjoyed the results. Nailing some assholes who thought they were the smartest people in the room was incredibly satisfying. His route to the Organized Crime Squad was a little unconventional. He'd been a homicide detective years ago before being assigned to the FBI by his department. But after several high-profile, professional hits on Russian organized-crime heads had taken place in Northeast and Center City Philadelphia, a task force was formed with the Philadelphia police department. First and foremost, the Bureau asked for a top-notch homicide detective to be part of it. Marc was sent up the street to the FBI and parked in a cubicle on the task force. He and Terri had been partners ever since.

Before coming over to the Bureau, all he'd known about Russian organized crime had come from the movies. What he discovered comprised an intricate network of financial institutions, straw owners, and boatloads of black money—generated from small-potatoes domestic drug sales, human trafficking, prostitution, and gambling all the way up to the international oligarchs who siphoned off billions of dollars in the gas business, sold military technology, and bought influence around the globe. The task force was close to putting in its crosshairs a Swiss national who had been setting up umbrella corporations and nested bank accounts for the benefit of some very nasty people. It was satisfying work.

Marc stood in the entrance to Terri's cubicle sipping his black coffee. He practically filled the doorway. He was a barrel chested man of about thirty-five. His dark hair was shaved close to his head. Had he let it grow, there would have been faint traces of gray appearing at the temples. He had an affability about him that relaxed everyone, a trait he used to his advantage in interviews. He came across as crude and unsophisticated at times but, in reality, was actually concealing a sharp intuitive mind. Many subjects had learned that the hard way when they underestimated him. He took another sip of his coffee and then spoke, "Um, I got word that the SOG surveillance on Schnoll next week got postponed. Said they got a higher-priority request. Sorry Ter." He didn't want to piss on her Cheerios right after she was so happy, getting the records she wanted, but he decided she needed to know now.

"Shit." Terri sat back in her chair. "Oh well, not like he's running all around the city, anyway. The guy's been living like a monk for months now." She understood there were competing priorities with surveillance requests, but she also felt like she was getting the short shrift treatment.

Marc nodded. "Dude hasn't left the house except to get groceries. Can't see why SOG isn't eager to bite into this job. It'd be a real short report: Surveillance initiated. Surveillance terminated. No target activity. Numerous sudoku and crossword puzzles completed. End of report." It was well known that SOG agents kept puzzle books in their cars for those long days with no activity.

Terri laughed out loud. "Right?! I still wonder if that breach at INTERPOL had something to do with Schnoll going quiet. They need to compartmentalize their cooperation with Russian law enforcement. I swear to God, if they screwed me on this, I will make it my life's mission to have someone's ass over there."

Terri believed, as did many of her colleagues, that Russian organized crime or OC as they called it, worked hand in glove with the Russian state—including the federal security service known as the FSB. It was reported that even INTERPOL had recently been infiltrated and sensitive target lists had been compromised.

Marc, like most good detectives and agents, wasn't fond of coincidences. "Yeah, it's a little weird that your man has an international ticket booked and then never travels. I know, shit happens, people's plans change, but it's just a little too coincidental for my likes. A week after we learn of the possible breach, your man there becomes a shut-in," he said.

He took another sip of his coffee as he watched Terri pop the first disc of records into a stand alone computer. "You want any help going through those records there? I'm not the fastest, but I'd be willin' to pitch in." Things were pretty light right now for him, and he felt guilty that she was going to carry most of the water on this part of the case.

"Thanks, but I've got this for now. No reason for both of us to go blind staring at a computer screen."

"Whew! Am I glad you said that! Could you tell my heart wasn't in it?" he said, grinning. "I'll follow up with the prosecutor on that TIII order. He thinks we should be able to go up on Dieter's phone in a few days, hopefully. He's gotta be doing somethin' in that house. Also, my shop wants me to help out on these recent murders in the city. Looks like there was another one a couple of nights ago. They found him yesterday."

Terri sat back while the search was running on the records. "Same MO?"

"Yeah. Not much left of the guy. Guess some stray dogs got to him pretty quickly. Found him in an alley near Fifth and Dauphin." He checked his notepad. "Name was, uh, Christopher O'Brien. Just got out of the joint two months ago. Did a stint for armed robbery. Had some priors before that, burglary and drug stuff."

"Did you say the dogs got to him? That's disgusting."

"Yeah, looks like a little karmic justice found him though. When the officers went to his address of record, they found his girlfriend and her son beat to death with a bat. Neighbors said they heard him fighting with her a few nights ago, and then they heard screamin'. A real prince."

"Can't argue with the outcome. How many is this? Is there any pattern?"

"So far, we know of five. They've all been bad dudes, but other than that, no connections. Some sources are sayin' that other ne'er-do-wells in our fine city have gone missing too. Not sure if they're related or not."

"You may have a serial killer on your hands, Detective Peterson."

"Don't even joke about that. If the press starts runnin' with it, my captain will shit a brick." He took another sip of his coffee as he turned to leave. "Alright, I'm gonna stop over at the US Attorney's office and then swing by the morgue. Happy huntin', Special Agent!"

Terri laughed and looked back to her computer screen. "Yeah, you too," she said, but her mind was already processing the data. The search produced a list of transactions in the name of Zhizn Holdings.

Dieter Schnoll sat in his living room, sipping his tea at his desk as he checked his email. It was the normal drivel. A tweak to a trust here, a modification to a beneficial owner there. One client was planning to divorce his wife and inquired if there was a way to hide his assets from her. All run of the mill and routine. Then he logged into his Swiss-based secure email. Now something got his attention.

His meeting was pushed back to the middle of next month. The email was in German, he read, "Greetings, Mr. Schnoll. I am pleased to inform you that I will be coming to Philadelphia on 10 June. I would like to meet with you on behalf of my client. Please have proposals prepared at that time. Respectfully, Sergey Rostovich, Esq."

This was excellent news. With this confirmation, he could now set about finalizing the authorizations to establish the trusts. He would also secure several shell company names and establish the ownership documents.

This client was substantial. And dangerous. Not to him, of course—unless he became a liability or a loose end that needed to be clipped. He had worked with some rough characters (or at least their attorneys) through the years. He rarely, if ever, met the actual clients—narcos and various organized crime figures, from the wrong side of the conventional moral line who prized their anonymity when it came to financial dealings. He never worked with terrorist organizations, though. God no. It wasn't that he felt ethically opposed to them, it was just that those dealings usually came with a heavier dose of law enforcement scrutiny. No need for that.

He hoped that one day he could stop this part of his business. Though he enjoyed the mental challenges that came with moving dark money, the moral gymnastics he increasingly had to do were becoming difficult. He justified it by telling himself that once he had amassed enough wealth, he could step away. The accounts at that point would be in the control of the clients. He would still do the legitimate wealth preservation work but from a tropical location. His estranged wife and two daughters still lived in Switzerland. The girls were almost grown now, and he only saw them a few times a year. That would change once he secured his fortune.

Marc arrived at the city morgue. It was an old brick building in a city filled with old brick buildings and very little money or inclination to upgrade them. In the hierarchy of budgets, a new morgue would be at the bottom of the list, if it registered at all.

Doctor Jerri Williams was in her office on the third floor when Marc popped his head in the door. "Yo, what's up, Doc?"

"Detective! How nice of you to grace us with your presence! It's been a while. I thought you might have given up this line of work for something with better pay and fewer hours."

"Sort of did. I'm over at the FBI on a task force. But something felt off lately. I figured I hadn't seen a stiff in a while and thought I'd come by here."

"And I thought you came here to see me," she said with a laugh. "Any particular case or will any body do, Detective?"

"This O'Brien character, from a couple of days ago."

"Oh, boy. You picked a doozy."

Jerri took Marc down to the coolers. She opened the stainless-steel door, pulled the slab from the drawer, and unzipped the bag. Marc was a seasoned homicide detective. He had seen corpses of people who had been slain in just about every way a human being could kill another human being—shot, stabbed, strangled, burned, hacked with all sorts of instruments, run over, plummeted from great heights, drowned—and in various states of decomposition. None were pleasant. But this one was particularly bad. For starters, the face had several parallel gouges on both sides that went to the bone. But even worse was that only about a third of the body— if you added up all the pieces—was present. The left arm was completely gone at the shoulder, the right was missing below the elbow, and neither had been recovered from the scene. The chest was torn open, the thoracic organs were absent—and that was it. Nothing was attached below the trunk. Jerri reached into the bottom of the bag and retrieved the right leg, which had been severed at midthigh.

"Wow. Do you have a cause of death?"

Jerri laughed, "Close your eyes and point. Any one of these wounds would be fatal. But there is one that I think might be the culprit. Wait for it."

Jerri turned over the torso. Marc's eyes went wide. He saw a gaping hole in the back of the neck where the vertebra should have been and what looked like some bone fragments in the wound.

"Holy hell, Doc."

"I think this is the one that killed him, and the other damage was post-mortem. But honestly, it's really hard to tell. They all occurred around the same time."

"Ok, two questions off the top of my head. A: How would somebody create a wound like this?" he said, pointing to the neck. "And secondly, why would that person then take an ax or something, hack this guy up, and cart off the parts?"

"To your first question, I have no idea; you're the detective, that's your department. We're running tests for any trace elements that might indicate a weapon, but so far we have nothing. There are no powder burns or ballistic indications. As to your second question, the conventional conversation is that he was partially devoured by stray dogs before he was discovered."

Marc turned to Jerri. "And, uh, you're not so sure, are you?"

Jerri looked him in the eye and paused a moment. "Look at this leg. The femur hasn't been cut with a saw or chopped with an ax. It's been crushed. The flesh is ripped straight—not cut, not gnawed. It appears that whoever or whatever tore through that leg did it in one motion. If we found him on the beach, I'd say it was a shark; or if in the woods, a bear. But we didn't find him on the beach or in the woods, did we? Last I checked, we don't have apex predators in the Kensington area of Philadelphia."

"The only apex predators in the city I know of hunt on two legs, Doc. How does this one compare with the others, the other open cases?"

"Similar for some of the wounds—deep gouges, though the others sustained attacks to their throats. The wound to the back of the neck on our boy here is new. The missing pieces and parts are consistent."

Marc rubbed his eyes, "Look, these guys were all found in some pretty rough areas of the city. There could be strays scavenging around, as fucked up and crazy as that sounds. So, unless we got a maniac taking chunks of flesh and organs as souvenirs or stock for stew, that dog theory might make some sense."

"If it was a dog, it had to be a big goddamn dog. A bite force powerful enough to slice through the flesh and crush the femur cleanly is tremendous. I don't know who or what did this, but 'stray dogs' as an answer doesn't pass my sniff test."

It was after 8:00 p.m. when Marc left the morgue. He was tired, but his mind was racing. Jerri's assessment kept playing on repeat in his head. Maybe there was some kind of serial killer shredding people. Even cannibalism was not out of the question. He knew the depths of human depravity had yet to be fully plumbed.

Surprisingly, given the gore fest he had just witnessed, he was hungry. Not surprisingly, he also had a throbbing headache. He realized he had almost no food at home—not uncommon since his divorce. He decided to stop for some Chinese take-out on his way home.

CHAPTER 2

I READ THE NEWS with casual interest. I don't have to teach my class until 10:00 this morning, so I allow myself the opportunity to catch up on current events. One benefit of my plight, in this form, food– good food, tastes divine. My latte with oat milk is particularly delicious today, and the aroma is heavenly. I suspect the beans come from Columbia; they are roasted to perfection. On the third page of the local news website is a short story about a dreadful homicide involving a Mr. O'Brien two nights ago. The story mentions that he was a violent criminal who is believed to have killed his girlfriend and her seven-year-old son before meeting his own demise. A slight smile creeps across my face, though I am not reliving the event. It's more like reading a positive review of a restaurant you like to go to. It simply reinforces your good taste.

Just below is a story of a corrupt judge who had been convicted of accepting money from the wealthy family of an accused teenage rapist in exchange for an extremely light sentence for the boy. The Honorable Louis DePalma has just been granted a presidential pardon. How nice for you, Judge DePalma. I know enough about corruption to understand how these things work, so I'm not surprised to read that a large campaign contribution had been made from a political action committee with loose ties to DePalma's family. Suddenly, I feel a wave of anticipation building in me. I take out a pad of paper, jot down the judge's name, and slide it under the blotter of my desk. I will think about this more later.

I don't want to get too excited before my class, so I distract myself and switch to a Russian-language page that I have bookmarked. It is a "Who's Who" of the Russian underworld and is fairly light reading for me. I am particularly interested in learning about the Russian scientists and oligarchs who have alleged connections to government agencies; it's kind of my hobby. There's a link to a site about the movement of dark money, and I bookmark that for closer reading as well. There is a chorus of birds among the noises of the city outside my window. There must be a wren nest nearby. I focus on the pleasant warble for a moment and enjoy the free concert.

When my phone buzzes, I gather my materials and head to class. Time to see what these young minds have retained about the history of Eastern Europe during the semester. One must earn a living in this dog-eat-dog world.

After several false starts and technical glitches, the Title III, or wiretap, as it is commonly called, was up and running. Typically, Marc and Terri spent hours every morning reading through the summaries of calls and texts and listening to the corresponding calls from the surveillance of the day and night before. Any calls or texts that were clearly non pertinent to any criminal activity, or were protected by a specific privilege (attorney, spouse, priest), were cut short by the personnel manning the shifts. Everything else was recorded in full, and anything in a foreign language received a translated summary.

The haul to date had been rather mundane. Terri was starting to wonder if Dieter had given up his dirty business then, she found it.

"I think we have something here," she said cautiously. "Take a look at this." She pointed to her computer screen.

Marc rolled his chair over and followed her finger as she spoke. "On May 30 at 13:35, Schnoll called a number in the British Virgin Islands and spoke to an unknown male:

Good afternoon, Charles, Dieter here.

Hello, my friend!

I hope you are good, and the Caribbean life is treating you well!

I am happy to report that the day-in, day-out sunshine and ocean air have not lost their magic on me yet.

Excellent! I won't take too much of your time, but I wanted to let you know that the matter I emailed you about several months ago appears to be moving again.

That is good news for you.

Yes, very good. I will need you to complete the trustee forms and FedEx them to me. Leave the beneficial owner page blank. In addition, I will need several shell companies established. We can use some of the names off the shelf, nothing special. I will need this by the first week of June. Can you do that?

Yes, of course. No problem.

Wonderful. Let me know your hours and fees and I will wire you the money. Swiss francs OK?

That is most thoughtful. Yes, francs are preferred. You know the account number.

I do.

End of call."

Terri then switched to the recorded text messages. "Right after that call, he texted a Belarusian number: 'We are all set for your arrival. Paperwork will be ready for the new project. Let me know when to expect you.'"

Marc grinned. "It sounds like they are coming to the States. Do we know who this Belarus guy is?"

"I don't have a clue. It isn't on any of our known associates lists, and I can't find it in any of our databases. I'm thinking of bouncing it off our 'cousins' upstairs and see if they can give us a name to go with the number. Are you comfortable with that?" Terri was referring to Dave Smith (probably not his real name), the CIA liaison who worked in the SCIF upstairs with the other secret squirrels. They referred to him as OGA Dave, OGA standing for "other government agency." He actually owed them a favor for pointing him to a potential asset in the past, though Terri wasn't sure if it had worked out or not. She had no need to know. That was the nature of this business, and she accepted it unquestioningly.

"Look Ter, I'm just a Philly homicide detective. This secret crap is above my pay grade, but if you are asking me, then yeah, I think it's OK."

Terri turned to Marc. "You're my partner," she said. "We're a team, and I will always ask for your input, Marc. I don't play that federal/local crap. Just realize that we are now moving into the other end of the pool. Dave's a good guy, but I will have to tell him why we are asking; and if this is someone they are interested in, we may get pushed out. Still good?"

"The way I see it, if we don't have a name, we're running blind. If we got a name, we can check airline manifests and get a heads up when he is coming in. I think we gotta risk the interagency poaching."

"All right, leave your cell phone at your desk and let's see if Dave is in his bubble."

The Special Compartmentalized Information Facility or SCIF, as it was commonly called, took up an entire floor of the building. This is where the counterterrorism and counterintelligence squads worked. It had the feel of a typical office environment—cubicles, computers, and conference rooms—with two exceptions. The entry doors were flanked by wooden cubby holes where you dropped off your cell phone before you entered, and the ceiling was dotted with several flashing red lights. If a visitor without the right clearance was escorted in, the red lights were activated. Ostensibly, this was to alert all the people working there to cover their papers, speak in whispers if they had to discuss anything sensitive, and do whatever other secret handshake they needed to do while uncleared ears were nearby. What it really did was give it a little life. Inevitably, everyone would poke their heads up from their cubicles to see who the new kid on the playground was.

Dave's office within the SCIF was even more locked down. Terri couldn't put her finger on it, but the air felt different in his space. Marc said it had the smell of being on a Navy ship. Maybe it was all the computers running in a room with poor airflow. Maybe it was the sound-suppressing material in the walls. Whatever it was, you could tell you were in a different world when you entered his realm. His office was sealed off in an interior room with no windows, only fluorescent lights. The unmarked door was ajar when they got there. Terri knocked lightly and walked in with Marc.

After a quick brief, Dave sat quietly for several minutes, staring at his computer. Then he looked up from the screen and announced, "Sergey Rostovich: attorney to the dark stars and a real asshole."

"Isn't that sorta redundant?" Marc couldn't help himself.

"Possibly, but as far as assholes go, he is in another league. Russian by birth but works throughout Eastern Europe. He's been tied to some members of the Kremlin in the past and is currently in the orbit of one Konstantin Kretzky," Dave finished, clearly happy that he was able to help.

Terri was familiar with Konstantin Kretzky. He was known as K2 to US intelligence agencies and was considered to be one of the most powerful criminal oligarchs in Russia. Before the breakup of the Soviet Union, however, he was just a lowly member of a regional crime family. He specialized in extortions, drug distribution, prostitution, and forgery. Once the USSR collapsed, he capitalized on the opportunity by brutally killing the head of the family and anyone that threatened his ascension. He seized control of the business and moved its primary interests to the control of natural-gas fields. Using threats and extortion, he bought what he could at fire sale prices. Those who were stupid enough to refuse to sell, he killed—and then forged documents granting him control of their companies.

He amassed huge wealth and was able to ingratiate himself with powerful political figures over the years through payoffs and the ability to make their problems go away. He likely maintained his political leverage through *kompromat,* lest someone get the idea that if he was arrested or killed, they could seize his operation.

Later, he expanded his network to include the pharmaceutical industry, where he siphoned off huge amounts of money through price gouging.

"Now, I have to tell you, since I ran this number and looked this guy up, my people will likely take a closer look at him as well," Dave said. "I can't tell you for sure, but I've seen it happen. Right now, he is just listed in a couple of footnotes, but that could change. Not my doing."

This was the interagency poaching that Terri and Marc feared could happen. If the Agency decided that they had an interest in Rostovich, or if they already had a working relationship with him, they could tell Terri and Marc to back off. Of course, then the FBI would protest, and it would turn into a full blown pissing contest. But ultimately, the claim of national security would win the day, and Terri and Marc would be out of the loop.

"We understand, Dave. We just wanted to identify the number. We're pretty much dead in the water without it," Terri answered.

CHAPTER 3

THAT EVENING, TERRI WAS wired from all the thoughts spinning through her head. She knew she needed a workout at the gym if she was going to have any chance of sleeping later, so she grabbed her bag and headed out the door. Only a few die-hards and oddballs like her were at the gym at this hour. Today was cardio day, and she had a good sweat going as she started her second mile on the treadmill.

Terri found that the steady footfalls and hum of the treadmill were almost hypnotic, allowing her mind to wander. Inevitably, she had thoughts about her dad and his painful end. This wasn't unexpected. She noticed when her mind was still it often went to this dark place. But she was ready for this and pushed the painful memories aside and replaced them with work.

Why was Rostovich coming over? How could they find out? Should they approach him, try to flip him? Should they approach Schnoll? Could she and Marc find out where the two were meeting and plant a bug? She would need to start working on an affidavit immediately, if that was the route they were going to go. All the aspects of the case twisted and floated in her mind as the treadmill registered three miles, and she started her cooldown. There were no epiphanies tonight, but she had ruled out a few things.

She left the gym, bag slung over her shoulder, and walked across the parking lot. About halfway to her car, she spotted him in the shadows. Immediately, her senses were heightened. Something seemed off. He stepped out and started walking toward her car on an interception path.

Her Glock 9mm was in her bag. Shit. Fumbling in a bag for her gun if he rushed her didn't seem like a great plan. She maneuvered the keys in her left hand so they protruded between her fingers. When he was about ten feet away, he darted toward her, his hand stuffed into his jacket pocket. But instead of running away, she ran toward *him,* closing the distance quickly. She unleashed a guttural scream as she jabbed the keys into his face, aiming for his eyes but gashing his forehead instead. That blow was followed immediately by another as she smashed the palm of her right hand into his nose, which immediately began spurting blood. He dropped a knife on the asphalt when he pulled his hand out of his jacket to clutch his face.

Stepping back, she executed a punt style kick to his crotch. He yelped and croaked out, "Bitch!"

As he hunched over, clutching his groin, she again let out a banshee scream and delivered another kick to his face, this time splitting his lip and snapping his head back. When he rocked back, she took a defensive stance and waited. He stumbled backwards a step, glared at her, and then ran.

It was over in a matter of seconds, but Terri sat in her car shaking as she waited for the police to arrive, the gun now in her lap. What had come over her? She had never reacted like that in training, and she had never screamed like that in her life. The shaking died down, but she was still pumped up. "Must be the adrenalin," she thought to herself.

Marc arrived about 20 minutes after the uniformed police officers. She had just given them her statement and a limited description of the assailant: male, about six feet tall, Hispanic or Caucasian, and wearing a dark gray or black hoodie, jeans, and work boots. "What a lousy description," Terri thought. "For chrissakes, I'm an FBI agent. I should've taken in more than that."

She pointed out the knife on the ground to the officers as Marc walked over. "You OK, kiddo?" he asked.

"Yeah, just shook up. I feel like a dumbass for letting this happen."

Marc reached out and gently took her shoulders. "Hey, stop it. You didn't do anything wrong. You didn't ask for this to happen. Just 'cause we carry a badge, doesn't make us superman, OK? Give yourself a break."

Terri looked up and gave a weak smile. "Thanks."

Marc looked at the officers on the scene. "They're going to pull security camera footage from the gym and stores in the area and see if they can get some leads. In the meantime, patrols are looking for your man, probably holding his junk and nursing a bloody nose. Description fits with a serial rapist prowling our fair city lately. You sure you're OK?"

"Yeah, I think I'm good."

"I talked to the officers. That was some fancy fisticuffs there. Remind me not to piss you off," Marc added with a laugh.

Terri laughed, too, but she needed to change the subject; enough of this "woe is me" crap. "So, before I had to kick that guy's ass, I was doing some thinking about the case. Let me bounce a few ideas off you. First, I think we should start working on an affidavit for a covert install in the event we find out where the meeting is. We can lay out all the probable cause now and leave the where and when blank. I'll get going on that. But I need you to reach out to the surveillance group and use that charm of yours to get us bumped up on the list for the week of–"

Marc listened intently, smiling a bit as Terri continued to rattle off the things they needed to get started on. She was OK. Back in the fight and fired up.

That night back at her condo, Terri struggled to calm her mind. Laying on her sofa with her four year old tabby Max curled up next to her, she surfed through channels. She liked the unexpected joy of finding a movie on an obscure channel rather than streaming one. She came upon the old Hepburn and Tracy movie *Desk Set*. An unconscious smile appeared on her face and her racing mind slowed. She remembered, as a little girl, sitting with her dad watching old movies. On Saturday nights he would make popcorn for them and find a classic movie to watch together. She remembered him rattling off the star's names and trivia about the movie. She could hear him telling her, 'Now, the computer in the movie was based on the government's computer at the time ENIAC, built at the University of Pennsylvania in the 1940's.' Before Google, there was dad.

She stroked Max and watched him stretch then curl up into a ball again. The smart banter between Hepburn and Tracy soothed her and she closed her eyes.

I arrive at the restaurant, a self-described Middle Eastern fusion place that had just opened last year. It is one of those trendy Center City places that Philadelphia is famous for fostering. Before I get to the door, the delightful mix of spices, hummus, fresh-baked pita bread, and succulent lamb fill my nostrils. I can tell that there's a respectable-sized crowd inside. A steady buzz of voices mingles with thumping music, a mix of traditional and contemporary West Asian styles. I walk in and immediately smell Jennifer. I see she is seated in a back booth.

When she called and suggested we meet for dinner, I thought her voice sounded tense. Now I notice that she looks distraught. She rises, gives me a hug, and kisses me on the cheek. I feel a slight warmth swell up my face. I look at her more closely and sense there is anger in her aura.

We order wine and read over the menu. We chat about normal coworker topics: the new dean, how our department chair is an idiot, and the changes in curriculum being proposed for the fall semester. It isn't until after she drains her second glass of Pinot Grigio that she opens up.

"I think Colin is going to leave me."

"Oh, Jennifer, I am so sorry to hear that. What makes you think so?"

"Things have been rocky for a while. Once he sold his company, he started using again." She must have seen my face register the shock. "He was clean when I met him, but I knew he had a history of addiction. I've never shared this with anyone before." She pauses and looks at me. "I think he met someone at his latest trip to rehab and—"

I honestly do not pay particular attention to most of what Jennifer is saying. The details of their relationship do not interest me except insofar as it might indicate that there is a possibility for me. She is one of the only people I feel a connection to. Perhaps it is simply animal attraction, but she has stirred something in me during our time working together.

"Look, I want him to be happy. I hope he gets clean and leads a fucking long and lovely life. If he wants to go back to London, fine. I really don't care to see him around anyway. I have no ill feelings for him at this point but—" The third glass of wine is gone.

I try to be a good human, or at least a passable human. I regularly feign interest in the trivial matters that occupy most people's daily lives. I listen to them complain about slights they perceive or the difficulties of balancing work and family. I convince them that I care about the same things. I don't. The truth is, I know I must live in their midst and therefore I must blend in with them. I know if they knew me for who I am, they would run in terror or try to exterminate me.

But there is something different about Jennifer. I see glimmers of myself in her. I recall the joy she tried to mask when she cut down a dissenting view during a debate about disciplinary policy last fall—she crushed the fool who dared cross her in the meeting. Even more important, she enjoyed doing it, and I could see that she took satisfaction in watching him squirm uncomfortably afterward. There is a vein of ice running through her, and I rather like that. Her presence gives me a heady feeling.

"So, what really burns me is that this guy—who I supported for years while he got his startup running, who I've gone to NA counseling with, who I shuttled to meetings when his license was revoked, who I took to rehab, and who I covered for with his family—*this guy* is now going to try to screw me out of the money! If that sonofabitch thinks I am just going to sit back and wait for his attorney to serve me papers and offer me 10 cents on the dollar, he will have a rude awakening." Fourth glass of wine gone.

There it was. I sensed that it wasn't the emotional loss but Colin's gross underestimation of her that had her seething.

"I found a card for a guy that does trusts and things in Colin's car. I logged into his email— dumbass never changed his password—and searched for the name on the card. I found an email in the trash to this guy—dumbass never emptied his trash; honestly, what did I ever see in him? Anyway, Colin said he was a client and was expecting to have a "life change event" in the near future and inquired about moving assets in an effort to make it difficult for a domestic divorce attorney to locate them if the life change event went forward."

She hesitates briefly, biting her bottom lip, before continuing, "I remember you mentioned in confidence once that you might have done some Anonymous computer hacking stuff in the past. Would you mind doing a little digging on this person?"

"Yes, that was a hobby of mine before I discovered the joy of academia. Please do not share that fact with anyone," I respond with a cool smile, silently kicking myself for sharing that. At least I had the sense to share it only with her. What I didn't share was that I still dabbled quite regularly.

"If you could, that would be great. I took a picture of the card and the email, too. I'll text them to you." She pauses and bites her lip. "I don't know what I expect you to do. I'm just a wreck. I think I just wanted to talk. You are such a good listener, Alex, and I needed to get this out. Thank you." Her eyes stare into mine and I feel an overriding desire swell in my chest. My mind suddenly feels foggy and all I want to do is help her.

"Absolutely. You can trust me." I reach across the table and hold her hand briefly. "Is Colin still living at home?"

"Yes. He hasn't said anything to me yet, but I suspect that will change soon."

"And you wish no harm to him, for this suffering he has inflicted on you?"

She gives me a slightly puzzled look. "No. Honestly, I would just be happy to have him out of my life."

Too bad. I would have relished a different answer, but I will respect her wishes. However, I see a flicker of recognition flash across Jennifer's face and she smiles briefly.

"Very well, Jennifer. You should contact an attorney and take care of yourself first and foremost. You have done all you can for him at this point. Ah, here is your text. I shall look into this Mr. Schnoll and let you know what I find."

The next morning, I settle back into my leather wingback chair. I have a plate of biscuits and a spread of delightful cheeses from my local shop. The Turkish goat cheese I purchased is divine. In my own space, all the smells are familiar, and I can easily focus on the details of the cheese without distraction. I revel in the pungent aroma. The honey I have paired it with is artisanal and unrefined. The sweetness of the honey and the bite of the cheese are exquisite.

I am rested from a peaceful sleep. I think of Jennifer as I read the text she sent me last night. Next to my cheese plate, my triple-screen computer array takes up most of the remaining desk surface. A quick internet search of Dieter Schnoll reveals almost nothing. He is an established attorney who specializes in trusts, estate planning, wealth management, and so on, with connections to several boutique European banks. Really quite mundane and completely expected. I cross-check some information with data revealed in the Panama Papers and other money-laundering data dumps, and something begins to emerge. If the reports can be trusted, then our Mr. Schnoll appears to have a penchant for working for some pretty unsavory characters: shell companies that he has helped to establish have been linked to drug cartel activity. Well now, this is taking a most interesting turn. I feel a twinge of excitement as I weigh the options.

I remove a thumb drive and a different laptop from my safe. The laptop runs a version of The Onion Router that will conceal my computer fingerprint and obscure even my nation of origin from any sniffer software. The thumb drive contains a bit of code developed by the NSA several years ago that found its way to the dark web. It isn't state of the art anymore, but for this task, it should more than suffice.

As I type the email and prepare the attachment, I can feel the anticipation building. I do enjoy the hunt.

Dieter rubbed his eyes. It took three tries to log into his email this morning. His hands were shaking, his mind was distracted, and he struggled to recall his password. After the second attempt, he resorted to checking the piece of paper in his top desk drawer. He heard the pleasant whistle of the teakettle call to him from the kitchen. Thank God. He needed some caffeine to clear the fog.

He prepared his cup of tea and stretched his arms over his head while it steeped. He'd had a fitful night's sleep. He couldn't get comfortable at first, and when he did finally drift off, he had the strangest dream: He was in a forest. It was dusk, and the shadows grew in the fading light. Something was out there, stalking him, but he couldn't see it. He ran, terrified, as the darkness closed around him—and then woke up to the sound of his alarm. How much had he slept? Clearly not enough.

In his inbox was an email from a potential client that looked promising. Without thinking, he clicked the attachment labeled Curriculum _Vitae.pdf. Very promising indeed.

It is early afternoon. I sit listening to a selection of music from Tchaikovsky's "Swan Lake" and reading Dieter Schnoll's emails and stored files. Very serene.

After a few hours, I feel I know what this man is about. As suspected, he helps rich people protect and hide their money, and he apparently has no qualms about where that money comes from.

Having accomplished what I set out to do today, I take some time to close my eyes and allow my mind to drift. I think of Schnoll and his like for a while, the evil they help propagate. But inevitably I return to the thoughts that have haunted me for so many years. How is it that I am here? How is it that I am what I am? I recall my earliest memories and replay, yet again, the events that got me here. I have gone over every detail numerous times.

CHAPTER 4

I REMEMBER WAKING UP in a room many years ago with blinding white lights burning my eyes. Five doctors, looking like specters in their biohazard suits, were staring at me through plastic face shields. I remember my terror as I tried to move, only to realize that my wrists and ankles were restrained. I could see what I guessed was a heart monitor, an EEG, and an IV rack slowly dripping a clear liquid into me. But as I watched the drops fall, I also realized that I could actually hear them plop every few seconds. What's more, I could hear heartbeats—not just mine, but the other people's, too. Fear rose in me by the second. Where was I? What was happening? I thought I was losing my mind. As it turned out, I was just losing my humanity.

The doctors consulted computer tablets and spoke to each other through voice emitters, their synthesized voices echoing in my head. They were so loud. Why were they so loud?

They lifted the sheet and peered at my torso.

"You see, the wounds have healed completely. The tissue damaged only yesterday has already regenerated. It is remarkable." They were speaking Russian. How did I know it was Russian? Was I Russian? I couldn't remember who I was or if this was my native tongue. My head was spinning as I struggled to put things into perspective.

After a few minutes of examination, one of the doctors spoke to me, "Can you understand me?" I nodded in reply.

"My name is Dr. Lavroski. You were involved in a military accident. You were believed to be near dead and transferred to my care as a last-ditch effort to save your life. You are in a lab, the Novaya Zhizn lab. You have been in a deep coma for three weeks. You have been given an experimental serum to aid your recovery. I am pleased to inform you that you have made remarkable strides. We will continue to monitor you for several days. Do you understand?"

I managed to croak out a yes. My throat was so dry. My tongue felt like a swollen lump. I tried to ask for water, but what came out was mostly unintelligible. Somehow, they understood me. Someone held a glass of water with a straw to my cracked lips. I drained the glass and could speak more clearly. I began to ask more questions, but the doctors told me to rest and left the room.

I tilted my head to the side and watched them leave. I had a vague memory of intense pain associated with them. I couldn't recall anything specific, but one word rang in my head: torture. There was a PIN pad by the door, and I could see the code Lavroski entered after scanning the ID badge on his suit. Good to know.

I looked around and studied the room more closely. There was a CCTV camera mounted in the corner by the door. Above the PIN pad was an intercom. On the wall opposite the door was a large mirror. And I knew there were two men on the other side. I could hear them.

There wasn't much else to discern from my limited vantage point, so I focused on the conversation I could hear behind the mirror.

"When does this one get the next dose?"

"In an hour."

"I don't like going in there. This one is strange. By all rights, they should be dead. Have you ever seen wounds heal that fast?"

"No. Our glorious scientists have created another miracle," someone said with a hint of sarcasm.

"I heard that the others all died before this point. I wish this one would, too. Maybe the next wound test will finish the job. I know the history, this one is a traitor."

"You shouldn't repeat rumors. If Lavroski learns that you are speaking out of turn, you may find yourself on the other side of the glass."

There was a grunt of acknowledgement.

I closed my eyes and dozed. I dreamt that I was back in grade school, and the teacher was angry with me. He drew his hand back to slap me but rather than flinch away, I reached up and caught his wrist. I squeezed and twisted it, bringing him to the floor, then sat on his chest and gouged out his throat. As I caught my breath, I looked around at the other children in the room. They were all in biohazard suits.

I was awakened by the whoosh of the door. A person in a white suit entered, carrying a metal tray with a syringe.

I asked, "What is that?"

The synthesized voice replied, "It is the medicine. That is all you need to know." Despite the transmitter, I recognized the voice of the man behind the mirror who was reluctant to enter the room.

"Can you tell me your name?" I ask.

"No." I could hear his heart rate accelerate.

"How did I get here? I can't remember."

"Doctor Lavroski has told you all you need to know."

"Can you tell me my name?"

There was a hesitation. He stopped tapping the syringe and looked at me. "You are no one. You are a traitor to the Motherland and deserve nothing. You are alive only to serve the purposes of science. When that purpose is met, you will die and no one will miss you. Do you understand?"

I could feel the venom in his words, but did I also detect nervousness—or maybe even fear?

The technician plunged the syringe into the IV port and pushed an amber-colored liquid into the line.

I watched anxiously as the liquid made its way along the tube and into my arm. At first, it felt cold as it entered my body. Then suddenly it was hot, and within seconds I was burning up.

My heart raced, and sweat poured off my body. My muscles started to cramp, wracking me with pain, and I jerked against the restraints. My bones felt like they were breaking. I let out a scream that my brain registered as completely foreign. My body convulsed, arching off the bed and crashing back down. I felt absolute panic. I thought I was going to spontaneously combust.

The bio suit clad technician backed away toward the door and shouted into the intercom, "This is the worst one yet! What should I do?" He yelled so loudly that I could hear his real voice come through the suit. Now I knew that I sensed his fear.

A voice replied, "You stupid ass! What did you do? I'll get my suit on and come in with a sedative. Check the restraints!"

"Fuck you and your restraints! Just give me the sedative now! Hurry up, something is happening!"

At that instant, I suddenly felt calm. I could hear the person on the other side of the mirror cursing and fumbling with something. I heard the person in the room with me begin to shriek in terror when I flexed my arms and snapped the restraints like paper bracelets. I sat up and, with a slight jerk, popped the straps around my ankles just as easily.

I felt a strength that I had never felt before. Every cell was alive, as if each mitochondrion was working on overdrive. I felt invincible.

The panicked technician was frantically trying but failing to scan his badge and enter his PIN code. I stepped from the bed, barely noticing the cold tile on my bare feet, and lunged. Somehow, I knew that I could cover the 3 meters in a single movement. He turned his masked face toward me just as I landed on him, his eyes wide and mouth agape.

With one hand, I gripped his head and tilted it back. With the other, I easily ripped through the suit and tore out his throat. Crimson liquid stained the pristine whiteness of his coverall, and he let out a feeble gurgle.

At that moment, the seal on the door broke as the other person I heard behind the mirror entered. I grabbed his arm, dislocating his shoulder with a sick pop, and tossed him across the room. He screamed as he flew over the bed, smashing his head into the wall. Then, slumping down, he was silent, lying motionless on the floor.

I stepped through the door into what looked like a decontamination room. I remember noticing that I had to duck my head to fit under the doorframe. The next door was locked, and I realized that it required a badge and a PIN code to open. Realizing I neglected to take one of the technician's badges and the door had now closed. I was trapped. Furious, I kicked the door and felt it start to give. After a few more well-placed kicks, the door buckled, and I found myself in the middle of a long hallway.

I listened. There it was, Dr. Lavroski's voice. It was faint, but I could tell it was him. I ran toward the sound, passing several doors before rounding a corner just as an alarm started blaring. It was so loud that it hurt my head, and I covered my ears briefly. Feeling disoriented, I paused for a moment. Through the roar of the clamoring horn, I heard a man shouting from behind a door, "What the hell is going on? What do you mean the subject got out? How?"

The door caved easily under my shoulder. I crashed into the office and sat back on my haunches. The man was still on the phone as my gaze met his. It was not Lavroksi but another doctor. I recognized the blue eyes behind wire rim glasses from his earlier visit. His surprised face turned into a mask of terror as I lunged at him. Covering the distance in one motion, I grasped his head between my hands and growled out "ID badge and PIN". His mouth moved, but no words would come. I squeezed his head a bit harder and asked again.

He spluttered, "On my coat, PIN 7985. Please let me—". But I was not in the mood to humor him. I tore into his neck with my teeth, relishing the warm, coppery taste of blood that filled my mouth. It was like mother's milk to me.

I found his ID badge clipped to his jacket by the door and discovered that it opened the remaining doors without a PIN code. Making my way out of the facility was a blur. I made short work of anyone I came across, leaving bright splashes of blood on the walls.

An armed security guard blocked the last exit. He saw me and swore, closing his eyes as he unleashed a barrage of fire from his Kalashnikov. A slug struck my chest, and I remember thinking, 'Well, that's it, I'm dead." But when I glanced down, I saw that the bullet had barely penetrated my flesh, and just a trickle of blood leaked into my fur—which seemed to cover most of my body. At that moment, I remember being more shocked by the hair covering my body than the gunshot. Holding up my hand, I saw that I had claws as well.

I looked back at the terrified guard and motioned for him to move aside. He obliged, wetting his pants in the process, and I strode outside. The night air was cool. Behind me, the alarms continued to wail.

Before me, the countryside under the inky black sky beckoned with a calm serenity. In the distance, I could hear what I somehow knew to be reindeer. I was ravenous. I leaped the security fence and disappeared into the dark.

I sit up and open my eyes to find that I am sitting in my house. Safe. Replaying the events of my escape from the lab have left me a little shaken and I try to slow my heart rate with some deep breaths. Who was I before I woke up on the table? I have struggled with this question for years but still don't know the answer. The only hints I find lie in vague memories of past lives, which I assume belong to others like me through the ages—a lineage of ravenous creatures. Somehow, I must have incorporated the vast data of their DNA into my own, because I seem to know more about my predecessors than I do about myself. Who were my mother and father? Do I have siblings? A wave of loneliness falls over me like a shadow.

Despite these troubling thoughts, I decide it has been a deliciously productive morning. Setting aside my troubling musings, I move on to more pragmatic matters: my dinner plans.

CHAPTER 5

THE SOG TEAM, 12 agents in total, assembled in the conference room. Terri sat on the edge of the table in front of the surveillance squad, holding a cup of coffee. To her left was a whiteboard. Marc sat on her right with his laptop. He had worked his magic and convinced the SOG supervisor to bump their physical surveillance request to the top of the pile. Every agent, of course, believed that they were working the "biggest case in the Bureau," but sometimes they really might be. Then they had to convince everyone else.

"Thank you, guys, for coming to the pre surveillance briefing. As you know, we have a TIII up and running on this guy Dieter Schnoll," she began. Schnoll's driver's license picture appeared on the screen. "We have communication that indicates he is setting up a money-laundering platform for some heavy hitters in Russia. To that end, this guy, Sergey Rostovich, is expected to arrive here in the area tomorrow." A passport picture of Rostovich appeared on the screen. "We have confirmation that he has booked a flight into JFK tomorrow. He purchased the ticket yesterday, so it is very short notice. New York SOG will attempt to pick him up and follow him to Philadelphia and pass him off to my squad, who will attempt to put him in a location and pass him off to your team."

"Schnoll has made a reservation at Viv's for tomorrow night. Two of you, Jack and Sarah, will have the luxury of dining there at the same time on Uncle Sam's dime. The rest of you will be mobile in the area." In the Bureau the joke was that we all had a rich uncle. But good old Uncle Sam was a cheap bastard. When you could convince him to spend some money, you were lucky.

A map of the greater Philadelphia area appeared on the screen. "Schnoll lives out here in Ambler. Pretty nice digs. The restaurant is here in Center City. We don't know if he is going to pick up Rostovich, either from a train at the 30th Street station or at a hotel, or meet him there. Also, since the reservation could be a total red herring and they end up somewhere unexpected, we will need to have you guys start tailing him at his house and see where he goes. Squad 1 has eyes on his house now and will stay on him until you get ready to pick up the surveillance tomorrow."

A hand shot up in the back. "If he goes somewhere else, and Sarah and I are already seated, do we get to finish our meal? I mean, I don't know when I will get back to Viv's." Laughter broke out in the room.

"If you've placed your order, yes finish what you ordered for chrissakes." Terri smiled and shook her head in exaggerated disbelief. "We are working on getting an installation of a camera and a microphone in the restaurant, but I'm not sure that will happen. The request will be sent to the judge today, but the time frame is tight. Regardless, you guys will be wired up."

Everything Terri had covered so far was standard and detailed in the OP plan provided to the team. She now got to the part that she wanted to emphasize in person. "Be on your toes out there tomorrow. We have intel that Rostovich works for Konstantin Kretzky. For those of you who don't know him, he runs one of the seven major crime organizations in Europe. He's a serious player in illicit oil money, arms trafficking, narcotics—you name an illegal activity, and he is likely getting a piece of it. He is also very close to the top echelons of the Russian government. Because of this and the fact that he is sitting on a mountain of money, there is the possibility of counter-surveillance on this meeting. It could be domestic PIs or a Russian team, or someone else entirely; they've used European teams in the past. We're checking with local PIs to see if they have been retained. No positive replies yet. Be aware of rental vehicles, cars with out-of-state tags, guys sitting in cars like us, whatever. If you see anything odd, call it out. We do not want to get burned on this, so stay loose. Weather permitting, we will have air assets working as well, so that'll take some of the pressure off when he's on the move."

Terri looked around the room. The sense of confidence had definitely been cut with some concern. No one wanted to be the one who blew a high-stakes surveillance. Which is exactly why she wanted to brief them face to face.

Another hand came up in the middle of the room. "Is Rostovich traveling with any security detail that we know of?"

"Good question. No tickets purchased on the flight at the same time he booked his. A crosscheck of the other names on the manifest didn't ring any bells. But if I was putting a surveillance crew or security detail in place for this, I would have flown them in on a flight before his. We'll keep looking, but nothing thus far."

Terri scanned the room. "No other questions? OK, on page eight of the OP's order is the communication plan. Everyone take a look at the channels we will be using."

My prey has made a reservation at Viv's, a nouveau French restaurant, for tomorrow. Excellent taste. I can feel the excitement building in me, like a small flame inching closer to the fuel that will cause it to explode. I take my time walking about the upscale neighborhood that the prey calls home until I come upon its house, a midsize colonial with an attached two-car garage. A white Land Rover is parked in the driveway. The property backs up to a large wooded area, and the landscaping is quite well done. Behind a lamp post in the front yard is a home security sign, but I don't see any motion lights or cameras. Nor do I hear or smell any indications of a dog in the house. From what I learned from the prey's computer, my quarry lives alone. My senses confirm it.

The air is filled with normal suburban sounds and smells. Most of the spring flowers have faded, and the summer blooms are beginning to erupt in a colorful explosion. Several yards with fresh mulch emit a heavy, pungent smell into the air. Down the street, a woman is walking an elderly terrier. As she approaches, the terrier yaps at me briefly. I fix my gaze on him, hiding my amusement when he whines and scampers behind the woman's leg.

As I round the corner, I see a parked van. The front seats are empty, but I can hear a faint voice on a telephone speaker coming from the back. A man whispers, "Copy." I am close to the van now, and I detect the somewhat sweet smell of gun lubricating oil. How interesting.

I continue my walk to my car, parked a mile away. I have learned all I need.

***

The following day, Dieter exited his driveway at 4:30 p.m. As he drove toward I-76, the first raindrops began to hit his windshield. The drive into the city on the Schuylkill expressway was always congested, and rain could double the hour-long trip. But he'd left himself plenty of time for this contingency; the reservations were not until 7:00 p.m. He had texted Sergey, who was staying at The Ritz only a few blocks from the restaurant, and offered to pick him up. But the Russian had said he would enjoy the walk to Viv's, rain and all, and meet him there.

Stopped at a red light, Dieter glanced at the folio on the passenger seat. He reached over and counted the three sealed manila envelopes inside. Everything was on track.

He approached the expressway ramp and came to an immediate stop. Red taillights sparkled on his rain-streaked windshield. As he nosed his way into the flow of cars, he still didn't see the sedan two cars back that had been following him since he turned out of his development.

The TIII room in the FBI office was almost empty. Judy Strasser sat at the monitor waiting for the alert to signal a call or text. She had her water jug, a pouch of trail mix, a can of Pringles, and a bag of Butterfinger Bites laid out on the desk next to her. Judy liked her snacks.

It was very quiet on the wire tonight. The target was driving, and she was glad that he wasn't one of those assholes who texted while they drove. To pass the time, she checked out the activity recorded during the preceding shift. There wasn't likely to be much else to do for several hours.

Terri and Marc were also in the TIII room, monitoring radio traffic in real time. Schnoll had left his home after texting Rostovich. The surveillance plane was a scratch because of the rain, so the cars on Schnoll had to stay a little tighter. The two listened as the mobile team tracked the

Land Rover on its way to Philadelphia. It was a very low-speed pursuit. Another surveillance team had already placed Rostovich at The Ritz, in Center City. An agent had radioed in about two UNSUBs who were loitering in the lobby and suggested that they might be part of a security or countersurveillance detail.

Jack and Sarah were wired up and ready to head into Viv's when either Schnoll or Rostovich arrived. Hopefully, they'd be seated nearby and possibly be able to pick up some pertinent conversation.

Terri's supervisor, Jim Martin, sat with them as well. He was an old-school agent who had become a bit of a legend in the field of organized crime during his 25 years of service. He had cut his teeth as a case agent investigating La Costra Nostra in New York and Philadelphia during some of their bloody turf battles, building case after case and bringing many Mafia families to their knees. The rise of Eastern European criminal organizations had complicated things, but he had managed to adapt. Throughout his career, one of his greatest strengths was the ability to match good cases with good agents. He loved to bring them together and watch the results. Given that the squad's resources were stretched thin tonight, Jim volunteered to lead the radio coordination.

"Looks like this caper is humming along pretty well. Nice job, guys."

"Good God, don't jinx us, Jim," Terri replied with a smile. "We still haven't gotten anything evidentiary yet."

"You will. You're on the right guy. This meeting tonight proves that. Schnoll is a player and you two will get him."

Marc stood up. "I wanna double check our car radios and make sure they're coded correctly. Where are your keys, Ter?"

"I'll come with you, and then we can head out to the residence. With the rain tonight, we should be able to park close to the house. Won't be many people out, and those who are will have bad visibility." The plan was for Marc and Terri to stake out Schnoll's house so the surveillance teams could break contact when he approached the neighborhood on his way home after the dinner meeting. He had seemed oblivious to them so far, and they wanted to keep it that way. No need to risk spooking him with a pair of headlights in his rearview mirror as he drove down the deserted residential streets.

"Happy hunting, you two. I'll stay here and monitor the teams. If anything hot comes in, I'll give you a call." He turned to Judy, who was giving him the side-eye, and said, "Don't worry, I brought my own snacks."

The restaurant was not crowded tonight, and Sergey was already seated when Dieter arrived. The two men exchanged handshakes across the small table. Then, over drinks and several courses of dinner, they talked. John and Sarah were just a couple of tables away, and Sarah had placed her purse with the camera on the chair closest to the targets. Nevertheless, they caught only snatches of the conversation; she hoped the equipment was capturing more. Overall, the conversation appeared to be generally innocuous—ordinary, polite discussion of Sergey's trip and the meal, with some laughter sprinkled in. But then the voices lowered, and they heard "client...asset protection...anonymity...". Just before the dessert drinks arrived, John saw Dieter reach into his folio, retrieve three large manilla folders, and hand them to Sergey. Sergey promptly put them into his briefcase. John sent a text message to Terri: "Package passed to SR appr 2200."

A round of vodka was delivered to the table, and both men raised their glasses in a toast. Just then, Sarah noticed two large men enter the restaurant and scan the room before moving directly to the target table. As the men sat down, it was clear from the expression on Dieter's face that this was unexpected.

The surveillance team outside saw the new guys enter and reported back. The team believed they were the same two men from the hotel lobby: both were about six feet tall with thick builds and were wearing jeans and sports jackets. One carried a briefcase.

Sergey looked at Dieter, "Herr Schnoll, these men are my associates. I believe you have had too much to drink tonight. They will take you home and ensure that you are safe. You are now a very valuable part of our club, and we do not wish to see anything bad happen to you."

Dieter looked left and right at his new companions, who met his confused look with blank stares. "Sergey, I don't understand. I will call an Uber and get my car tom–"

Sergey leveled his eyes at Dieter, "Herr Schnoll, this is not a request. Please provide them with your valet ticket."

Jim Martin listened intently to the surveillance radio traffic. Unexpected things often happen during a surveillance: civilians get mixed up in the events, other crimes happen, car accidents occur, people miss turns or get lost. Shit always happens. But this was different. Something was starting to feel very wrong and dangerous.

The radio crackled. "Land Rover is pulling out, UNSUB 1 is driving. Target and UNSUB 2 are in the back seat. Heading north on Broad."

"He's turning right on Spruce; I'm going with him. Whoa, he's making another right. I think he's trying to clean himself. I'm going straight. Someone else try to pick him up."

As the Land Rover circled the block and got back onto Broad Street, another car pulled in behind them.

Jim got on the radio, "He's checking for a tail, and he's got a sweeper car following. Everyone back off. Don't get burned." This was getting very dicey very quickly. He needed to let Terri and Marc know.

Terri and Marc sat in their cars looking out the rain-streaked windows, oblivious to the scramble that was unfolding on Broad Street. Schnoll's neighborhood fell into a radio repeater dead zone, which meant that all radio traffic with the main office was broken. They could talk car to car, but that was about it. To use a phrase that all agents come to utter at some point in their careers, "Comms suck."

Terri got off the phone and immediately called Marc. "I just talked to Jim. We have a situation coming our way. Everything's gone off the rails. Remember those two guys in the hotel lobby?"

"Yeah, possible security team."

"Well, they showed up at the restaurant and took Schnoll for a ride in his car. One of them is driving, the other is with Schnoll in the back seat. They did a bunch of countersurveillance moves and have another car following. Registration for the chase car comes back to a rental company in Virginia. They finally got on the highway and are heading this way, about 20 minutes out. SOG has backed way off. We're flying solo out here right now."

"So much for a routine meeting. What do you think?" Marc asked.

"I don't know. Maybe I'm being paranoid, but this has all the hallmarks of a hit."

"Yeah. That's what I was thinking too. I'm gonna call the locals and give 'em a heads up on this. Let 'em know if we call, they need to send the cavalry in a hurry."

"Copy that." Terri reached into her back seat and pulled her ballistic armor out of the carry sack. Her hands were shaking slightly as she pulled the Velcro straps apart and slipped it over her head.

I have parked on the other side of the wooded area from the prey's house. Suddenly, flashing lights illuminate the inside of my car. A policeman gets out and approaches; I can hear his radio squawking as I roll my window down. He asks if I need any assistance. He wants to seem helpful, but I can see him smelling the air for alcohol and scanning the car for contraband. I explain that I have lost a pet dog and am searching for him. The poor thing is terribly frightened of storms and bolted from my car. He advises me to be careful and returns to his car. How trite.

I watch as his taillights fade away down the road. It is very dark now, and the rain is constant, keeping everyone from the park—perfect hunting weather. I leave my clothes in my car and wear only a large black poncho. The rain makes little popping sounds as it pelts the Gore-Tex hood. I pause, listening intently: no sound other than the rain. I sniff the air deeply, invigorated by the fresh, damp smell. There are no other scents. I scan the area one last time, eyes piercing the darkness. I detect no movement. I am at last alone, and I move into the trees. It all feels very natural.

Seated in the back seat of his own car, Dieter feels helpless. He has tried to talk to his unwanted companions, but they are unresponsive. The driver watches the road, following the directions from his phone, and occasionally checks his rearview mirrors. The man sitting to his left only looks at him. When they were still in the city, he thought about bolting from the car at a stoplight, but his hands and feet would not move. They are approaching his neighborhood now. His panic is intensifying. "I can walk home from here," he offers.

No response.

"Look, I have money, I can pay you," He blurts out.

The man only looks at him impassively. The driver says something in Russian and the other man glances out the front window and turns to Dieter. "We are approaching your home. We will all go inside." Dieter notices for the first time that both men are wearing gloves.

I have been crouched in the woods behind the fence for about 30 minutes. The sound of the rain plopping on the leaves and ground has been steady and comforting. I have removed the poncho and savored the water running along my skin. I don't feel any chill. My blood is hot with anticipation. I see lights on the street through the fence, and I hear a car approaching. The car slows, and I see the headlights swing in an arc toward the garage. I stand and let the transformation happen. I am prepared for the pain as my body changes; I welcome it. When it's done, I can see over the fence. With little effort, I vault over it and charge across the yard.

Terri watched in her mirror as the white Land Rover approached up the street. She couldn't see into the car, but she knew it was them. She slumped lower into the seat as it approached and eventually passed her, turning into the driveway. She saw the headlights of the second car turn up the street behind her. Through the running water on her windshield, she saw a man exit the driver's door silhouetted against the headlights. It was not Schnoll. A flash of lightning revealed a shape moving fast around the corner—something big. She keyed the radio handset to ask Marc if he saw it, too, but it was already at the Land Rover.

The driver of Schnoll's Land Rover put the car in park and opened the door. Schnoll knew that he should run, but his hands were shaking so badly that he couldn't even unbuckle his seat belt. As the lightning flashed, he glimpsed a shape rushing toward the car. He froze.

I round the corner of the garage and see the prey exiting the car. He looks up just as I slash my claws across his face, ripping through his skin. The force of the blow sends him to the ground. I hear a curse in Russian from the back seat of the car. This is unexpected. I lean down and look through the window as a man pulls a pistol from under his jacket. I smash the glass and reach in, grabbing his neck just as he raises the pistol and fires into my chest. The impact is only a slight sting, but I let out a roar of disapproval. I yank the man out through the window and hold him off the ground by his neck. Swatting the pistol away, I bring his face to mine.

The terror in his eyes feeds my rage. I disembowel him with one hand and break his neck with the other. Then I drop him on the asphalt.

The first man, my prey, is still unconscious on the driveway. I retrieve my prize under my arm and start to move to the back yard when I hear footsteps splashing quickly through the puddles. I turn and see a young woman with a pistol drawn and the letters FBI on her chest. She is screaming, "Don't move!" I can sense there is fear in her but not panic. I hear another set of feet approaching. It is a man with another pistol and the letters POLICE on his chest. This is most unexpected. I do not wish to harm them; I don't need the kind of attention that killing them would bring. Besides, I have what I came for. I turn toward the wooden fence and the forest beyond. But then there is gunfire, and I flinch slightly from the impact of the rounds. I spin around, enraged. How dare they shoot at me after I let them live? In the distance, I hear sirens and more cars approaching swiftly. I study the pair before me, memorizing their faces, and then turn away again. I toss my meal over the fence and hear it land with a wet thud on the muddy ground. I vault the railing, pick up my package, and trot into the dark trees.

***

Marc turned to Terri, who was just staring at the fence, gun hanging at her side. "What the fuck was that?"

Terri simply shook her head, still staring toward the forest.

"Should we go after it?"

"Nope."

"My thoughts exactly."

Misha sat in his car stunned. "What have I just seen?" he thought. His team was dead, killed by...something. And now the FBI and police were on the scene. Suddenly, self-preservation kicked in. He put the car in drive and sped away.

CHAPTER 6

T ERRI SAT UNCOMFORTABLY IN front of Jim Martin's desk. He had closed his door, which was usually a bad sign. Marc, equally uncomfortable, was in the chair next to her. Across from them, Jim was leaning on his elbows reading her draft 302 regarding the events of the previous night. The wall behind him was filled with an assortment of family pictures, plaques, awards, and a hand-drawn portrait of him created by his daughter when she was 5 years old. Martin was old school and preferred to read paper versions of reports instead of electronic. He set the document down, leaned back in his chair, took his glasses off, and rubbed his temples.

"OK, I know we went through this before, but humor me as I wrap my head around what we have: two dead Russians."

"Yes, sir. Actually, one Bulgarian, Anatoly Vichin is confirmed dead. His body was discovered in the driveway. The remains of a second person, who we believe was part of the pair observed in the hotel lobby, were discovered in a wooded area, approximately half a mile from the rear of the Schnoll residence. There was no identification located with the remains, and we are working to ID him. Vichin was Bulgarian intelligence," Terri confirmed.

"Great. Just great. One confirmed dead operative; a pile of parts that we think is a second; plus a third who fled the scene and was stopped by Pennsylvania State Police on the turnpike heading to New Jersey."

"Yes, Misha Popov is a Russian from the embassy in DC. We're holding him on a material witness warrant, but he's claiming diplomatic immunity and refusing to cooperate."

"Oh, I know all about that. The State Department is badgering the shit out of the SAC, who in turn is badgering the shit out of me. This is turning into an international incident. We also have— or rather *don't* have—Sergey, who caught a red-eye flight that night and is back in Europe by now."

"Yes, sir. That is our belief as well."

"And we believe these guys were there to kill Schnoll but were interrupted by—I'll get to that later," Jim continued.

"Yes, sir. We recovered two hypodermic needles containing an unknown substance from the victim's briefcase, and we sent them to the lab this morning for testing. We're pretty sure that the operatives intended to kill Schnoll."

"So now we have Dieter Schnoll, the intended victim and our investigative target, who likely witnessed the killings from the back seat of the car, and thus far is unable or unwilling to talk about it?"

"Yes, sir. He is currently hospitalized. We will try to talk to him in the next couple of days if he seems communicative."

"And then we have you two."

Terri stiffened at what was coming next.

"I have a senior FBI agent and a decorated Philadelphia police detective on the scene of a double murder. They witnessed the murders, attempted to intervene, discharged their weapons—to no avail, I might add—yet still can't give a good goddamn description of the perpetrator or perpetrators of said murders." Jim was practically screaming at this point. "Did I miss anything?" he asked rhetorically.

Terri and Marc both looked at their laps instinctively. When it was put like that, it did sound very bad.

"I mean, for chrissake, what you describe sounds like an eight-foot tall Ninja wearing body armor and a fucking bear suit!"

"But remember Jim, it was raining like hell, like your proverbial dark and stormy night," Marc added, trying to lighten the atmosphere.

Jim was not in the mood. "Shit. Based on what you guys have given me, I'd say it was raining Jack Daniels. Look, I'm not telling you to change the material facts of your report. But we cannot put this into an official document. Yes, it was raining like hell, maybe you only thought you saw this person or persons, as you described them. Rewrite it and give me something that's scaled back and fuzzy on the details, no pun intended. Maybe something like 'an unknown subject with an unknown weapon.' In the meantime, I will hold this version in my safe."

As they left Jim's office, Anthony Jackson—AJ, as he liked to be called—leaned back in his chair. "Well, there they are, the team that couldn't shoot straight." Jackson had come to the Organized Crime squad about a year ago. He had transferred to the Philadelphia division from Boston, where he had worked on violent gang cases. He still hadn't proven he was a competent agent but he had shown he was a raging, misogynistic asshole.

Terri didn't look at him and kept walking.

"You might need some extra firearms training, Terri. Or maybe just stick to the office and avoid the street," he continued.

Terri had had enough. "Hey Jackson, remember last week when I told you to F off? Just consider that a standing order anytime you think of talking to me, OK?"

"Someone is feeling touchy today. Maybe it's that time of the—"

"Yo. Knock it off, Antony," Marc cut him off. His normal affable persona gone, replaced with one of cold stone. "Maybe you should spend some more time to makin' a case of your own and less time worryin' about other people's cases. Capice?"

AJ glared at Marc for the moment and then went back to his computer to shop for holsters.

As they walked back toward Terri's desk, she whispered to Marc, "Thanks, but I can handle that jerk on my own." Her father made sure she learned how to tackle bullies and jerks at an early age.

"I got no doubts on that, but I think we got more pressing things to do than get into a slam battle with God's gift to law enforcement over there," Marc whispered back. His phone alerted and he checked his text messages. He stopped walking and turned to Terri. "Feel like taking a ride?" he asked.

"Yeah, know any cliffs I can drive over?"

"Funny. Nah, I was thinking of the medical examiner's office. I got a message from Jer, she asked me to stop by. Said she had something on the O'Brien case. Based on last night, I think it might be relative."

Terri looked at him, "O'Brien was that stiff the dogs got to, right? Are you serious?"

"As a heart attack, Ter. I saw O'Brien's body. There's some striking similarities to our dead guy in the woods."

"Canis lupus," Jerri said as she handed over the report to Marc.

"What is that, a disease?" Marc asked.

"It's a wolf," Terri said woodenly.

"Bingo! Someone paid attention in biology class," Jerri offered. "We found some hair samples around the wounds on O'Brien. DNA sampling came back with *Canis lupus* as the closest match, about 90%."

Marc's mind was racing. Could it be that what they saw last night was real? It seemed like something from a nightmare.

Terri studied the report for a minute, then handed it back to Jerri. "My DNA analysis reading is a little rusty. What was the other 10%?"

Jerri paused a beat, "It came back human, of Eastern European descent. I'm assuming the sample got corrupted in the testing."

Marc leaned forward in his chair, "I wouldn't be too quick with that assumption, Doc. Let us tell you about last night. But you gotta swear that this conversation doesn't leave this room."

Jerri's eyes went wide as Marc and Terri conveyed the events from the previous night.

When they finished, Jerri leaned back in her chair and looked at the ceiling tiles for a moment. "So, if I believe what you told me—though it's a helluva tale—and combine that with the forensic evidence I have, it would appear that we have three possible scenarios: a psychopath with an animal fetish wearing some kind of biomechanical suit covered by a wolf skin; an actual wolf; or something unknown to any of us."

Terri had taken out a notepad and started writing the theories Jerri rattled off. It was an almost unconscious action. She had worked this way her entire life, creating lists, taking notes, compiling data to support or refute a theory. "I think we can rule out actual wolf. What we saw was on two legs, at least eight feet tall."

"Plus, we shot it at close range four times. I'm sure we hit it," Marc added.

"OK, wild wolf is least likely. That leaves 'psychopathic killer' or unknown. What do we know about any such biomechanical or exoskeleton suits?" Jerri asked.

"Only what I've seen in the press," Terri replied. "I know that DARPA, the Defense Advanced Research Projects Agency, has demonstrated some of them. They help soldiers carry loads, lift heavy stuff. I haven't seen anything publicly that could move like this thing, though."

"Don't mean it doesn't exist. My question is, how would your man there get his hands on that technology, if it exists? I gotta think that those things have to be locked down in a lab somewhere. If one of their supersuit things went missing, they'd know, right?" Marc asked.

Terri closed her eyes, trying to remember in detail the encounter from the night before. "I don't think it was a man in a supersuit, either. It was huge and muscled, it moved smoothly, and the face...it—it growled and bared its teeth. There'd be no way a guy in a wolf skin would be able to do that. It was too organic, like a real animal."

"That was where I was heading as well: unknown", said Jerri. "But before we go any further, I want to be perfectly clear about one thing." She sat back in her chair and placed her hands on the desk. "I will not be writing any of this in any reports. I have worked my ass off to reach where I am, and I will not jeopardize that. I was the only Black woman in my medical school class. I have had to put up with more shit than either of you can imagine through my career. There are people who would love to see me sidelined, and I will not give them any ammunition by writing any of this stuff down officially. If anyone comes to me and asks about this, I will tell them you two have lost your damn minds. Clear?"

Terri and Marc nodded.

"Good, now let's get to work. In medical school, we are taught that if you hear hoofbeats, think horses, not zebras. In other words, the most likely explanation is usually the correct one. Well, in this case, all the conventional explanations don't fit. I'm afraid we are looking at a very rare zebra indeed."

They now shifted to what they could do to identify their zebra. Jerri was going to reach out to the county coroner and ask if she could examine the bodies given the cases previously found in Philadelphia.

Marc was going to ask the Ambler police department for every traffic citation, parking ticket, jaywalking violation, animal complaint, and anything else he could think of for the past two weeks in a three-mile radius of Scholl's house.

Terri was going to check the surveillance logs for the agents on Scholl's house and talk to them about everything they saw.

They all agreed that, given when and where—miles from the other killings—this attack took place, they could rule out coincidence. If the killer had, in fact, targeted this group, that would indicate planning. Planning meant preparation. And preparation likely meant gathering intelligence. Hopefully, the killer had made a mistake.

The legal consultation room at the federal detention center was small and sterile. The table and chairs were bolted to the gray floor. The fluorescent lights gave everything a bluish hue—perhaps by design, since blue is known to be a calming color. But that would be giving far too much credit to the persons designing detention centers.

"The FBI and the Department of Justice are trying to hold you as a witness. We are certain that your diplomatic status will prevail, and you will be released soon. Our ambassador is aggressively pushing the matter.

You need only to be quiet and remain patient," the Russian consular representative said as he sat across from Misha Popov.

Misha nodded his acknowledgement. He had not spoken to anyone yet, not even his fellow inmates, and he would stay silent.

"I need you to tell me what happened last night. I don't know what the goal of the operation was, but it was obviously a failure. Both of our men are dead. Many people in the embassy are asking questions. Many people in Moscow are asking questions. I do not need to know what the operation was, I assume it was classified, but I need to know who killed our men," the consular representative said.

Misha looked at him blankly. "I will tell you what I saw, but you will not believe it. First, let me say it wasn't a 'who', but a 'what' that killed the men."

My meal last night left me unsatisfied. The unexpected circumstances soured my dining experience. The flesh was succulent complete with an aura of violence and evil. But it was not the prey I had expected. Very disappointing.

There was much to consider today. First, the prey was not who I sought. I only learned of this after I perused its belongings. Nikolai Draganov was the name on the passport.

Second, I rushed my attack without checking to see how many people were present. I shall have to be more patient in the future.

Third, and potentially most troubling, I was seen by law officers. Why were they there? Were they suspicious of me? No, the computer virus I sent was virtually untraceable. They must have been following the prey. Perhaps they had their own interest in the prey. I remember the smell of gun oil emanating from the van when I walked by. Yes, that must be it. Where was the prey I sought? Why was Draganov driving the prey's car? And the other one in the back seat, the fool who shot me, what was his role? Were they associates of the prey? Too many questions.

I stretch my arms over my head and feel the slight bruises from the bullet impacts. Very sloppy on my part last night. I will be more careful, as well as patient, in the future. My next hunt, a month or so from now, will be domestic beef or wild venison. I can control the cravings of the beast to an extent, but it will have to be fed at some point. I do not wish to further antagonize the police and become a focus of their attention. The hunting grounds of Philadelphia will have to be off the menu for a time.

I will consider these events over a long walk after I finish my scone. It is a lovely day. The rain has cleared the air and the sky is bright and cloudless. Perhaps when I return, I will see if Jennifer would like to have dinner this week. I can use the pretext of having information for her. Of course, I will have to research more on the prey. Very troubling, but I will not let it overshadow my day. I savor the last bite of my scone. The butter is from Ireland and is extra creamy. Delicious.

CHAPTER 7

T ERRI WAS IN THE office early. She had read all the logs related to the Schnoll residence. Nothing jumped out at her, but she wanted to talk to the agents alone and pick their brains on anything they saw that might not have seemed important at the time. The last couple of days had been rough. Putting up with the ribbing of her squad mates. Watching a case she had worked on for over a year go up in flames and set off an international incident. Questioning her own memory and sanity. But the worst of all was getting chewed out by Jim. He reminded her of her dad.

Terri's father was an FBI agent, and he had been so proud of her when she reported to Quantico. He died of cancer shortly thereafter. She remembered that, even though he was weakened from the chemotherapy, he insisted on driving with her to check in at the FBI Academy. He gave her a big hug and whispered in her ear, "Give 'em hell, kid. You're going to do great." It sure didn't feel that way now.

Terri and her father had been very close. He was steady and nurturing, tough when he needed to be, but always with a purpose. What would he tell her now? "It's going to be OK. Sometimes bad things just happen. We can't control that. All we can do is control how we react to it." That was what he had told her when he was diagnosed with cancer, and she could still hear the words in her head. She desperately wished he was sitting there with her this morning.

Inevitably, whenever she thought of her father, she thought of her mother. Terri recalled her early childhood being consumed with trying to win the approval and love of a mother who had none to give. Although Terri's mom never received an official diagnosis, her behavior was consistent with narcissism. Terri remembered that everything she did when she was a child was cast in the light of how it affected her mother. She realized early on that if she did well at something, it made her mother look good, and Mom was happy. But if she did poorly at something, her mother pointed out how bad it made her look, and she was unhappy. And for Terri, life was not good when Mom was unhappy.

She remembered vividly what her mother would say whenever Terri would cry as a child. Regardless of the situation, the woman would look down and say, "Stop crying, Theresa. You know when you cry, it makes me upset, and you don't want to make your mother upset, do you?" As a little girl, Terri didn't understand how this simple phrase encapsulated her childhood. But later in life she looked back with a discerning eye. She read about the traits of narcissistic personality disorder and the effects of narcissistic behavior on people close to someone with the disorder. It wasn't physical abuse, but it was hurtful and damaging nonetheless.

When she was ten years old, Terri's parents divorced, and her mother moved to Minnesota. But when Terri's dad passed away, her mother never even sent a card—forget about coming to the funeral. In fact, Terri wasn't sure if her mother was still alive or dead. In Terri's mind, it didn't matter. Her mother was just an unpleasant memory, a ghost.

Her father never remarried after the divorce. He always told her he was a father first, an FBI agent second, and that was all he had time for. And he made that clear to everyone in the Bureau. As an adult, Terri came to the conclusion that her father had divorced his wife to save his daughter.

Terri's mind drifted, and she wondered what her mother would say about the royal fuck-up she had unleashed last night. *'Theresa, what have you done? What will the neighbors think of me when they hear this? This rashness clearly comes from your father's side,'* she mused. That gave her a slight chuckle.

Failing Jim felt like she was failing her father. It was the look of disappointment in his eyes that hurt the most. She pulled out her badge and rubbed her thumb over it. It was the same badge her dad had carried. Remembering her father, missing him terribly in this moment, she so wanted to cry, but she would not. Not here. Not now. She sipped her coffee and willed the tears away.

She had decided to plow into work and try to get back to some kind of normal, if that was even possible. Work was always her solace.

Michael McNeill was an early riser and she hoped she could catch him before the rest of the squad rolled in. Like clockwork, he rounded the corner into the squad area at 0730.

Mike was a good agent, very diligent and smart. She asked him about the time he spent in the van sitting surveillance on the Schnoll house.

"I didn't see any gorillas in turtleneck sweaters and leather jackets, if that's what you're looking for," he replied. Mike was referencing the stereotypical Bulgarian henchman from movies, but he wasn't that far off from describing the actual hit team. Their passport photos looked like Bond villains.

"No, I didn't think you did. What was the level of street activity?"

"Pretty normal suburban stuff. Guys mowing lawns, women walking dogs. Women walking. Men walking. Women running. Men running."

"Did anything seem off with any of them? Like maybe they weren't from the neighborhood?"

"Not really, except—this is going to sound weird."

"What was it?"

"There was this one person who stopped by the van and seemed to sniff the air. Just struck me as odd."

Terri looked up from her notes, "Can you identify them?"

Marc was at the Ambler police station in a conference room. He had greased the skids by bringing in a couple of loaves of Stock's pound cake. Cops love donuts, it's true. But Marc knew that cops around Philadelphia love pound cake even more, and Stock's Bakery made the best. It's a documented fact.

A mound of traffic tickets, parking tickets, suspicious-person calls, burglaries, break-ins, motorist assists, and reports of stray dogs and lost kittens was piled up in front of him. It covered everything for the past two weeks. He started making a list of possible suspects, focusing on anyone who didn't have a home address within a five-mile radius of the township.

Detective Weaver stopped in, cradling a piece of pound cake on a paper towel. "How's it going?"

"So-so. Big pile of hay, and I'm still not sure what the needle looks like."

"I hear ya. Gotta say, I am really glad you guys are taking this double homicide federally. We'll help out anyway we can, but I don't need that kind of pressure bearing down on us."

"Don't blame you one bit. I think it's gonna get ugly. By the way, has, eh, Officer Pincheko come in yet? I think he's the last one from the shift that night I gotta talk to."

"Yeah, I think I saw him come in. He's been on nights and just switched to days today."

A few minutes later, Pincheko stuck his head in the conference room and introduced himself to Marc.

"Come on in, and please sit down. This is very informal. I just want to talk about the other night. I've been reading all your reports that you and the other patrolmen submitted. Great work, very detailed. What I'm looking for is anything that, uh, didn't rise to the level of making a report. Anything you might recall."

"It was raining heavily that night, as you know. There wasn't much happening until, well, you know."

"Yeah, all hell broke loose. I was there. Before that, did you notice anything? Anyone loitering'? Any cars out of place?"

The officer thought for a moment and pulled out his notebook. "Earlier in the evening, I had one car in the park. A blue Volvo wagon, PA tags. I spoke to the driver, and they said they were looking for a lost dog. I didn't think anything of it until now."

"About what time was that?"

"I'd say 10:30 or 10:45 p.m."

"Can you tell me what the driver looked like"

"She looked to be in her mid to late 30's, short dark hair, slim build. Very pretty. 'Bout it. Sorry I don't have more. Really didn't seem important at the time."

PART 2

CHAPTER 8

Marc and Terri met up for lunch at Pho Cali, a Vietnamese restaurant in the Chinatown area of Philadelphia. They had both agreed that any conversations about project Zebra would take place outside the office.

Terri said, "I went through all the logs again. Not surprisingly, there weren't any descriptions of any eight-footers lurking around the neighborhood. I caught McNeill when he came in this morning, though. He had one thing that jumped out. He said there was a—"

"Woman, dark hair, early 30's?" asked Marc.

"How the hell did you know that?"

"I talked to a cop at Ambler PD this morning who said there was a woman matching that description sitting in her car in the park the night of the... whatever we're calling it. I had him show me on the map where she was parked. It was directly in line with Schnoll's house and the remains of the body we found in the woods."

"Holy shit." Terri dropped her spring roll into her pho bowl.

"It's great, except it doesn't make any sense. Do we really think a woman did this?"

Terri shot him a look. "And just why the hell couldn't it be a woman? Too docile? Too weak? Too maternal?"

Marc laughed and raised his hands. "Sorry, I didn't mean to insult your gender by excluding them from the realm of serial killers out of hand," he said. "I just got a vision of a man as the doer here. Guess I was thinkin' 'horse'. My apologies."

Terri rubbed her forehead, "I'm sorry. I'm just a little tired." She hated snapping at Marc but she felt herself fraying at the edges.

"Yeah, I'm not getting much sleep, either. I mean, if we're looking for a werew—"

Terri held up her palm. "Don't say it. Don't say the 'w' word. I am not prepared to utter that word. It may be the case, but this isn't the *X-Files,* and I am not going to be Dana Scully to your Fox fucking Mulder, all right?"

Marc laughed, "Yeah we are gettin' into *X-Files* territory here." He watched Terri try to wrestle her spring roll out of her bowl of pho with her chopsticks. "You may need a fork, Ter," he suggested playfully.

She shot him a glance and speared the roll with a chopstick. "More than one way to get ahold of them."

"So where do we go next with this?" Marc asked.

"I think we talk to Dieter. He's our best—and only—shot at this point."

Dieter sat in the avocado-green chair, sipping orange juice through a paper straw in his room at the University of Pennsylvania Hospital. Though the television was on, he wasn't really watching it. He was replaying the events in his head again. He was startled when a nurse showed two visitors into his room.

"Hello, Mr. Schnoll. I'm FBI Special Agent Terri Watson. This is my partner, Detective Marc Peterson. We'd like to ask you a few questions about the other night. May we sit down?"

Dieter nodded. Terri and Marc pulled over a couple of chairs and sat down.

"Thank you for talking with us. I know you have been through a lot." Terri wasn't going to go easy with Dieter. He was obviously fragile, but she was not in the mood to beat around the bush with him. "The two men who were with you in your car. Did you know them?"

Dieter shook his head.

"Did they tell you why they were driving you to your house?"

Dieter shook his head again.

Time to play her first ace. "We have identified them. They were foreign intelligence agents, either working for your client or a foreign government." She saw his expression change; a look of fear appeared in his eyes. Terri paused before she played the second ace. "We recovered some items from their briefcase that lead us to believe they intended to kill you."

Dieter's eyes went wide as he listened to Terri. He had suspected that was the case, but to have a complete stranger say it out loud was jarring. Dieter was not a man of violence. The idea that someone tried to kill him was unsettling.

"We have a duty to inform you that we believe your life continues to be in danger. Do you have any reason to think that someone would want you dead?"

Dieter shook his head, but his expression belied the gesture.

Terri continued, "Mr. Schnoll, I'm going to be frank with you. We know a lot about you and your business dealings. We know that you have been engaged by numerous people on the wrong side of the law. We are offering to help keep you safe, but you must be honest with us. Do you understand?"

Dieter nodded.

"We would like to have you help us with our investigations into some of these people. I don't think I'm exaggerating when I say that we are probably your only lifeline at this point. When the people who wanted you dead the other night find out you are still alive, they <u>will</u> be back. If you work with us, we will do everything we can do to keep you safe. Will you help us?"

Dieter took another sip of his juice, set it down, breathed deeply, and said, "Yes." He broke quickly.

"Very good. Mr. Schnoll—"

"You may call me Dieter."

Terri reached out and took Dieter's hand. "Thank you, Dieter. Now, who were you having dinner with that night?"

"Sergey Rostovich."

"He wasn't the proposed client, was he?"

"No."

"Who was?"

"Konstantin Kretzky." Dieter shivered when he said the name.

Terri was satisfied that Dieter was now telling them the truth. The trick she always followed during an interview was to ask many questions she already knew the answer to. It was a way for her to gauge the truthfulness of the subject. She could read nonverbal cues pretty well and could usually tell when people shifted from truthfulness to deceit. Dieter was onboard as of now. And even if he changed his mind later, it would be easier to get him back on the straight and narrow.

"Thank you, Dieter. I know you're tired. We will go into more detail on the areas you can help us with later, maybe in a day or two. But I also want to ask you about what happened at your house that night."

Dieter closed his eyes and looked down. "I cannot tell you what I saw. You told me to be honest with you, but you will think I am lying or crazy."

Marc leaned in, "Dieter, we were there too. You may not remember, but Agent Watson and I were there."

Dieter looked up. "Then you saw it, too. The wolf."

I am tempted to bite her fingers off at the knuckle. I am used to pain, especially dental pain, during my transformation. But having this sausage-fingered woman rummaging in my mouth with whirring tools and sharp hooks is very unpleasant. Finally, the cleaning is complete and the doctor of dentistry comes in.

"Everything looks pretty good. No cavities. In fact, you are blessed with fantastic teeth. I don't see any wear on them. Remarkable. You clearly take very good care of them. Now, are you flossing after meals?"

"I do try, Doctor, but there are times I eat very late and may not have floss with me."

"Completely understandable. Just try to floss when you can. See you in six months."

I think to myself, *Not If I see you or your tormenter on the street first; it will be a very bad day for you.* But I smile and say thank you instead.

I leave the office and enter the street. It is 4 p.m., and I am to meet Jennifer for a drink. I look forward to seeing her.

The walk to the bar is quite pleasant. Despite the tempting odors of the city in the summer, I am able to focus on the warm sunshine on my face. Hidden behind my sunglasses, I take in the people around me. I like the anonymity of the city: no faux pleasantries to exchange, minimal eye contact. I am a predator mingling with my prey, and they have no idea. As with flocks of birds and great schools of fish, there's a degree of safety in numbers. A lone predator has to single out its prey from the group. They are fortunate that I am very selective.

I arrive at the bar early, but a crowd is already forming: local office workers—some young, some old—a few couples, and the old men perched on their stools at the end of the long wooden bar who have been here since opening.

I select a high-top table near the back and watch the door.

Marc and Terri left Dieter at the hospital. They were feeling good about the interview. Convincing someone to come onboard can be a risky pitch, and there are many ways it can all go south quickly. If you approach person A for cooperation against person B (your target), A can in turn go to B and tell B that the Feds are after them, hoping that curries favor with B. Or person A can be arrogant and decide to face their fate alone—terminal bravado. They can also choose to play stupid and hope the whole thing just goes away—terminal stupidity. Preparing to pitch someone involves a bit of a guessing game combined with amateur psychology. But in this case, Marc and Terri held all the cards, and Dieter had nothing to even bluff with. Terri wasn't lying when she said they were his only hope. Getting someone to cooperate immediately after someone else has tried to kill them is generally a good plan. Throw in the added trauma of what Dieter had seen, and the thought of protection in exchange for opening his books can seem like a pretty good deal.

Dieter was now a cooperator, so he was no longer their target. He might be a target again someday; cooperators often attempted to play both sides, though the lifespan of a snitch typically isn't long in prison. But for the moment, it was all good. They hoped to use his knowledge to pry the lid off of several criminal organizations. All in all, it had been a productive day. They decided to celebrate with a drink downtown.

I see her come in, and my heart begins to beat harder. She spots me and comes over. Above the fragrances of brewed and distilled concoctions, I can smell her scent. It is heady. Then, as she removes her sunglasses, the world feels like it falls in on itself. I can feel my blood begin to boil.

"What on earth happened to you, my dear?"

"I could tell you that I walked into a door or something, but I won't lie to you Alex. I confronted him. We had a fight. I think he was high. And he hit me. He didn't even remember doing it the next day. He got so angry when I brought up the drug use. I've never seen him like that. It's getting very scary."

Jennifer continues, but I'm barely listening. A rage is building in me, and it takes every bit of self-control not to fly out of here and find him. The air suddenly feels stale, and the expansive room becomes claustrophobic. I can hear toasts being made, jokes being told, laughter, and jovial conversation. The barrage of sensory input is too much, and I want to leave.

Jennifer, my lovely Jennifer, has been hurt. This will not stand. My mind is consumed by fury and vengeance.

I try to maintain my composure as I reply. "Oh, love, I feel so bad for you. Is there anything I can do?"

"I'll be fine. I've asked so much of you already. I think I need a clean break. I honestly just want to be rid of him."

"So where is Colin now?" I ask as casually as I can, not letting any hints of my intentions slip out, though they are barely contained.

"I threw him out. He is staying at the Transcontinental Hotel, I think." She pulls her phone out and checks the tracking. "Yes, it says he is at the Transcontinental. I wonder when he'll disable this feature on his phone. Honestly, he is not very good at sneaky stuff, thank God."

From her phone I see his phone number and memorize it.

Jennifer changes the subject, and we finish our drinks over more casual conversation. I sense that she feels embarrassed and hurt. As we make our way through the growing throng of patrons toward the door, a couple enter, and I smell gun oil again. I study their faces. Yes, it is the FBI agent and the police officer from several nights ago. Of course, they do not recognize me. Or do they? Are they following me? If only I didn't have Jennifer with me, I would deal with this tonight. I wait for her Uber to arrive. Then, as I think about it, I realize that it's good that Jennifer is here. There are too many people now, and I cannot afford to be rash again. Plus, I have an appointment at the Transcontinental that I very much want to keep.

Before Jennifer gets into the Uber, she takes my hand and kisses me on the lips. The spontaneity of the moment catches me off guard. I feel my face flush as I inhale all the aromas I can get. I want to remember every detail of this moment. It has been so long since I have been touched or kissed tenderly. My mind is suddenly cluttered. It clears as I watch Jennifer driven away. I refocus and start to walk toward the Transcontinental Hotel.

"That was some fancy work today, partner, getting Dieter onboard with Team America at the first meeting." Marc was legitimately impressed. Convincing someone to turn on their former life is not an easy process. Often, it takes several meetings and a fair amount of arm twisting.

"Sometimes the program sells itself. Timing is everything. A week ago, he would have told us to piss off. Today, he knows he's a hunted animal. We really are his only refuge at this point."

"What about his family? Are they in danger?" Marc asked.

"Possibly. The bad guys sent a pretty strong message that they want him dead, for whatever reason. I imagine that when they learn he's still alive, if they don't know already, they will do everything they can to get to him. Going after his family would be a huge risk on their part, but it could be really effective. I'll reach out to our guys in Bern and give them a head's up about the attempt on his life. We'll ask for the Swiss police to provide some beefed-up protection on his family over there. We can't do much more than that to protect them overseas."

"What about bringin' 'em over here?" Marc asked, as the drinks arrived.

"We'll talk to Dieter about that. If his family is open to it, and he shows that he is producing good stuff for Uncle Sam, we can be very generous."

"And what about the…uh, other stuff? He pretty much corroborated everything we saw. I thought I heard a gunshot as we were running up to the car, which would explain that spent shell casing in the back seat. He said the Russian shot the thing at point-blank range. Then we put four more slugs into it, and we saw what that did." Marc paused. "What are we dealing with here, Ter?"

Terri looked down at the creamy head on her dark glass of stout. "I don't know. My whole life, I have focused on facts. If something can't be proven in a lab, it isn't real. But in this case, I just don't know. We were witnesses to facts and evidence that point to a conclusion flying in the face of science." She started holding fingers up as she listed what they knew.

"We have a string of dead people that don't fit into a conventional category for method of death. We have an eyewitness who saw the thing smash a car window, yank a man out, and tear him to pieces."

"After being shot at point blank range," Marc added.

"Yes, and we also saw it with our own eyes, shooting it several times before it tossed what was probably a 200-pound man over a 7-foot fence like he was a bag of trash. Then we watched it vault over that fence like it was nothing and disappear. And the only suspect we have is described as a female with dark hair who was driving a blue Volvo. I'm open to any and all suggestions at this point."

"I'm no scientist, but it seems to me that a good scientist, like a good investigator, follows the evidence wherever it leads." He took a sip of his Scotch, swirling the ice, and then continued. "Plus, if this, uh, thing's smart, and everything points to that, you might have something that science doesn't know about, partly because the thing is actively trying to *not* be discovered."

Terri thought about that for a moment. "Good point. If, and it's a big goddamn if, something like this did exist, it will do everything it can to stay hidden." Terri's mind was thinking through the implications of this train of thought.

"What if these things have been around for centuries? If they existed in the past, any references to them today would have been written off as myth or folklore. I think every culture has some type of shapeshifter legend. It hasn't been confined to any one area or religion."

Marc nodded and listened as Terri continued.

"All these old myths had religious overtones from the societies in which they emerged. But what if they were real? The people of the past would have tried to make sense of what they had seen, but couldn't explain, by associating it with religion. As those religious beliefs withered and died out, the things they were trying to explain would be lumped in with the defunct religion and written off as lore. It's the perfect cover for a creature like this."

"Anybody who even brings it up is immediately called crazy. Hell, I feel a little nutso now, just talkin' about it," Marc pointed out.

"Exactly! Anyone giving it some credibility is considered a lunatic and discounted outright," Terri said a little too loudly. She lowered her voice and continued. "So an intelligent creature that didn't want to be found could hide in plain sight."

"Like the proverbial wolf in sheep's clothing," Marc said quietly as he sipped his Scotch. "Um, you know, we can never let this get out. I mean, after I got the surveillance van stuck against the roof in the parking garage two years ago, I found that sign 'CAUTION LOW CLEARANCE (and IQ)' hangin' over my desk the next morning when I got in. Can you imagine what the squad would do if they heard of *this?*"

Terri laughed. Their squad was notorious and ruthless with jokes. If you couldn't handle it, this was not the squad for you. "Oh my God, I cannot even!"

They both sat quietly for a few minutes, sipping their drinks and mulling over the implications. Then Terri said, "I should have Dieter's forensic computer report back from the lab tomorrow. I'm going to dig into it this weekend. You're welcome to come in and join me if you want."

"As tempting as that sounds, Ter, I have my kids this weekend."

"Oh crap, I forgot. Sorry. I'll start cranking on it alone." She totally forgot that Marc was out of pocket this weekend. But she was fine going it alone and was actually looking forward to the quiet of an empty office and a couple of terabytes of data to peruse.

Marc hadn't seen his son and daughter for two weeks and was relishing their time together. He had already bought their favorite cereals (which they had polished off during their last visit), the ingredients for home-made Bolognese sauce, fresh pasta, and salad. He was planning to take them to the zoo on Sunday. David was 10, and Madelyn was 12.

The divorce had been hard on them. Harder than it had been on Beth and him. To her credit, Beth never attempted to trash-talk him to the kids, like he had heard happened in other divorces. They still idolized him, though he knew that that would likely change as the teenage years approached. He could already see Maddie getting more interested in texting her friends than playing a board game with David and him. It was normal, but it still stung.

Beth was doing all right. They talked almost every day, usually in the evening (if he wasn't working late), and they were still close. He suspected they always would be; the separation was amicable. They had both realized that they just could not be happy together, largely as a result of his job. As a new hotshot homicide detective, he was trying to make his mark in the force, so he worked crazy hours. He had a home, but he was rarely there. And even when he was there, he was exhausted and wanted to be alone. Beth had had a husband in name only. The expectation of more had been killing them both. When Beth said one day that she wanted a divorce, he agreed. They cried together that night, but they both knew it was right. The hardest part was explaining it to the kids. That was three years ago, and they had settled into a good routine since then.

Marc looked at Terri. "You ever thought about having kids? Gettin' hitched? I only ask because you gotta have a life outside of work. This job can eat you alive, Ter. You're smart as hell and one of the best investigators I've worked with, but you have to take care of yourself."

Terri looked down at her drink. "I have thought about it, but it never seems like a good time to start a relationship. It's hard to meet people outside of the office and dating one inside the office can be... complicated." Terri had attracted the attention of several single agents in the office over the years. She was very attractive, blonde with blue eyes. She had always politely but firmly put aside their requests. She had since developed a reputation for being somewhat aloof.

Marc nodded.

Terri went on, "I would love to have kids someday. I see you with yours, and it's really nice."

"Don't be fooled, they're a colossal pain in the ass, cost a ton of money, and break my heart without even tryin'. But they are also the greatest thing I've ever known. Look, I'm not telling you how to live, but think about taking care of yourself in the big picture. At some point, this job ends. We will all wake up one day and find out we are no longer a cop or an FBI agent. For people who have nothing else in their life, that is a dark, dark time."

"Noted. Thanks, partner."

Terri had always been circumspect with details of her life. The walls she built as a child were still in place. It started when her father instructed her to not tell strangers what he did for a living for security reasons. Then when her parents got divorced, she didn't want to talk about that part of her life and avoided it as well. Add the bouncing from city to city, school to school as her father's career dictated, and you wound up with what she was known to be now–a loner.

Marc finished his Scotch and got a water. Terri was just finishing her stout. "Have a good weekend with David and Maddie. I'll fill you in on what I find on the computers when I see you Monday."

"Thanks. Have fun with that."

Terri flashed a weak smile. "You know I will." She thought about what Marc had said. Spending her weekend reviewing case work was the highlight of her plans, and that was fucking pathetic. She really did need to get a life. '*Put it at the top of the list when this case is done,*' she thought.

I approach the entrance to the Transcontinental Hotel, noting the presence of security cameras. I already have my sunglasses on, but I add a scarf for good measure as I near the door. Like most higher-end hotels, the Transcontinental is well appointed, with stuffed chairs, some artwork on the walls, a vase or two, and an overly enthusiastic desk clerk. I can smell her pleasant perfume and freshly washed hair. Light classical music—Mozart—plays from speakers hidden in plastic flowers. The lobby phones are in the rear. I don't want my number on Colin's phone. That would be very careless. I call Colin's number and he picks up.

"Hello, Colin. This is Alex. Can we talk? I just left Jennifer, and there are some things you need to know."

"Is she OK?"

'*Like you care*', I think to myself. Out loud, I respond, "Yes, but very distraught. I would rather talk to you in person. I am in the lobby."

"OK, I'll be right down."

"Actually, if I can come up to your room, that would be best. I'd rather not speak in public. It's sensitive." I chuckle quietly as I think that what I have in store is definitely not for public viewing.

"Right. I understand. I will come down and get you. You need a room key to operate the lifts."

"I'll meet you at the elevators."

CHAPTER 9

T ERRI GOT INTO THE office about 8 a.m. on Saturday. It was deserted except for the switchboard operator and the duty agent, who was just getting off his overnight shift and was going over any turnover notes with his replacement. Weekend shifts in the radio room were entertaining, to say the least. The switchboard operator handled the radios, running vehicle checks, criminal background reports, and the like for anyone who needed information. The duty agent assisted in running tags, doing computer searches, and fielding telephone calls.

Everyone joked that the main number to the FBI must be prominently displayed at every in-patient mental-health facility in the surrounding area. Some callers were regulars: the mumbler, who you could not understand; the screamer, who just yelled obscenities; the Captain, who claimed to work for the government and wanted to talk about UFOs. Sometimes these individuals would call several times a night. Other calls varied, from people who suddenly realized—at 2 a.m.—that they needed to get their fingerprints taken for a job or people who had been overserved at the bar and decided to tell an agent about something they saw last month. When someone called in and said, "I've been doing some thinking," the reality was more likely to be "I've been doing some drinking." The duty agents were there just in case something real came in, which was almost never.

Each agent got scheduled for weekend duty about twice a year. It was shared pain.

Terri popped her head in the door. The outgoing agent was packing his bag and preparing to go home. "How did it go last night?" she asked.

"Eight hours of my life gone, never to be seen again and with nothing to show for it."

"In other words, normal."

"Yup."

"I'll be working in the Squad 1 area. Anyone else in?"

"No, you're it so far."

Terri found one of the standalone computers used to review files; they were not connected to any Bureau computer systems. She took a removable hard drive out of her bag. It was an exact copy of Dieter's seized computers, created by the computer forensic squad. She connected it to the standalone computer.

She started by going through Dieter's email. She compiled a list of contacts and sorted them into categories—clients, business associates, family, friends, and so on. She then searched the emails for any relevant contact names and grouped them together, revealing conversations that took place over days and weeks.

Searching for keywords like "money laundering" was useless. No criminal worth their salt would utter the words, let alone put them in writing. The communications were much more nuanced. She needed to understand the flow of the relationships first. Then she and Marc would sit with Dieter and discuss each client in detail to learn how the person acquired the income that they needed to conceal and determine the current status of the accounts.

Next, she delved into the Swiss-based emails. The server itself might be out of reach for US law enforcement, but the emails that Dieter had read and written were stored on his own computer. As expected, this was where he did the bulk of his illicit work. There would be plenty of topics of discussion with him going forward from this batch.

One email in particular caught her eye; it had been marked "Quarantine" by the forensic computer team. The email appeared to originate in Budapest, Hungary. The attachment, a résumé, apparently carried a sophisticated virus. 'This is why we use standalone computers to review these things. God knows what's on here that they didn't catch,' she thought.

Terri was startled when OGA Dave appeared suddenly in the doorway.

"Jesus, do they teach you that at The Farm?"

"I can neither confirm nor deny that I have been trained by the CIA to walk quietly," Dave said with faux sternness.

"Guess I was just engrossed in these files. Might be some stuff in here that we can share with you guys once we flesh it out. Plenty of foreign contacts, guessing some narcos and PEPs." PEPs was short for politically exposed persons. They were usually foreign politicians, government ministers, or some type of royalty. If they were using the services of one Dieter Schnoll, they were likely stealing money from somewhere. Through Schnoll, they could layer their ownership of bank accounts and evade the scrutiny their positions entailed.

"Sounds good. Keep me in the loop, if you don't mind." Dave came in and sat down. "Hey, I want to let you know that I had no inkling that there was a hit team in the country. I hope you know me well enough to believe me when I say that. I would never hold that kind of information from you guys and potentially put someone in danger."

Terri noted that Dave said "he" didn't know. It was possible that, somewhere in the Agency, someone else knew and didn't share it with him in time or decided—for operational security—not to share it at all.

"Thanks, Dave. I know."

"But I do have some background that I *can* share. You may already have most of this already, though."

"Shoot," Terri replied.

Dave opened a notebook. "Nikolai Draganov entered the US at JFK two weeks ago. Anatoly Vichin entered the US at Miami three weeks ago. Misha Popov is assigned to the Russian embassy in Washington, DC."

"Yeah, that's what we have as well. We checked their travel status and arrivals. We believe that Draganov went to the consulate office in New York two days before the attempted hit. Looks like lots of coordination."

Dave nodded. "The two Bulgarians were linked to an attempted murder in the UK a couple of years ago, too. Poisoning seemed to be their MO back then."

Terri agreed. "Apparently, they didn't want to take any chances this time. We got the report from the Bureau lab. The syringes they had with them contained some chemical agent that I can't pronounce. Would have caused a cardiac arrest that looked like natural causes to any coroner who wasn't specifically looking for it or who missed an injection bruise."

"I think I know the chemical you mean. Nasty stuff. Induces the classic 'Russian heart attack'," Dave confirmed.

"The question I have for you, Dave, is, why Dieter Schnoll? Why a government-backed assassination? I mean, yes, he's worked with a ton of dirt bags, including the Eastern European variety. But this seems a bit extreme. We'll look through everything and ask him who he thinks he pissed off at this level, but I'm scratching my head a bit on this."

"Yeah, that is the million-dollar question. With Sergey Rostovich's involvement, there is a strong likelihood that K2 was part of it."

"Right, but I mean who's the dog and who's the tail here? Was K2 setting up Schnoll on behalf of someone in the Kremlin who wanted him dead, or was he using government resources for his own hit? I'm currently leaning toward the Kremlin using K2 and Rostovich to get to Schnoll, given the level of coordination involved here: the trip to the consulate by Asshole Number 1, the use of an embassy asset for a driver, and the sophistication of the chemical agent we found. This seems to be outside of even K2's capabilities."

"I agree, Terri. This seems like a government-directed hit. They usually shy away from this stuff on US soil, but somebody powerful wants your guy dead."

"Sure looks that way. The question is, who?" Terri asked.

"Maybe the answer is in there somewhere," Dave said, pointing to the computer's external hard drive.

"I'll do my best to find it, if it is."

Dave nodded. "I know you will. I'm sure you guys already knew that Rostovich hopped a flight to Vienna that night."

"Yes, we tried to grab him, but he was gone before we could get the warrant signed."

Dave leaned back in his chair. "There has also been a lot of strange chatter overseas on this, above and beyond the normal ass-covering and deflecting. Look, I don't know what happened at Schnoll's house that night—don't need to know, don't want to know. But whatever did happen there has triggered a lot of conversation within a tight circle of the Russian government."

"What kind of conversations? What circles?" Terri started to feel a pit form in her stomach.

"Medical research mostly, scientists and their handlers. This is going to sound strange, but something about 'the beast'. It's probably code for something, but damned if I know."

Terri's stomach turned. She wanted to ask more questions, but she didn't want to have to explain to Dave why she believed they weren't, in fact, speaking in code. What the hell did the Russians know about the thing she and Marc saw?

"That is odd. You're right, must be code for something." She changed the subject. "Hey, speaking of code, I have an email here that was quarantined by our guys. Some fancy virus in it. I don't know anything about this stuff. Can you take a look at the name and see if it rings a bell? The email says it's from Hungary."

Dave leaned in and looked at the screen. "Hmm. That name appears to be a piece of NSA code," He said pointing to the monitor. "This was one of the dirty little secrets that got dumped by that insider a couple of years ago. Pretty sophisticated. Maybe your guy here wasn't running a current antivirus software or maybe the virus has been tweaked to avoid them. Either way, this is a pretty capable little monster you have there. I'm not a cyber guy, but that's what it looks like to me anyway."

"Based on that assessment, I doubt the email came from Hungary, then, either."

"Good bet."

"Who wants to see a wolf t'day?" Marc asked the kids at breakfast.

David's eyes lit up over his glass of orange juice. "For real?" he asked excitedly.

"Yup. I set up a private tour for us at a wolf sanctuary."

Madelyn stirred her cereal. She really wanted to watch YouTube videos and text with her friends, but deep down, she was kinda excited too. She just didn't want to show it.

The drive to the wolf sanctuary took about 90 minutes. Once they got on the turnpike and headed west, the suburban sprawl quickly gave way to farm and forest. They talked about their summer plans. David was looking forward to meeting up with his friends at the swimming pool when he wasn't at camp. Maddie was looking forward to sleeping in and hanging out with her friends.

"How about you, Dad? What are you looking forward to this summer?" David asked.

"Eh, when you reach my age, summer ain't what it once was," Marc replied. "I'm afraid it's mostly just work with heat. But I am lookin' forward to taking you guys down the shore for a week in August."

"Awesome!"

"When in August?" Maddie asked.

"I got the house booked for the second week."

"But that's when Kaitlyn's birthday party is! It's going to be epic. I can't miss it. Everyone is going!"

"Oh, I thought your mom said that week was good. Let me know the date of the party and we'll work around it. I can drive you back for it."

"Or I could skip the shore and just stay with Mom," Maddie suggested.

"Alright. We'll see how it all shakes out." Marc was a little annoyed and hurt. Their week at the shore was becoming a tradition—or so he thought. This is nature's course, he told himself. She'll pull away from her mom and him for a number of years, but then, when she is ready, she'll come back and reestablish a relationship. At least he hoped that would be the case. All he could do was give her some space to grow and be there if she needed him. Forced family fun was a sure-fire path to resentment.

Marc pulled into the preserve and parked. They met their guide, a 60-something volunteer named Helen, near the sanctuary's entrance.

The facility was expansive, with several enclosures for rescued wolves. The enclosures were large and designed as natural habitats. It wasn't a zoo; the wolves could avoid the visitors at any time. But most were curious about the two-legged creatures gawking at them, which made everyone happy.

Helen was extremely knowledgeable about the wolves. "Here is Luca. She just came to us from Montana. Beautiful animal," Helen pointed out.

"What can you tell us about wolf behavior, like how do they act?" Marc asked as they walked toward another enclosure holding several wolves.

"Let me answer your question with a question: where do domestic dogs come from?"

"Wolves!" David yelled.

"Right. So, many of those behaviors and characteristics that we love in our pet dogs can be found in wolves," Helen said with a smile.

"Like, which behaviors?" Marc asked.

"Loyalty, for one. It's the fabric of the pack. Wolves are extremely loyal to one another. They form lifelong bonds, raise the pups collectively, and even care for the old or injured members," Helen said happily. She was enjoying this tour a great deal. "And there is some evidence to suggest that pack members go through a form of mourning process when one of their own dies. Interestingly, herding dogs that tend cattle and sheep have similar instincts as wolves. A wolf has to understand its prey, and it quickly learns how to maneuver a herd to single out the sick, weak, or young. Herding dogs use the same principles when they work."

"I never thought of that," Maddie exclaimed, revealing her enjoyment despite her best efforts.

"When we bring a dog into our families, we are establishing a pack. We want that dog to see us as part of their pack and draw on the fierce loyalty that defines a wolf pack," Helen continued.

"How 'bout hunting. Can you tell us more about how wolves might go about selecting their, eh, prey?" Marc asked, drawing a quizzical look from David.

"Well, research shows that wolves and herd animals have evolved together over thousands or even millions of years. Deer, moose, elk, and so on have developed effective countermeasures to avoid succumbing to the wolves. They have excellent hearing and smell, for example. White tail deer, in particular, are very agile, and they have sharp hooves. Elk and moose have antlers and strong legs. Because of these defenses, wolves will usually select the old or sick for predation. This, in turn, saves resources for the fittest members of the herd, which are more likely to reproduce and thus keep the herd healthy. Sometimes, wolves will take a robust and healthy animal, like if it is in deep snow and cannot run away, but generally, the culling is beneficial for the herd. The expression "You won't find a starving deer in wolf territory" rings true.

Marc considered this. Clearly, his motivations at the wolf sanctuary were not entirely for family fun today. He had one last question. "What about lone wolves? People talk about them all the time. Is there anything to it? Do they exist?"

"Well, wolves, like people, are social animals. Lone wolves do exist, but we have found that they don't tend to be alone for long; they are usually seeking a pack," Helen stated as they approached the main building. The tour was almost over. She left the group with one last thought.

"We need to ask ourselves, why have humans vilified wolves to the degree we have? All throughout history, wolves are seen as evil. In reality, they exhibit many traits we consider to be noble. After all, with no wolves, we would have no domestic dogs. So why do they trigger some deep fear inside us? Is it simply that, as early humans, they competed with us for scarce food resources, and this fear of them has persisted, even now that the competition is over? Or is there something else? Do we see ourselves in them—devoted, loving individuals, living in a complex structure, that kill to survive? If so, then perhaps that reminds us of something else about ourselves, something we may not want to look at, something primal and vicious?" Helen finished, looking at Marc. "Anyway, thank you for coming today. Be sure to stop by the gift shop on your way out."

It was Tuesday, and Terri was almost at the office when she got Marc's call. She turned around and drove to the medical examiners' office. Marc's car was already there when she pulled into the lot.

As she walked into Jerri's office, Marc handed her a Wawa coffee. God bless that man.

"Morning, Jerri. What have we got?"

"It may be nothing. I was just telling Marc that a guy came in on Monday. Cleaners at the Transcontinental Hotel found him in the bathroom of his room around 11 a.m. that day. Time of death is estimated to be between 10 p.m. Friday and 2 a.m. Saturday. Looked like a slip and fall at first."

"But…"

"But something wasn't right. He definitely had massive trauma to the back of his head. But when I looked closer, I found bruising around his neck, like someone picked him up. You can clearly see five pressure bruises: four on one side and one on the other."

Marc spoke up. "After Jer called me, I did a little checkin' with the detective on the case and took a look at the photos where the body was found. The tile on the floor, where he hit his head, was shattered."

Terri nodded. "Wow. That must have taken a lot of force."

"Yes, it did." Marc checked his notes. "The last call he got on his cell was from a lobby phone, Friday at 10:12 p.m. Security cameras recorded a woman, possibly brunette, wearing sunglasses, using a lobby phone and then meeting our victim at the elevators."

"Oh, shit. Did they try to get prints off the phone in the lobby?" Terri asked.

Marc shook his head. "Yeah, no luck there. It's a fancy hotel and the cleaning crews are very thorough. They cleaned that phone three times already before the body was discovered."

"What are the thoughts at the PD?"

"Operating theory is that he summoned a working girl, had a little fun, went to take a shower, slipped, fell, and died. End of story."

"You're not buying that any more than Jerri is, though, are you?" Terri asked.

"No, I am not."

"How long was the woman there?"

"About 50 minutes. She took the fire stairs back down to the lobby and exited. Last seen on video walking east." Marc handed her a group of stills from the cameras. It showed a woman about 5 ′10″, with a trim, athletic build, wearing a red dress and heels, a patterned scarf on her head, and sunglasses.

"How is the detective who has the case?"

"He ain't bad, but he'll look for any way to clear it that he can. He has a hefty workload, as Philadelphians continue to kill one another day and night throughout our lovely city. Look, if there is the slightest chance of this being an accident, he's going to write it up that way and move on to the pile of conventional murders waiting for him on his desk."

Terri remarked, "That might work in our favor this time." They didn't want to take a chance on bringing in someone to the party who might not be able to keep this investigation confidential. Best to let this sleeping dog lie for now. "Who is—or was—the victim?"

"Colin Miller."

Terri almost spit out her coffee. "Address?"

Marc checked his notes. "Uh, 1247 Ricketts Lane, Ambler, PA. Why?"

Terri sat back in her chair, "I think I was just reading some emails from this guy on Dieter's hard drive over the weekend."

CHAPTER 10

ST. PETERSBURG, RUSSIA

Dr. Peter Lavroski sat uncomfortably in the waiting area. The leather seat squeaked as he shifted his weight. He had been sitting for thirty minutes. He wished people valued his time as much as he did, but this was not a meeting where he could show any annoyance. He glanced up at the attractive blonde assistant. She was exactly what Konstantin liked: young, beautiful, and immodest in her dress code. He always seemed to have these women orbiting him. At last, the assistant opened the door and ushered him in.

Konstantin Kretzky was seated behind his desk. He was larger and balder than the last time Peter had met him in person, about seven years ago, at Peter's retirement from government service. He remembered that Kretzky shook his hand, congratulated him on his accomplishment, and handed him an envelope stuffed with cash. Why in God's name had he asked Peter to come meet him now?

"Dr. Lavroski, you are looking well!" The large man stood with some effort and shook his hand.

"Thank you, Mr. Kretzky. You are looking well, too."

"You are too kind, Doctor. If I look well to you, you need to have your eyes checked. I eat too much. I drink too much!" Kretzky chuckled and patted his ample belly.

"You live well, sir."

"I do indeed, sometimes too well. But enough of this. I do not wish to take too much of your time." Kretzky had had enough pleasantries. "Do you remember your project Lazarus?"

Peter blinked several times. "Of course, I recall it. It was the last project I worked on at the lab before I was moved—I mean before I moved to an administrative position." Shortly after the incident, the entire lab was shut down, demolished actually, and Peter was forced into a bureaucratic posting in Moscow. His career as a research scientist had come to a sudden and inglorious end. He lasted three years in the Moscow office before he was asked to retire. He left the scientific community as an object of curiosity and pity, the central figure in a cautionary tale of a once-promising scientist who got careless and was now disgraced.

"Yes, the circumstances of the lab's closing were truly unfortunate. Such a shame. But there is renewed interest in your work there by some scientists from Moscow."

"Why would there be renewed interest? The project was a failure. All the subjects died." Peter was getting more uncomfortable. The details of the incident usually hovered at the edge of his memory. But now they had kicked in the door and were rushing into his mind.

"Well, it seems, good doctor, that you may have declared failure prematurely."

"What do you mean?"

Kretzky pulled a cigar from his humidor and clipped the end. He ignited the tobacco with a jet lighter and pulled the smoke. "A report has found its way to me implying that the beast—you recall the beast, yes?"

Lavroski nodded silently. Of course. How could he forget the images of that creature on the security cameras—the wrecked bodies, the carnage? So much blood.

"This report implies that the beast was not in fact killed, as you stated at the time, but is still alive. A government man claims he saw it kill two of our men in Pennsylvania. Now how could that be?"

Peter began to sweat. He could feel a cold trickle running down his back, and he tried to calm his voice before he spoke. "I was told by our head of security at the time, that the...the subject was located a day later in a village and terminated. A burned body was returned to the lab. I had no way of knowing if he was telling me a lie."

"And yet, here we are." Kretzky held his hands open wide. "I took you at your word when you said that this had been cleaned up. But now I am having questions asked by idiots in the Kremlin who have heard the rumors of your fuck-up."

"Maybe it is a mistake. Maybe there is another."

"Perhaps, but it seems highly unlikely, doesn't it?"

Peter hung his head. It did indeed seem very unlikely.

Kretzky pulled on the cigar again, blowing out the smoke before he spoke. "So, at the direction of the government, we have recovered all the files from the storage facility and turned them over. As of today, you are recalled as a special consultant to the government team researching your, uh, missing pet. You will work with Dr. Demikhov, the team lead. Svetlana will provide you with the details. You will report to me on their progress and plans, as before. Do you understand?"

For just a second, Peter thought about protesting, but he wisely decided against it. He felt nauseated as the blonde assistant handed him a manila envelope and showed him out of the office. He had tried for ten years to forget the events of that night and now he was being forced to relive it all. What had he done to deserve this, he wondered. But instinctively, he knew the answer. He had sold his soul and turned his back on any principles he had held decades ago. The ripples from those decisions continued to wash over him and, he feared, would eventually drown him.

CHAPTER II

MILLER RESIDENCE, AMBLER PA

DETECTIVE SIMMONS AND HIS partner, Detective Russel, parked on the street in front of the Miller home. It wasn't a mansion, but it wasn't insignificant, either. The large red-brick colonial had an attached garage with three bays. Simmons saw no cars in the driveway and guessed, given the immaculately manicured lawn and gardens, that the Millers kept things in good enough order to actually fit their cars in the garage. Unlike his own home, where the small garage was used to contain overspill from all the crap in his basement. God, how he hated people like this.

They rang the doorbell and were soon warmly greeted by Jennifer Miller. They had both looked at her driver's license photo before arriving, but it did not do her justice. She looked radiant, despite the fading black eye she'd tried to conceal with makeup. She welcomed them into the sitting room and offered them something to drink. They accepted some coffee, which she brought out on a tray. (A tray, really? Who does that anymore?)

"Thank you for meeting with us today, Dr. Miller," Simmons started.

"Please, call me Jennifer. How can I help you?"

Russel took a sip of his coffee and set it on the table. He began taking notes as Simmons talked.

"As I mentioned on the phone, we are looking into the death of your husband."

Jennifer's pleasant smile disappeared from her face. "Yes, of course. I'm still in a bit of shock. It doesn't seem real, but anything I can do to help, I will."

"Thank you. Now, first off, why was your husband staying at the hotel?"

"We were having some issues, marital issues. He'd been there a few days while we were sorting things out."

"I see," Simmons said, as Russel jotted on his pad.

"These issues, were they related to your eye?" He said, nodding toward her yellowing bruise.

"This?" she asked, pointing to her eye. "No, not at all. I was unloading groceries from the store and left a cabinet door open and caught myself," she said with a laugh. "No, our issues were of a different nature." She looked Simmons in the eye as she spoke. *Just ordinary husband and wife issues. Nothing bad,'* she thought to herself.

"Just ordinary husband and wife stuff?" he asked.

"Yes, that's it," she agreed, smiling slightly.

"OK, I have to ask, where were you the night he died, Friday?"

"I had drinks in the city with a coworker, Alex. We were at that old bar near City Hall."

"McGillin's?"

"Yes, I believe that was the place."

Russel looked up, "Very good place for a drink."

"Yes, it is. I have a credit card receipt from there," she said as she placed the small paper slip on the table. "I left there and caught an Uber home. I spent the rest of the night here," she stated as she intently watched Russel writing his notes. *'It was only a co-worker. There is no reason to look at that any further,'* she thought.

Simmons didn't see any reason to follow up on her alibi. It was drinks with a coworker and she had receipts.

"Can you think of anyone who might have wished your husband harm?" Simmons asked.

"I honestly cannot think of anyone. He was such a wonderful man. Everyone who ever met him enjoyed being around him. It is such a shock. I just feel it is my fault, this horrible accident," she said convincingly, with a hint of tears. *'It was all just a terrible accident',* she thought as she stared at Simmons.

Simmons stared down at his folder. The CCTV stills of the woman in the lobby of the hotel stared back at him; likely a high-end call girl summoned by Colin Miller. He glanced up and was initially startled when he saw she was staring at him. It felt like her eyes were peering into his soul. Suddenly his head felt foggy and he felt a strange warmness toward her. He couldn't place it, but he believed her and–*liked* her. Definitely an accident. There was no point showing her these photos. She had already admitted that they were having marital trouble. There was no foul play here. The whole thing was an unfortunate accident. She had been through enough, he decided, and there was no reason to hurt this wonderful woman further. He closed the folder.

As they drove back to Philadelphia, Detective Russel reviewed his notes. "Seems like an accidental death to me."

Simmons glanced at him as he approached a red light. "Yeah, I think we can put this one to bed. I'll tell you what, if I wasn't married, I'd be giving that woman a call. I think she was giving me a vibe."

Russel laughed and said, "What are you talking about? She was into me!"

"Who are we kidding, she is way out of both our leagues," Simmons said with a shake of his head.

"Yeah, she probably isn't looking for a balding, middle-aged cop sliding into his pension years. But you never know!"

Terri walked into Marc's cubicle. "Do you know how much Colin Miller was worth?" she asked. His death had been ruled an accident by the police, but Terri and Marc were pursuing their own investigative ends. She had just returned from asking Dieter about his former clients, Colin and Jennifer. Dieter believed that Colin made the bulk of his $35 million when he sold a software company several years back. The cash portion was held in a Swiss bank connected to a brokerage account. Colin did some light trading but had invested most of his wealth in several European funds. Dieter didn't believe that Colin was into any nefarious financial dealings and noted that he thought he paid his US taxes appropriately. But Dieter also admitted that he had a limited perspective.

Marc looked up. "I'm gonna say $10 million," he ventured.

"Not bad. Try tripling that, and you're in the ballpark."

"Whoa. That kinda money can definitely buy you some enemies. Also, I talked to the detective that had the case. He interviewed the wife and established that there was some sort of marital strife and that was why he was living at the Transcontinental. As expected, they are writing off his death as an unusual accident."

"What's the wife's story?"

Marc checked his folder. "Eh, Jennifer Miller. No kids. She's a tenured professor at the University of Pennsylvania. She came up clean for criminal records; nothing on her in either our system or yours. I pulled her driver's photo and registration." Marc handed the hard-copy printout to Terri. "Notice anything?" he asked with a grin.

"Son of a bitch. Slim brunette with a blue Volvo wagon registered to her. I'll start a full work up right away."

Within an hour, Terri had gathered a substantial amount of intelligence on Jennifer Miller by searching public records. Jennifer Wysocki was born in Maine and is now 35 years old. Her Social Security number cross-checked to Maine as well. Her parents (now deceased) were Polish immigrants, and she has no known siblings. She graduated from Smith College and then received her master's and her doctorate from the University of Vermont. She is currently a professor in the history department of the University of Pennsylvania.

She and Colin had married seven years ago, and they owned a house in Ambler, on the Main Line, an affluent area named for the train line that ran into Philadelphia. The Main Line was an old-money suburban area of the city, back when there was a lot of old money in Philadelphia. For example, Grace Kelly, who ultimately married the Prince of Monaco, grew up on the Main Line. Though the golden age of Philadelphia wealth had come and gone, it was still one of the most exclusive areas to live in—if you had sufficient means.

Overall, there was nothing remarkable about Jennifer's background. What was remarkable was that this highly educated woman was now linked to several murders.

Marc and Terri decided to discuss their investigation outside the office, so they headed out to Khyber Pass, a small restaurant and bar that had some of the best Louisiana cuisine in the city. It was also only a short walk from the FBI office and was loud enough that they could go over case work and not have to worry about anyone listening. Even so, they sat at a back table and spoke in hushed tones as the tattooed server brought their order of cornbread and bowls of jambalaya.

Terri started first. "OK, let's lay this out. We have an email to Dieter from Colin describing marriage issues and inquiring about hiding assets."

"Marital strife confirmed by the homicide detective's interview," Marc added.

"Right. We have the attack at Dieter's house that neither of us believe was random. Dieter confirmed that Colin and Jennifer were clients."

Marc nodded as Terri continued.

"We have police interaction with a female in the vicinity of the attack who had dark hair and was driving a blue Volvo. The police said she was parked on the other side of the wooded area behind Dieter's house. It is a direct line from the house through the recovered remains of one of our dead Bulgarians and where that blue Volvo was parked."

"And we have a blue Volvo registered to one Jennifer Miller, who happens to be a brunette," Marc added.

"Exactly. Then, a few days later, Jennifer's husband has either a nasty slip-and-fall or a grabbed-by-the-neck-and-head-smashed-into-the-floor incident—take your pick. Either way, she is tied to both incidents through relationships. What was her alibi for the night of Colin's death?"

Marc took out his notebook. "Uh, says she had drinks with a coworker, Alex, last name not given, at McGillan's. Christ, we may have just missed her there. Anyway, she had receipts from the bar that matched up with her story. Then she gets an Uber home and stays there the rest of the night."

"Not exactly an airtight alibi," Terri offered.

"The detective thought it was tight enough and didn't follow up on any more details. Like I said before, he was looking to clear this one quickly and move on. Accidental death."

"She had plenty of time to get home, get in her car, drive to Philadelphia, park a few blocks from the Transcontinental Hotel, do her business, and get home again. Also, if you look where she lives, it isn't that far to Dieter's house either."

"And you got upwards of $35 million in motive," Marc pointed out.

"As you said, that kind of money can buy a lot of enemies. So, if we run this out, we have Jennifer, a hard-working professor by day and bloodthirsty killer on occasion. Killing her husband for money after he threatens to divorce her. It's flimsy, but there is a connection." Terri leaned back in her chair. "I can't believe we're even having this conversation. It's nuts."

"It is that. Do we really believe Jennifer Miller is a... you know?"

"We don't know that. What we do know is that she is our most promising lead." Terri was appreciative that Marc didn't say the "w" word. So why the attack at Dieter's house? I can't believe she was there for the hit team. There's no way she would have known about that. Dieter must have been the target."

"Maybe just to clear up loose ends? Maybe she knew Dieter was on notice from Colin about problems with the marriage. If she was planning on taking out her husband, maybe she didn't want Dieter bringing up those issues," Marc suggested.

"It's thin as hell, but it's the best we have. Let's spot-check surveil Jennifer. We have her license plate and her address. Let's just see if we can pick her up doing anything... odd."

"You mean like eatin' a neighbor or somethin'?" Marc asked with a grin.

"Yeah, that would fall into the odd category," Terri replied with a laugh, glad for a little levity, dark as it was. "In the meantime, I'll continue to debrief Dieter on his other client list, hopefully ones that aren't dead. That'll keep the boss happy." Terri paused. "You know, these debriefings of Dieter and the follow-up investigations are going to quickly become all-consuming. There's enough work here for a full squad. No way can we keep up with it and continue to run this other stuff down. I think we'll need to bring someone on board to help. But only on the Dieter piece. Not Project Zebra."

"You got someone in mind?"

"Sarah Holmes, from SOG, just transferred over to the squad. She was an analyst for several years before getting into a new-agent class at Quantico. She seems really sharp and eager to dig in. I'll talk to Jim, if you're cool with it, and see if we can't get her detailed over to us to help on the Dieter investigation."

"She was in the restaurant with Sergey and Dieter that night, wasn't she?" Marc asked.

"Yes. She's done some good work."

"I'm good with that. Um, we're gonna have to tell Dieter to keep the, uh, wolf talk on the down-low when Sarah is involved, though."

"Absolutely."

I have not yet decided whether to have beef or venison for my meal this weekend, so I take a trip to Hershey, Pennsylvania. The sweet smell of cocoa from the candy works is overpowering, and I do not really care for it. I am not a fan of artificially sweet things. But there is a thrill park here with lots of tourists. It is very easy for me to blend in.

I have been here before to dine, sampling cattle from a nearby farm. It was satisfying, but farmers generally frown on their livestock being eaten by predators and take many precautions to discourage it. I understand. It is their livelihood, and I do not begrudge them attempting to protect their animals. Also, I do not want to kill a farmer in self-defense. I decide upon venison.

I much prefer wild prey, anyway, whether from the forest or the streets. I enjoy hunting, not just harvesting. My thoughts drift, and I consider a society in which less concern is placed on the disappearance of people from a city than the loss of an animal from a farm. Even if it works to my benefit, that is problematic. What does that say about the ethical and moral state of those people? Too philosophical for this moment. I can feel the excitement growing in anticipation of the hunt tonight.

The sun set hours ago. I have entered the forest, and it is glorious. I feel at home. I allow myself a moment to absorb the sounds of the insects and tree frogs. I can hear the faint flapping of bats' wings, as they, too, search for prey. I smell the pleasant aroma of honeysuckle, the sickly sweet smell of a decaying tree, and the myriad of other scents nature has to offer.

I leave my clothes in a pile just inside the edge of the tree line and transform. Strength surges through my limbs. As I flex them, I can feel the massive muscles ripple. My senses multiply, and my brain is more alert. I watch a raccoon move toward a creek, and I can hear the gentle running of water. You are safe tonight, small fry. I smell a white-tail stag in the distance.

I make sure to be downwind of the prey. Unlike the urban variety, these animals are constantly on alert for danger. I begin to trot in the direction of the scent. Hopping fallen logs and leaping over uneven terrain, I feel more alive than I have in months.

I pause. I can hear the animal nearby. It has heard me as well. I move slowly, listening, scanning the dark—and then I see it. It's about 60 meters away, looking at me. The breeze has not yet carried my scent to it, and it is unsure what I am. I crouch and move slowly toward it. I will not run until it does. It continues to stare at me, bewildered. Suddenly, it turns and bolts. I sprint after it, crashing through the branches. The buck is trying to make it to an area of thick undergrowth, but I close the gap. With a lunge, I am on it. I sink my claws into the ribs of the animal and bring it to the ground. It tries to regain its legs and escape, but I quickly bite into the back of its neck, ending the struggle. I take a moment to admire the creature before I eat.

CHAPTER 12

DR. PETER LAVROSKI FELT like he was being interrogated rather than assisting a colleague. He was not wrong. Dr. Vladimir Demikhov, dressed in a white lab coat, pressed him for details. "I have read *your* reports on the incident at *your* lab." Vladimir's emphasis made sure that Peter understood that he was responsible for everything that took place there. "They are amateurish, vague, and self-serving. I want you to tell me everything you did leading up to, during, and after the incident."

"You understand the serum we were working with?"

"Yes, I am familiar. I have reviewed the files recovered from storage. Apparently, it was all destroyed in the hasty and ill-advised effort to cover everything up."

"Yes, the remaining samples were incinerated. I was ordered to destroy them. I was following orders!"

"I'm certain you were, Doctor," Vladimir said with a hint of menace. "Tell me about the subjects. How were they selected?"

"They were not selected. They were provided to us. They consisted of 20 individuals, 10 male and 10 female. They were prisoners. All were determined to be in reasonably good physical health."

"What was your impression of your results?"

"Promising, initially. Of the 20 we started out with, 7 died immediately after the first administration of the serum. The remaining 13 were able to withstand it and began to show regenerative properties."

"When did you start to see problems?" Vladimir asked as he wrote notes without looking up.

"It was after the third round of dosing. The subjects began to experience psychological problems—amnesia, specifically. They did not know where they were or who they were. We created cover stories to keep them in a workable state, but the dissociation persisted and accelerated."

"What do you mean by accelerated?"

"Several of the subjects became extremely violent. At one point, two of them were passing each other in a hallway, and there was an... altercation."

Vladimir looked up. "What type of altercation?"

"The two subjects attacked each other. Afterward, I spoke to the nurses escorting them. They said there were no words exchanged between the subjects. They just lunged at each other and tore each other apart. Both died from massive blood loss."

"Go on. What happened to the rest?"

"Most died as we continued to administer the serum. We were left with three. We wanted to investigate the regenerative properties, so we conducted, uh, tests on the subjects. We hoped these tests might give us a clearer picture if the project was worthwhile continuing."

"And by tests, you mean inflicting various wounds and injuries?"

"Yes."

Vladimir scribbled in his notebook. "You may proceed. What happened to the final three subjects?"

"All the subjects recovered incredibly well from intermuscular cuts. One subject succumbed to a 7.62 mm gunshot to the chest from 10 meters. The other two recovered. The second subject succumbed to a stab wound penetrating the heart. The remaining subject recovered. The remaining subject is obviously the one in question."

"Yes, I presume that is the one we are most interested in. Was there anything remarkable about her prior to the administration of the serum?"

"No."

"Then tell me about the final day."

"The subject was very distraught. She was scheduled to receive her fifth dose of the serum. The next day she was to be exposed to various degrees of fire for more testing. Upon receiving the serum, the subject experienced an unexpected physiological change, killed several staff members, and escaped."

"Yes, the escape. I have reviewed the CCTV footage. Quite impressive. Tell me about the recovery of the subject."

"Our director of security, Colonel Dimitry Astov, set out the next day with the remainder of our security detail—approximately 15 officers, if I recall correctly. I cautioned him that the subject was extremely dangerous, though he was well aware of that already, and I told him that she was unlikely to be killed easily by firearms. As a result, Astov and the team took phosphorus grenades and an improvised flamethrower with them. We believed they were the only means to stop the subject. The following day, Astov returned, alone, with a charred body, claiming it was the escaped subject."

"And the rest of the security detail?"

"He explained that they were killed in the fight with the subject."

"Well. Now that all appears to be called into question doesn't it? Unfortunately, Colonel Astov's whereabouts are currently unknown, so we are not able to ask him to account for his actions. The FSB is attempting to locate him as we speak."

Peter wished his own whereabouts were currently unknown, as well.

"Did you attempt to positively identify the remains?"

"No. I did not. Look, I understand there was some sort of sighting of the subject in the US. How can we be sure this is the same creature? It is possible that it is different, yes?"

"All things are possible, yes. But the only confirmed existence of this creature we know of is from *your* lab." Again, the emphasis. "It is possible that such a creature may exist in some corner of nature or that the Americans pursued a similar line of study as yours, but that would be a remarkable coincidence. I am here to determine if the burned remains you recovered were in fact the subject or if, as I believe, your incompetence has left us exposed. What did you do with the remains when you received them?"

"They were buried on the lab grounds."

"Would you be able to locate the location of the grave?"

"I am not sure. It was a long time ago, and the lab was razed to the ground. There was no marker placed to identify it."

Sarah Holmes was a fast learner, growing up as an Army brat, she had to be. She had always excelled in school and attended Princeton University majoring in computer science. When she told her parents she was joining the FBI as an analyst out of college, her retired colonel father was not too pleased. He protested that with her degree from Princeton, she could certainly find a more lucrative career. But, she pointed out that he had taught her the value of service, duty, and country. He knew it was his own damn fault and did what any father in his position would do, really the only thing he could do. Agree.

Terri hated giving her grunt work—database checks, financial data review, name checks, subpoena tracking, and all the other administrative tasks—but it was the best way to get Sarah up to speed with the investigation. To Sarah's credit, she didn't complain. She tore into each project like it was a personal challenge, and it quickly became apparent that she was a very skilled investigator.

"I've cross-checked all the client names with classified reporting. Here are all the matches and pertinent file numbers. Definite hits are tabbed in green, possible hits are tabbed in yellow. They are broken down by US citizens and foreign nationals." Sarah set the stack of folders on Terri's desk.

"That's great. We'll go over them and draw up targeting plans. First we'll work with Dieter and see what he knows about each one and whether he can fill in any blanks. Are you free this afternoon to meet with him?"

"Sure. It'll be good to meet him in person and start getting the raw intelligence." Sarah felt a slight charge of excitement.

"Good. I've reserved a small conference room. We're on for 3 p.m., so we'll pick him up at 2. I'll drive, you ride shotgun."

Dieter had been living in a rented safe house since the attempted hit. For security reasons, Terri and Marc did not want him coming into the federal building through the public entrance. The protocol was for Terri or Marc to pick him up outside his door or at a coffee shop near his new residence and drive him into the building's underground parking garage, known as the Bat Cave. It was safe, secure, and discreet. From there, he was escorted up the service elevators and brought into the FBI offices to avoid any public exposure.

If he was valuable enough to be targeted for murder by a foreign government, he was damn sure valuable enough to protect. In addition, his value as a cooperator would be greatly diminished if it were revealed that he was meeting with the FBI. Terri and Marc had spoken with him earlier and instructed him not to bring up anything remarkable about the attack he had witnessed when in the company of anyone but them.

It was 6 p.m. when Terri and Sarah began wrapping up the interview with Dieter. The conference room table was covered with folders, documents, and drawings. Dieter was a very visual person. He drew out line diagrams of the various structures for each client illustrating the layered ownership. Often, there was a trust held somewhere in the Caribbean or South Pacific. The beneficial owner held the original trust documents. Any copies of the trust documents held in the originating country, however, had no listing for the beneficial owner; the section was simply left blank. The trust structure usually showed ownership shares held by several shell companies incorporated in other countries. Those shell companies then held bank accounts in still more countries. Some of those banks had relationships with other banks that allowed them to nest the accounts in larger Swiss banks.

The byzantine structure was intended to obscure who ultimately owned the money. Individuals who went to these lengths to hide assets were doing so for a reason. Sometimes it was for simple tax evasion from whatever country they resided in. But more often, it was because they acquired the money illegally.

Dieter's artworks illustrating the financial structures were collected and put in a corresponding client folder. Sarah had taken 15 pages of handwritten notes; her hand ached from the task, and her head was spinning as she tried to grasp the intricacies of the schemes.

Dieter seemed to be energized by the discussion. He enjoyed talking about his world of money movement and ownership layering and was quite proud of it. He had the air of a professor illustrating a complex concept to students. "Moving money offshore is relatively easy. Any idiot can do it," he stated with his Swiss accent. "Next time, we will talk about the really interesting part: getting the money back onshore cleanly and without drawing attention from you FBI people and the IRS!" he said with a grin.

"Can't wait," Sarah replied, flexing her hand.

Terri noticed. "Don't worry Sarah, I'll take the notes next time. We'll try to save you from carpal tunnel syndrome. Dieter, I want to hear about the retrieval of the money offshore, but I also want to talk about Konstantin Kretzky next time. Put together anything you've heard about him. Now let's get this packed up and get you home."

Dieter's enthusiasm vaporized with the mention of Kretzky. "I will try to have some material prepared for our next meeting," he said lamely.

After dropping Dieter at the safe house, Terri and Sarah drove back to the office. "I haven't seen Marc around the office much the last week," Sarah said.

"He's been pulling some PD hours on these murders. Task force officers have two bosses, and it's hard to please them both at the same time." Marc had been running leads for the PD. But Terri didn't mention that he had also been loosely surveilling Jennifer Miller.

"Terri, what happened at Dieter's house that night? I've heard people talking about it here and there, but I want to hear it from you."

Terri paused. "What have you heard?"

"That the Russian hit team got clobbered by some maniac, possibly the same person responsible for the spate of strange killings in Philadelphia that Marc is working on."

"Well, that isn't wrong. Look, you're a young agent. You have a long career ahead of you. I don't want to pull you into something that could derail that. Let's just stick to the financial investigation right now."

Sarah pressed the issue. She didn't like being out of the loop. "Terri, I know we haven't worked together for a long time like you and Marc have, but you are going to have to trust me. I think I need to know what is really going on. I am involved in the work with Dieter—I mean, we are driving him together from a safe house right now! If someone out there still poses a threat to him, I need to know."

'Damn it, she was right,' Terri thought. She couldn't in good conscience have Sarah interacting with Dieter and not be aware of the risks. "OK," she said. "You think you really want to know?"

"I do."

"Hit Marc on his cell. See if he can meet us in the office. Tell him I'm buying Chinese takeout; that should bring him in. If you're going to hear it, you're going to hear it from both of us."

The office was deserted except for the radio room crew. Terri, Marc, and Sarah sat in the squad break room. By 9 p.m., the three of them had polished off most of the dim sum and brought Sarah up to date on Project Zebra.

"We warned you, it's as crazy a damn story as you'll ever hear," Marc said as he expertly popped the last shumai dumpling in his mouth with a pair of chopsticks.

Sarah had been mostly quiet while Terri and Marc had relayed the events of the attack at Dieter's home and the subsequent information they had gathered. She was now waiting for the punchline. "Wait, you're serious? I mean, this is some sort of 'screw with the new girl on the squad' crap, right? 'See if she'll fall for this'."

"No, we're not screwing with you Sarah," Terri countered.

Sarah shook her head. "Look, I don't know what you guys saw that night, I wasn't there, but I cannot accept this. There must be a reasonable explanation, or an unreasonable explanation that doesn't include some kind of she-beast."

"Wait here. I'll be right back." Marc got up, went to his desk, and retrieved a folder. He returned and set it on the table. "These here are the autopsy reports and photos of O'Brien, Nikolai Draganov, and Anatoly Vichin." Marc opened the folder. "You can see there wasn't much left of O'Brien." He pointed to the pictures. "Here is the leg wound that Jer showed us. Here is the wound to the back of the neck we mentioned."

Sarah wasn't a doctor, a pathologist, or a homicide detective. She felt a little nauseated looking at the graphic wound photos.

"Here is the ME report on Anatoly Vichin." Marc read out loud, "Subject has died from a massive hemorrhage caused by a large abdominal wound. Additionally, Subject has suffered a crushed trachea, which would have been a mortal wound as well." He flipped the pile of photographs to those of Vichin. "Here's your man where we found him in the driveway. He was ripped wide open. You can see, in this one here, that the window of the Land Rover is smashed."

Sarah nodded as she fought her stomach trying to flip over.

"Here are the photos of Nikolai Draganov's remains, which we found in the woods a couple of hours later. Like O'Brien, there wasn't much left. The county ME couldn't determine a clear cause of death because there wasn't enough to examine. He listed it as likely due to a massive hemorrhage from several wounds."

"OK, no mas. If you're kidding, you can claim victory. I'm officially spooked." Sarah kept waiting, actually hoping, for them to say, 'Gotcha!' and have a good laugh, but it didn't come. "Jesus Christ, you're really serious, aren't you?"

"Sorry, Sarah. Unfortunately, we're not kidding," Terri said with resignation.

"Just so I am clear, we collectively now believe there is some kind of a werew—"

Marc cut her off. "Eh, hold it. Don't say the "w" word. Ter doesn't like it."

Terri laughed, "He's right. I won't let him say it out loud, but yes, that is essentially what we, the two of us and Jerri, now believe."

Sarah nodded slowly. "Ok, I'm not ready to be fully included in that group but I am leaning that way. So where do we go from here?"

Terri started, "Well, we have to make a few assumptions. Mrs. Miller is the best lead we have. If she is the doer in these attacks, it seems unlikely to me that she suddenly developed a taste for fresh flesh. She may have done this elsewhere. I think we should take a look at her address history and check for any reports of odd deaths, missing persons—anything that might tie in with our current MO. Sarah, I would like you to tackle that piece. Marc and I will try to keep some eyes on Jennifer Miller as much as we can. If anyone gets anything interesting, give a call to the others. No text messages. We are going to have to keep this off-book, obviously."

Sarah and Marc looked at each other. Terri had obviously been thinking about this, a lot.

CHAPTER 13

T HE OLD ADAGE STATES that it's better to be lucky than good any day. The corollary to that saying is that hard work creates luck. The next morning, as Marc drove past Jennifer Miller's house, he hoped the hours they had been pouring into this case might translate into some luck.

It did. He saw Jennifer pulling out of her driveway. Her powder-blue Volvo wagon slowly maneuvered the streets and highways to a Volvo dealership. He stayed back several car lengths and allowed vehicles to get in-between them as they drove. When he saw her pull into the dealership, he stopped on the street. He watched as she pulled up to the service area doors, parked, and walked in. A short while later, she emerged from the lobby and stood on the sidewalk; it looked like she was talking on her cellphone. He took out his notebook and jotted down the activities and times.

As he looked up from his notebook, he saw a darker-colored blue Volvo wagon with PA tags drive past him and pull into the lot. He glanced over and caught a glimpse of the driver. She was an attractive brunette with expensive-looking sunglasses. Something seemed familiar to him, but he couldn't place it. The Volvo pulled into the lot and stopped in front of Jennifer. He watched as she walked to the passenger door and climbed in. He couldn't be sure, but he thought Jennifer leaned over and gave the driver a kiss.

He followed the women into Philadelphia. The car turned west on Market Street and parked in a lot at the University of Pennsylvania. He saw them get out of the car and start walking toward a red-brick building. The driver was about 5'10', a little taller than Jennifer. She was still wearing her sunglasses as she walked across the parking lot.

And then it hit him.

"Ter, I need you to run a tag for me. I'll be at the office in 30 minutes. I'll fill you and Sarah in when I get there."

After parking, Marc called Terri and asked her to meet him in Old City with Sarah at the usual coffee shop. He also asked her to bring the registration and driver's-license information from the tag he called about, as well as the security camera footage from the Transcontinental Hotel lobby. He was seated at an outdoor table when they arrived and had taken the liberty of ordering them coffees. Terri could see in his eyes that he was excited.

Sarah handed the folder to Marc. He skimmed the contents and set it on the table. The photo of Alexandra Stepanova stared back at him. "I think we've been on the wrong person." He pointed to the photo. "I saw this woman here pick up your girl, Jennifer, at the Volvo dealership and drive her to UPenn. She caught my attention because she was driving a blue Volvo."

"Look guys, I know I'm new to this case, and I don't know how many brunettes drive blue Volvo wagons in the Philadelphia metropolitan area, but there are probably more than two," Sarah pointed out.

"Yeah, but she was wearing these sunglasses." Marc pointed to the Transcontinental lobby picture. "I'm sure it was her."

Terri looked at the photo and information on the license and compared everything with the Transcontinental stills. It certainly was a possibility. "What do we think her connection is to all this?'

"Don't know, but if I hada guess, I'd say some sort of love triangle." Marc's experience had taught him that passion was a powerful emotion and could drive people to kill as easily as anger.

"Didn't the wife say that she had drinks at McGillan's with a coworker named Alex the night of her husband's death?" Terri asked.

"Sonofabitch, you're right!" Marc exclaimed.

Terri closed the manila folder and tucked it back into her bag. She turned to Sarah and said, "I'll run the background checks on Alexandra and get you the results. We need you to take a crack at her address history and see if we have any odd unsolved deaths."

"You got it. I've come up dry so far with any oddities in Jennifer Miller's address history."

"Still doesn't rule her out, it just doesn't rule her in."

That evening, they reconvened at Terri's condo on the Delaware river to assess what they had found. Max sat perched on top of one of the large shelves in her living room filled with books. Novels and scientific texts alike were lined up neatly in rows. Marc and Sarah sat on her sofa, and Terri pulled a chair to the coffee table between them, where all their reports were arrayed. Max jumped down delicately from his perch and walked around the three of them, tail curled up into a shepherd's hook as he rubbed his face on their legs. He was claiming them all for his own.

Terri started, reading from the reports she had run earlier in the day. "Alexandra Stepanova is a naturalized US citizen. She emigrated from Russia to New York City about ten years ago. She moved to Brighton Beach, where she lived for a couple of years—no surprise there; that neighborhood has a huge Russian immigrant population. From there, it appears she was accepted into Penn State, State College campus. She majored in History and graduated in three years with honors. From there, she attended Drexel University, right here in West Philadelphia, for her master's and doctorate. She completed them and was hired as faculty at the University of Pennsylvania, where she teaches today. She resides in a house in the 2100 block of Pine Street. No FBI history or foreign-national inquiries. When I ran her known phone numbers through our system, no suspicious foreign or domestic calls popped up, either. She's pretty clean."

"We got any information prior to her arrival in the US?" Marc asked.

"No. We are mostly blind to anything before she touched down at JFK."

"Well, I struck out with the city records as well. No police interactions. Nothing anywhere except for home sale information and vehicle registration. A model freakin' citizen," Marc said as he set his records back on the table.

Terri turned to Sarah, "What did you come up with based on the address history I gave you?"

"Well, tracking odd murders or missing people in New York City is like looking for a needle in a needle factory. Their numbers are bigger than ours, as you would expect. I couldn't tease out anything specific. But State College is much smaller, so any fatalities there would jump right out." She paused. "Zero unsolved deaths or deaths matching our suspected MO."

Marc and Terri's face fell a little on that news. They knew they were back to square one if they couldn't find a correlation.

"However, there was a story in a local paper during the time she was at State College about some cattle mutilations!" Sarah held up the article triumphantly.

"Well how do ya like that!" Marc yelled.

"You can put me in for an incentive award at your earliest convenience," Sarah informed Terri, as she handed her the article.

Terri scanned the story and read portions of it aloud: "Local Farmers Report Multiple Strange Cattle Deaths Recently. Several farmers and ranchers in the Centre County region have reported unexplained cattle deaths and mutilations over the past two years. Otherwise healthy animals have been found killed and apparently scavenged. The Penn State Veterinary School and local officials stated that the attacks appear to be predation, as the animals did not die of natural causes."

"Like I said, the dates match up to the time she was living in State College. Shortly after the publication of the story, the cattle deaths stopped," Sarah added.

"So, she's been in Philly for about five years. Why would her activities suddenly get law enforcement attention? Wouldn't we see more homicides going back further?" Terri asked.

Sarah offered a thought. "Like New York, we have a ton of missing persons—homeless people who just vanish and no one is looking for them. It's possible that she has been active here but no one noticed."

"Good point. We only got onto this caper 'cause Jer happened to catch one case, O'Brien, and got suspicious. Another examiner might have just written it off with the dog theory. I'll follow up with her and see if she can look at any old cases in her records that might match what we're looking for." Marc hesitated. Here he was getting ready to piss on everyone's Cheerios again. "Eh, this is great stuff and all, but where we goin' with it? What's our end game? If we find Alexandra is our suspect, yipee, then what?" Marc asked.

Terri had been thinking about this for a while. What was the end game? How far could they go with their investigation? They couldn't go to a prosecutor and seek a subpoena for information like telephone records or banking records. What would they tell them the investigation was related to? All advanced investigative techniques were off the table without a legal justification. They did have an open case on the attempted murder of Dieter Schnoll, but how could they explain that Alexandra was even related to it—much less a suspect? And what could they do about it if they were able to prove Alexandra was the killer? Prosecute her? *'One step at a time,'* she told herself. *'No sense getting too far down the path.'*

"That is the tricky part, isn't it?" Terri said.

"It seems we are wading into a real gray area here," Sarah confirmed.

Silence fell over the group as they each worked through the available options.

"This may sound crazy, but what about a cold interview?" Terri finally said.

"You serious?" Marc asked. "You want to just walk up, knock on her door, ask to talk to her about—Lord knows what—and eventually just confront her about being a werewolf? There, I said it!"

Terri laughed, "Well, gosh, when you put it like that, it sounds worse than it did in my head. But yes, in a nutshell, that is what I was thinking. I'm open to any and all suggestions here."

Sarah offered her thoughts. "Marc has a point. *If* she is what we kinda sorta think she is, she may not take kindly to being confronted about it."

"*If* she is what we kinda sorta think she is, we've shot her several times and we saw how well that worked. We're pretty defenseless here if she, as Sarah says, 'doesn't take kindly' to our meeting. I'm not gonna lie, I ain't interested in being on the menu," Marc responded as he sat back and folded his hands on his head.

"Good point. We have to have something to protect ourselves," Terri agreed.

"Whatya mean, like garlic cloves or a cross?" Marc asked with a little sarcasm.

"I think that's for vampires," Sarah deadpanned.

Terri thought for a moment. "What is it that she needs the most?" she asked. Then it hit her, "Anonymity."

Marc leaned forward. He was now intrigued. "Go on."

"Ok, just spitballing here. Look, if she is our girl, then it's reasonable to believe that she stopped killing cattle and shifted to some other targets because she didn't want to draw attention to herself. We can tell her that if anything happens to us, there is a full dossier on her, prepared and sitting in the hands of an agent—that would be you, Sarah. We'll also give a backup copy to Jerri, in case Sarah buys the farm too."

Sarah looked up, "Wait, what?"

"Just kidding. You won't be involved in the interview, if we do it. I think we will want to keep you as clean as possible. But I do want some redundancy in our insurance policy with Jerri as well."

"That should make her day. We might not have to worry about Alexandra; Jer might kill us herself for putting her in that spot," Marc pointed out with a laugh.

"We'll let Alexandra know that this dossier contains all the findings we have and notes that we took while interviewing her. If we go missing or wind up on the dinner table, the dossier will be sent to every three-letter government agency around and several press outlets. Her quiet existence will be over, and she will be hunted relentlessly."

Sarah nodded, "Not bad. Think it will be enough?"

"If it isn't, we'll always wish it was. Before we pull the trigger on an interview, I want to get some more surveillance on her and continue to dig deeper for records. Sarah and I will keep at that and compile the 'Oh, Shit' dossier. We want to have everything we can get before the knock and talk."

"Colin's funeral is tomorrow. I'll try to get some pics and video. Maybe we can pick something up."

"If you can get some shots of her with the sunglasses on, we can show them to her along with the Transcontinental security stills and ask her if she visited Colin Miller before he was found. Might spark some conversion."

"Christ, I hope that's all it sparks," Marc said under his breath.

CHAPTER 14

I T IS STILL DARK, and Jennifer has just left. She came over last night and let me seduce her. My head is in a fog as I have my coffee and a scone. I find it difficult to savor the tartness of the cranberries baked into the dough. It is like she has a spell on me. I replay the events in my mind. I feel satisfied—and maybe even happy. Very little in life gives me joy. I gain satisfaction from the selection and stalking of my prey. But joy and happiness? They are elusive.

Jennifer explained that she needed to get home and get ready for her husband's funeral. I will be there. I have never attended a funeral (that I can recall)—much less for a person whose death I caused.

The rites of death are strange to me. Dying is as much a part of life as birth; you cannot have one without the other. And we all die eventually. Death is as relentless and unconquerable as the tide of the ocean. You can't control it; you just have to learn to live with it. It is the dark shape that hides in the shadows, always present but unnoticed—until it comes for you.

Mourning the passing of a person seems like a waste of time. Perhaps if I lost someone I cared about, or remembered losing someone, I would feel differently. Do I still have enough humanity left to feel sad about such a loss?

Clearly the impending funeral has triggered these thoughts. I will not let them cloud the memory of the time I have spent with Jennifer. I do recognize that my musings about life and death indicate that some residual humanity still lies somewhere inside me. However, I also know that this drivel about living, being, and dying has no consequence for me or anyone else. It changes nothing.

My head begins to clear as the sun breaks over the buildings to the east. I will take a walk in the fresh morning light and remember Jennifer's soft caresses and sweet lips.

Several hours later, I find myself sitting in the back of the church. Many coworkers of Jennifer and mine are there. I greet them or nod in acknowledgement. We exchange some pleasantries, and they move on, settling in a pew several rows ahead of me. I choose to sit alone. I can hear some of their conversations; they are talking about how sad this must be for Jennifer, the shock of it, the senselessness of it all. Others question why Colin was at the Transcontinental at the time of his death and offer their ideas—in hushed tones, of course.

The priest speaks, reciting old words, written centuries before by old men, that are intended to help everyone sleep easier tonight. I do not believe in these words or the god they profess to originate from. Jennifer speaks, describing what a good man Colin was. I know these statements are for the benefit of the uninformed. Jennifer and I know the truth. There is singing, much of it off key and grating, but the organ is well tuned at least. Despite my lack of faith in the entire pageant, I enjoy the musical interludes to a degree.

At last, the ordeal concludes. I see Jennifer walking down the aisle, wearing a fitted black dress. She has tear tracks streaking her cheeks, but I don't sense any real sadness in her aura as she passes and glances at me. Outside the church, she motions for me to come over. She wants me to ride with her in the limousine to the burial. Accompanying us in the limousine is Colin's brother, John, who flew in from London for the funeral.

During the ride to the cemetery, I do not speak. I see that John is truly bereaved and shocked. He and Jennifer discuss the senselessness of the accident. In earlier conversations, I felt that Jennifer was not particularly surprised by the news of Colin's so-called accident. Did she expect this outcome? As she talks with John now, I detect that it is an act to ease his grief. Behind my sunglasses, I coolly watch the procession of vehicles pull into the cemetery.

Jennifer, John, and I get out of the car and walk to the gravesite. It is a spectacular summer day. The sun is high in a clear blue sky. The manicured grass is dark green with hundreds of stoic and solemn monuments to the dead jutting up all around. I can smell the recently cut grass. The hushed conversations of the mourners grow louder as they approach. The birds are very active and loud. There is traffic noise, but it is in the distance and reduced to a muted hum. It all seems very tranquil—as intended, perhaps. I do hear a strange faint sound, a clicking somewhere in the distance that I cannot place.

I watch as Jennifer and John stand together at the foot of the open grave. After more hollow words, the mourners line up and toss cut flowers onto the casket. I do not understand this rite, but I follow along and dutifully throw my carnation into the gaping hole. I can smell the pleasant sweetness of the flowers as they accumulate on the casket lid.

I am reminded that a luncheon follows afterward. Will this never cease?

Marc had parked about 80 yards away on the parallel road across from Colin Miller's gravesite. He had seen the area reserved for parking near the freshly dug grave and chosen his vantage point on that basis. When the limousine arrived, he focused the telescopic lens and began snapping pictures. He could see Jennifer and Alexandra step out of the black car with an unknown male. When the graveside service ended, he continued to snap pictures as everyone returned to their vehicles. He waited 30 minutes after the last car left before he, too, left the cemetery.

CHAPTER 15

RUSSIA, NEAR THE TAJIKISTAN BORDER

DIMITRY ASTOV HAD JUST finished his morning chores. He milked his goats, fed them, and changed their water. He tossed cracked grain for his handful of chickens and collected a few eggs. He didn't used to be a farmer, but he had learned how to become one over the years since he had moved here. There was a routine and a cycle to this life that required hard discipline—the one attribute from his army career that had translated to his new lifestyle. Every year, crops had to be planted at roughly the same time and then cared for properly in order to produce grain to be harvested when it was ready. Fruit trees bloomed and bore fruit according to their own rhythm. Animals were born, raised, and slaughtered on a cycle. He found that the daily, weekly, monthly, and yearly routines provided a comforting familiarity. If one did not have the discipline to do everything on the proper schedule, the crops would fail, the fruit would spoil, and the animals would sicken and die.

He had purchased this small plot with cash through his cousin after he left the security position at the lab. He had no electricity, no phone, no internet, no obvious ties to the modern world. He wanted to vanish and be forgotten, a goal that he had largely achieved.

He had a long list of things he intended to accomplish today. He was thinking about this list as he sat in the shade of his small porch and drank his midmorning tea. Then he noticed dust clouds appear on the dirt road that led to his modest home. He watched with increasing dread as the black SUVs came into greater focus. He knew who they were and why they were coming.

In a flash, his mind took him back to the lab.

Immediately after the creature escaped, he assessed the situation. Nine staff members had been killed, and seven more were wounded. His training kicked in, and he directed that the cafeteria be converted to a triage center for the wounded people. The medical personnel did what they could, but the two most severely injured died within hours. He assembled his remaining security team in the garage for a roll call. To call them a "unit" would have been an affront to any military organization that was ever fielded. They were mostly untrained, save for the three weeks of private-security contractor school they had attended when they were hired. They were taught how to write reports, do security checks, maintain access control to sensitive areas, and check the credentials of visitors. Ironically, their primary function was to prevent any unauthorized person from entering the facility, not exiting it. As for firearms training, they were taught which end of the gun was dangerous and how to pull the trigger. So, essentially, they were completely untrained in anything that would be useful now.

Only he and his number two, Pavel Yemenov, had any military training. Astov had a background in Special Forces; Yemenov had been in the Russian Navy. But again, neither experience offered much in the way of skills for the situation they were now facing.

He met with Dr. Lavroski to discuss the escaped subject. Astov had no idea what kind of work they were doing at the lab and was shocked when the doctor gave him a brief overview of what they were up against. Apparently, bullets had very little, if any, effect. This confirmed what his officer at the rear exit, who had encountered the creature, told him. The officer claimed to have stood his ground and shot the creature, to no avail. Astov initially dismissed this claim and berated the youth, but it seems that the account was true.

Dr. Lavroski suggested that intense fire was the only way to destroy the creature. With that in mind, he worked with Yemenov and some of the engineers at the lab to create a makeshift flamethrower from pressurized propane gas. He also took ten phosphorus grenades from the storeroom.

With these unproven men and unorthodox weapons, Astov set out to capture or kill the creature.

He had an idea of the general direction the creature was headed in when it left the facility, and he knew that there was a small, mostly deserted village on that route about 25 kilometers away. He decided that that was the best place to look. He would later wish he had gone somewhere else instead.

It was early evening by the time they arrived at the village in their three-vehicle convoy. Most of the homes and buildings were abandoned; there couldn't be more than four families living there. The sun was low in the sky, and the shadows were beginning to lengthen. Even in the twilight, it was obvious right away that something was not right. The dirt streets were deserted. All the doors and windows were shut tight. He approached a house that appeared to be occupied and rapped on the door, the red paint now faded and peeling. He shouted that he was from the army and demanded that someone answer. An old man opened the door, clearly shaken. He said he was glad the army was there. He said a devil had appeared last night and killed several animals. Astov asked him if he knew where the "devil" had gone, but before the man could answer, the first scream pierced the quiet evening.

More screams followed, and Astov heard a prolonged burst of automatic rifle fire accompanied by panicked shouts. The noise was coming from where the vehicles were parked. He ran toward the sounds, and when he came around the corner of a barn, he saw two officers lying on the ground. From one man's neck, a small geyser was shooting thick crimson liquid into a low arc that splashed on the dusty ground. The other one lay face down in the dirt, a dark pool forming around his head and shoulders. Yemenov had drawn his pistol and was threatening some of his men, who were trying to snatch his keys to the trucks. Yemenov and Astov knew that if the men got those keys, they'd be gone in a flash, leaving everyone else behind.

The men were wide-eyed and terrified. Astov started grabbing them, one by one, and pushing them to form a rough perimeter around the trucks. He had just positioned the fourth man when he saw something leap from the roof and land in the middle of another group of men who had huddled together near a building. The attack was fast, vicious, and efficient—a blur of camouflage uniforms, terrified shrieks, glimpses of brown fur, snarls, and snapping jaws. Astov instinctively raised his rifle but could not find a clear target. The security officer next to him was not so discerning, letting loose a sweeping barrage of fire into the mass of bodies, cutting down several of his compatriots in the process.

The creature turned from the frenzy and bounded toward the vehicles, moving unnaturally fast. Yemenov raised his pistol and got off a shot before a claw tore into him, reducing his face to a bloody mask. He dropped to his knees and toppled over on the dusty ground. The creature darted behind a truck and disappeared. The remaining security officers scattered and ran. Astov simply stood there, stunned. Over the next several minutes, he listened to the shrieking of his men as the beast ran them down and killed each one. He didn't see a point in running. He stood and waited for his turn.

At last, the screams ceased. Astov turned around slowly and was shocked to see a naked woman walking toward him. He shouldered his rifle immediately but held his fire when she raised a finger and shook her head. As she drew closer, he could see that she was covered in blood—the blood of his men—and that her short-cropped hair was matted to her head with gore.

She asked, "Are you the leader?"

He nodded.

"Are you a smart man?"

He hesitated but then nodded again.

"Then listen to me. I will spare you on one condition: that you say I am dead. Do you understand?"

"Yes."

She reached out and clasped his throat with her hand. Her grip was a vise around his neck. "If you betray me, I will find you,..." she looked down at the name on his uniform, "...D. Astov." She leaned into his face and inhaled deeply through her nose. "I will track you and kill you. I will kill everyone related to you; I will end your bloodline on this planet. Do you understand?" Her grip tightened.

"I do," he managed to croak out.

"Good. You are smart. There is a young woman in that house." She pointed to the house he had knocked at earlier. You will go into the house and find the identification papers for the young woman living there and provide them to me. I will also need clothes. I will give you five minutes before I come and break your arm."

She released him and he ran to the house. He indeed found a young woman, Alexandra Stepanova, hiding with her family. At gunpoint, she provided him with all her identification. He also took possession of a dress. He returned, winded, and handed them to the woman, who had hastily washed off the blood in a horse trough. She dressed herself, put on a pair of boots from one of the men, and retrieved a set of truck keys from Yemenov's body.

Before she climbed into one of the trucks, she turned to him and said, "Remember, D. Astov, I am now dead."

He sat for several minutes and watched the truck move down the road and then disappear into the gloom. It was dark now. He thought about the rest of his orders. There were to be no witnesses to the creature. That included civilians.

He retrieved the phosphorus grenades, collected fresh ammo clips for his rifle, and walked toward the small cluster of houses.

When the final barbarous act was done, he gathered up the burned remains of Alexandra Stepanova, placed them in the back of his truck, and started driving back to the lab.

Dimitry snapped back from the horror of that day. He watched the ominous vehicles approach and knew his past was quickly catching up with him.

He looked up at the religious ornaments and talismans hanging from the roof of his small porch, including an orthodox crucifix, a star of David, a pentagram, and a swastika. He had tried to ward off any evil that might approach his humble home. He knew that evil existed because he had seen it. But now, in reflection, he realized that the real evil had been living in his house the whole time. He had too much blood on his hands to ever be clean again. The old man had been wrong that day, a decade ago. The devil hadn't come the night before; it had arrived in a three-truck convoy.

The dust cloud bringing the FSB men was now getting closer. He walked into his house, entered his bedroom, and retrieved a box from his dresser. He took out an old photo of his wife and daughter, whom he had sent away long ago to live in England on his modest pension. He propped it up carefully on the side of the box. He then retrieved a pistol. In one fluid motion, he inserted a magazine, racked the slide, inserted the barrel into his mouth, and pulled the trigger.

CHAPTER 16

Terri, Marc, Sarah, and Jerri Williams helped themselves from two large pizza boxes on Jerri's desk. Marc had picked them up at a little place in the Italian Market. It had been a week since Marc got the photos at Colin Miller's funeral. It seemed like a good time to take inventory of where they stood.

Terri had been able to scratch out a bit more information on Alexandra Stepanova. According to her immigration records, the area in which she was born was practically a frontier area in Siberia—very harsh, unforgiving, and with very little access to formal education. How did this woman make her way to the US and become a professor at an Ivy League University? Each piece of new information seemed to lead to more questions.

Sarah had attempted to do a deep dive on the history of shapeshifters. "To avoid curious questions from anyone passing my desk, I ended up doing this research on my home computer. God only knows what's going to pop up on my Google news feed now."

She continued, "Shapeshifting is mentioned throughout human literature and folklore. The most well-known examples are of werewolves and such—sorry, Terri—from Europe and North America."

"I'm past that now, but thank you," Terri offered with a nod.

"The Navajo tribe in the US has the myth of the Skinwalkers. Greek and Roman myths are littered with references, which include animals, plants, and rays of light. The ancient Celts and Scots have them, as do the Norse. Interestingly, in Scandinavia, there is a myth about a group of she-werewolves, the Maras, that stalk humans by night. Seemed oddly relevant. Anyway, there are legends of these types of phenomena in literally every culture around the world. I had no idea until I started researching this stuff. A person could get lost in that rabbit hole for days."

Terri had been furiously taking notes as Sarah spoke. Without looking up, she offered, "There are also Judeo-Christian references. Satan took the form of a serpent, and God took the form of a burning bush. Just saying."

Sarah continued, "I decided it was best to focus on the case at hand. Lycanthropy specifically refers to a person turning into a wolf. I obviously decided to discount any research references made after the 1930s movies due to pop-culture influences. One historical reference in particular jumped out at me: The Beast of Gévaudan, in France. It's one of the best documented, and it seems to be pertinent to our situation. Between 1764 and 1767, more than 100 people were attacked by an unknown creature. The attacks were often on men and women tending flocks of sheep or herds of cattle. Several victims were discovered partially consumed. Various hunting parties attempted to kill the creature, and some claimed to have shot it with muskets. But the creature ran off, apparently uninjured.

The beast was described as wolf-like but not a wolf. Conventional theories are that it was a lion or hyena that may have escaped from a nobleman's menagerie. Others say it was a rabid wolf—a nonstarter, since none of the surviving victims contracted rabies. Contemporary accounts described it as being very large and covered in gray, brown, and reddish hair with talon-like claws. Finally, in June of 1767, a local man, Jean Chastel, shot and killed the creature, allegedly using a silver bullet."

Marc almost choked on a bite of pizza. "Seriously? That's what finally killed it?"

"Yes. Some of the documentation of the time indicates that," Sarah continued, "And, also allegedly, human remains were found inside the creature. Anyway, the attacks stopped after that, so they claimed victory and moved on."

Jerri chimed in, "Historical references are very useful. Good work, Sarah. But what are we going to do about our particular situation here and now?"

Terri and Sarah had completed the dossiers earlier that day. Hard copies were printed and supporting reports, photographs, and other material were photocopied and placed in the two large manila envelopes. Thumb drives with video statements by Terri and Marc, stating who they were interviewing and why, were included as well. The envelopes were sealed with evidence tape, and labels that read Project Zebra were affixed to the outside. Sarah retained one copy of the package locked in her desk at the FBI office. Terri handed over the other one to Jerri while explaining its contents and the plan to confront Alexandra.

"You're really going to do this?" Jerri asked, looking first at Marc and then at Terri.

"Against my better judgment, I think we are, Jer," Marc answered.

"You're just going to go ring her doorbell and ask her if she is some kind of mythical creature and hope for the best? I swear, you two have more balls than brains sometimes. If she doesn't tear your fool heads off immediately, then what? What if she tells you to fuck off? What are you going to do then?'"

"Well, first, I think going to her house would be a mistake. I think we'll call her and ask to meet in a public place. We'll put our heads together and come up with a location that has the right mix of public exposure and discreet atmosphere," Terri added. "As to what happens if she tells us to pound sand, maybe we will have at least spooked her enough for her to move on."

"Uh-huh. And if she decides to roll the dice and take you both out, that leaves young Sarah and me here to spill the beans. I knew I shouldn't ever have gotten mixed up in this," Jerri said, shaking her head.

Marc shifted uneasily in his seat. Terri saw it and knew something was eating at him.

Terri tried to ease Jerri's concerns. "Yeah, I'm sorry about that. We've tried to minimize your role in the dossier. We explain that you presented us with the information, and we drew the conclusions."

Jerri smiled. "Look, I'm just blowing off steam. Do I want to become the new poster child for *Cryptozoology Monthly?* No. Do I want to risk my professional reputation? No. Do I want to open my family up to ha-rassment and ridicule? No. Do I think we have a likely suspect and need to do something? Yes." Jerri paused, then continued, "Every decision has consequences. And doing nothing is a decision. It is the coward's path. If we do nothing, we will likely see more deaths."

"That seems right. There would be no reason for her to change her behavior or move," Sarah agreed.

Jerri continued, "I don't know about you, but the guilt of that will eat at me. Any action we take will have ramifications, and we don't know what those will be. But they have to be better than doing nothing, right? At least we will have tried."

"I agree, Jerri," Terri confirmed. Marc said nothing.

After the group broke up and Sarah left, Marc caught Terri by her car door. "Um, I don't know if I can do this, Ter," he said. "It's just hittin' me now."

Marc was no coward. Terri had known him for several years, and she had never seen him shy away from his duty. "What's getting to you?"

"I can't stop thinking about my kids. What'll happen to them if she comes after me? Or if she goes after them?"

Having a family as a law enforcement officer is always a risk, though instances of bad guys going after that family are rare. They seemed to understand that if that line were crossed, the gloves would come off. Terri thought of a story told by old timers in the Bureau who had heard it from even older timers, though its veracity had never been proven. The story was that many years before, when agents got word of a threat to another agent's family member, they essentially kidnapped the bad guy. He was handcuffed, blindfolded, and driven into the woods. There he was told that if anything happened to the family he'd threatened, he would disappear. Message delivered. No further threats to any families. It might have been just FBI lore from back in the day, but it did make for a good story.

This situation was different. There was no way to predict what Alexandra might do. She was so clearly off the charts compared with every other subject they had ever pursued, that assigning any conventional motivations to her appeared futile. And what if she really was a wild animal? A cornered beast usually doesn't react well.

But Terri had no children or close family who could be threatened.

She looked Marc in the eyes and replied, "It is dangerous, I'm not going to downplay that. This is not a normal situation, with normal actors. I get that. Honestly, in the heat of the hunt, I hadn't considered your family, Marc. I'm so sorry I didn't think of them in this equation. But I can't go in there alone. I need a partner. If you really can't do this, I understand. I can talk to Sarah."

"I don't like that either." Marc paused and rubbed his eyes. "Tell ya what, lemme think on it."

That night, when he got home, he called his ex-wife. "Beth, I got somethin' to tell you, and I need you to listen to me carefully. I am workin' on a case. The person we're going after is–really freakin' dangerous. If anything happens to me, I need you to take the kids and go. Don't tell me what plan you're thinking of, OK? Don't tell me where you might go. I just need to know that you'll do that. Also, if I ask you to go, you gotta go immediately, with the kids. No delay. Immediately."

"Marc, what the hell are you talking about? What are you working on?" Beth asked.

"I can't tell you that. I am so sorry to put you in this situation, Beth. But I wouldn't ask ya it if I didn't think it was important."

"I'm scared now."

"Yeah, I get that. We never talked about anything like this before, but I need to know you'll do it if necessary."

"Jesus. OK, If I had to, I suppose I could take them to—"

"Don't tell me! I don't wanna know what you're thinking. If I don't know, I can't say." Beth went silent at the other end of the line. He needed to comfort her. "Look, I'm sure it'll work out fine, and I'm just being an overly cautious idiot."

When the call ended, he stared up at the ceiling. How the hell did it get to this? He couldn't tell if he had fully reassured Beth, but she had agreed to get the kids out of the area if called upon. And he'd needed to know that before agreeing to confront Alexandra with Terri. Seriously, what the hell were they getting into?

PART 3

CHAPTER 17

Terri and Marc sat at a back table in Scarpetta, an Italian restaurant on Rittenhouse Square. It was adjacent to the Rittenhouse Hotel and offered an unexpectedly private setting in a very busy public area. They tried to appear calm as they sipped water waiting for their invited guest to appear.

At exactly 1 p.m., Alexandra walked through the door. She wore a sleeveless forest-green dress that ended at her knees. Her thick, dark hair was cut fashionably short. She removed her sunglasses and scanned the room intensely with her piercing green eyes. Her 5'10" stature gave her a sense of almost regal sophistication that attracted the attention of several patrons and service staff as she paused in the entryway.

Terri spotted her and started to motion her over to their table, but Alexandra was already striding toward them. It was as if she recognized them.

As she approached the table, Marc and Terri rose to shake her hand. Alexandra did not return the gesture, and they awkwardly returned their hands to their sides.

"Thank you for meeting us today, Professor Stepanova."

"Please call me Alex. It is not every day that one is invited to lunch by the FBI. I must admit, I am a little curious about why you would like to speak to me," she said with a slight Russian accent as she sat down.

Terri and Marc each produced their credentials. "I am Special Agent Terri Watson, and this is my partner, Detective Marc Peterson. As I said on the phone, we're hoping you can help us with a particular matter."

"Certainly. My afternoon is free, and my time is yours," she offered with a cool smile that did not reach her eyes. Marc couldn't help but notice that her teeth were the whitest he had ever seen.

"Thank you for that, Alex. Would you like to order anything to eat or drink before we get started?" Terri offered.

"Yes, I will have an iced tea."

Terri summoned the waiter and ordered three iced teas. Marc ordered an appetizer of salamis, flat bread, and cheeses for the group as well. Another server dropped off an assortment of fresh bread and olive oil.

Terri started. "We would like to talk to you about Colin Miller."

Alex casually tore off a piece of bread and dipped it in the seasoned olive oil, letting it soak. "What would you like to know?"

"How well did you know him?"

"He was the husband of a friend of mine. I did not know him otherwise and only met him a handful of times."

"Did you see him on the night of his death?" Terri asked. "That would have been last Friday."

Alex took a bite of the bread, appearing to savor the flavor as she fixed her eyes on Terri. "I was told the investigation into his death had concluded, and that it was a tragic accident."

"That was not my question. Did you see him that night?" Terri pressed.

Alex again gave a slight smile and took a sip of her tea. "No. I had drinks that night with his wife, Jennifer."

Marc opened a folder and retrieved the photo from the Transcontinental Hotel security camera. He slid it across the table to Alex. "This was taken on the night he died. The person in this photo had the last known interaction with Mr. Miller before his body was discovered."

Terri leaned over and pretended to examine the photo, "It certainly appears to be you, doesn't it?"

Alex said nothing.

Marc retrieved another photo, this one of Alex and Jennifer at the cemetery. "Now, here you are with Mrs. Miller, at Mr. Miller's burial." He placed it next to the previous picture.

Terri again leaned over the table and looked at the photos side-by-side. "The resemblance is striking, wouldn't you say?"

Alex glanced at the pictures, then at Terri and Marc. "Well, you do seem to enjoy—what is the expression?—'show and tell', don't you?" Alex sat back in the booth and folded her hands together in front of her chest, steepling her index fingers toward the ceiling. Staring at Terri, she said, "Let me tell you what I think from my perspective, may I?"

Terri nodded.

"If you are trying to implicate me somehow in the death of Colin, as it appears you are, you have a distinct and obvious lack of evidence, don't you? These photographs will prove nothing."

"I wouldn't be too sure of that. Let me ask you another question. Do you know Dieter Schnoll?"

"No, I do not."

Marc decided to bluff. "You know, Alex, your car was spotted in the vicinity of the killings that night at Schnoll's house." He watched as her demeanor changed slightly. Her confidence seemed to waiver. He had hit a nerve.

Terri saw it as well. She leaned in and looked directly at Alex, "You *do* recognize us, don't you?"

Alex unclasped her hands and set them on her lap. She glanced down at the table and then back up, focusing her steely gaze on Terri. "I feel there is a question you would like to ask me, but you haven't the courage. Am I right, Special Agent Terri Watson?" Her tone was almost playful, but it had a strong undercurrent of menace.

Terri was a little rattled by this. When she and Marc had role-played how this interview might turn out, "go ahead, ask me if I'm a lycanthrope" was not one of the options either of them had envisioned.

"Before we go further, I want you to know, Alex, that we have prepared an evidence package pointing to you. If anything happens to either of us or to our families, the people holding this package will distribute it to multiple government agencies, news outlets, and social-media sites." Terri played her only ace: "You will not have a moment of peace if we are harmed." She now prayed that that card would be enough.

After a moment of silence, Alex smiled broadly and clapped her hands together. "Well, this is getting very interesting now, isn't it? It seems we are at a standoff. I cannot harm you unless I am willing to face much scrutiny and be hounded by dogs. You cannot charge me because you have no evidence that anyone will believe. How exciting. I must admit, this was not how I thought this would go. You are very surprising, both of you."

Alex continued. "I will also tell you both that I know you are afraid of me." With that, Alex leaned in and sniffed the air deeply. "I know the smell of fear. And yet you sit here across from me. How admirable. I know many in your positions who would have turned away long ago. So, do you still have the courage to ask your question, Special Agent?"

Terri looked at Marc, who gave her a slight shrug. She turned back to Alex and asked the question.

I knew the question they wanted to ask. When I said I admired them, I meant it. Despite the fear running down their spines, this agent and police officer remained in place, striving to do their jobs. They didn't ask for payoffs to remain silent, as I thought they might. In my home country, or at least the country I lived in before, that most certainly would have happened.

"I think you already know the answer, don't you, Special Agent Watson?" Strangely, Alex felt a sense of... what? Relief? For years, she had borne this secret life alone. No outlet. No release. It felt liberating to at last be able to open up with someone.

Terri and Marc were now in unknown territory. Terri struggled to find words and form a coherent question. "Um, OK, so—you're OK if we talk about this?"

"As I see it, we are in a neutral status. I can tell you anything I wish to tell you and you are powerless to bring charges against me. Who in their right mind would ever believe it, right? You can ask me anything you like, gain any information you want, but cannot use it. I, in turn, cannot harm you because I will be exposed. You have set up a very nice scenario,

Agent Watson and Detective Peterson. Kudos." Alex seemed extremely engaged, almost giddy. "So, where should we begin?"

Terri defaulted to her training. Start with the background, establish a basis. "Why don't you tell us where you're from?"

Alex's brow furrowed. "That question is harder than it would seem. I can tell you only as far as I remember. I have no recollection of anything before I became... what sits before you today. I know I came from Russia, and I speak Russian, among several other languages. But I do not know if I was born there, who my parents were, if I have any siblings. Nothing."

Marc gave a quizzical look, "Whatya mean, like you got amnesia?"

"Of a sort. The first thing I remember is waking in a room in a facility. I was told I had been in an accident and given a drug of some type." Alex relayed the events of her origin, sparing some of the details of her escape, saying only that she made her way out of the facility and into the wilderness.

"What was the name of the facility?"

"Novaya Zhizn."

Something in that name sounded familiar to Terri, but she didn't react. "Tell us more about this place. Do you remember any names, where it is—is there anything at all you can remember?" She and Marc listened intently and took notes as Alex relayed all she knew about the lab. Terri looked up from her writing. "And that was the first time you recall the... transformation, as you call it?"

"Yes."

"So, you don't remember anything prior to that day?" Terri asked.

Alex looked perturbed. "I have memories from before, but they aren't mine. I recall scenes. I assume they are from others of my line that came before. It is jumbled and difficult to put into words. They are like dreams;

if I focus my attention on them, they evaporate." Alex explained some of the memories she had.

Terri and Marc were quickly sailing deeper into uncharted waters now. They each had talked to people over the years who claimed all sorts of special attributes: clairvoyance, ESP, time travel, prior lives. It came with the job. Normally, they would say a kind word to the person, explain that they would file the report, and walk away. This was the first time they believed the claims of such a person.

"This is not my birth name. I would like to know what I was before. I have a curiosity," Alex concluded.

Terri took note of this, underlining it in her notes. "I understand. Having no past can leave one feeling untethered," she said with a soft tone.

Alex studied Terri for a moment. Untethered. What an interesting concept. There was something about this woman that made her feel at ease, as if she really was trying to get to know her. Was it simply a ploy or was it real compassion? There was more to this person than met the eye, she suspected. She inhaled deeply. The pleasant aroma of the food in the restaurant filled her nostrils. There was also the soap and shampoo that Terri and Marc had used this morning. And the gun lubricating oil from their pistols, discreetly concealed beneath their jackets. Those scents were all to be expected. But there was also something unexpected; something familiar that she couldn't place.

Marc broke the silence. "So, um, are you the only one, you know, of your kind or are there others?"

"I am the only one I have encountered like me. That doesn't mean there aren't more, just that I have not found any."

"How do ya, eh... select your targets?"

Alex grinned, "Haven't you figured that out, Detective?"

"Well, most of 'em appear to have some sorta criminal element, with eh, violent tendencies."

"Most? If you look closely, you will find that they were all bad actors." Alex seemed pleased with herself as she continued. "In the wild, predators are known to provide an ecological benefit. They cull the weak, the slow, and the sick, which then no longer compete for resources or contribute to the gene pool. The herd is stronger, healthier. I have chosen a similar path. I select those that are holding the human 'herd' back, weakening it, draining resources that could better be used by more beneficial members of society. And, as I'm sure you noticed, they were all men, Detective."

She spoke the last sentence with a certain icy glee. Marc shuddered.

"What about Colin?" Terri asked. Since Dieter was now cooperating with them, she did not want to bring him up again with Alex.

"What about him?"

"He wasn't a violent criminal, as far as we can tell. His wife didn't mention any abuse or anything," Marc countered.

"Hmm. That is odd, isn't it? How many abused spouses never report their abusers? I guess it never happens," Alex mocked. "And the drug abuse wouldn't explain his behavior behind closed doors?"

Marc looked confused and turned to Terri, who replied, "Alex, there were no indications of substance use in the toxicology report from the medical examiner." Terri knew she shouldn't have said it, but it slipped out.

Alex had already read Marc's expression and knew that something she said didn't correspond with the information he held. She quickly hid her confusion. "Interesting. So, tell me about that worm, Dieter Schnoll. Why were you both there that night?"

"We can't discuss that matter with you. Just as anything you say to us today will not be discussed with anyone else we talk to," Terri stated sternly.

"I see. And you cannot tell me why those other men were there with Schnoll, the Bulgarian? Were they both Bulgarians? I only got... familiar... with the one."

"No, we cannot discuss it. In these situations, we ask the questions."

"Well, what is the fun in that? I feel you owe me at least something; you did shoot me that night after all," Alex said with a laugh.

"Those are the rules, Alex." Terri was becoming uncomfortable, as was Marc. They needed to get away and regroup. Alex was pressing them on areas that were too sensitive to even dance around. She was obviously smart and intuitive. Terri wondered, was there more? Could she read their minds? By asking the questions, was she drawing out the information she sought, even without them ever speaking it?

Marc sensed the need to get off this topic as well. "Alex, may I make a request, on behalf of this fine city and my department? Could you please stop eatin' people from the streets of Philadelphia? Can you try cows? You like beef, right?"

"Oh, my dear Detective, you are so blunt and funny! Yes, I have eaten cows as you say, but you might be surprised to know that farmers and ranchers do frown on disappearing livestock."

"How about deer or rabbits or something else? I have to ask."

Alex looked at Marc. His humor shielded a sharp mind. He was no fool. She turned to Terri, her eyes focused and intense, "Do you care for this man? Do you trust he is a good man?"

Terri was taken aback and stammered.

"If you tell me you think he is good, I will believe you." Alex pressed.

"Yes. He is a good man and I trust him with my life."

Alex turned to Marc, who was dumbfounded by this exchange. "Then, yes, Detective, I will try to not leave any bodies on your streets." Alex chose her words carefully.

There was silence for a moment, and then Terri spoke up, "Alex, I think we have covered a lot of ground here today, and I appreciate your candor. We would like to meet again. Would that be OK?"

"Yes. I enjoy talking with you both. I would like to do this again. Should I call you, or would you like to call me?"

"We know how to reach you."

Sarah watched from her car as Alexandra Stepanova walked out of the restaurant and crossed Rittenhouse Square. She texted Terri and Marc that Alex was gone, and they could come out. They didn't want Alex getting any license plate numbers from their cars.

They all arrived at Terri's condo simultaneously. Marc immediately laid on Terri's sofa. Terri sprawled in a reclining chair, head back and eyes closed.

Sarah sat on the floor. "So, you guys didn't get eaten. That's good, right?"

"I feel like I've been through a mental meat grinder," Terri groaned.

"That was the weirdest thing I've ever experienced. Was she playing with us?" Marc asked.

"I don't know. She is smart, charming, and very dangerous. By the end, it felt like we were the ones being interrogated," Terri replied.

"She copped to it all. She admitted everything. I didn't know where to go. I've never seen that before," Marc commented, staring at the ceiling.

"She admitted to everything because she knows what we know—that we can't do a damn thing with it," Terri pointed out.

"Wait, she admitted she was a... you know?" Now Sarah had a hard time saying it.

"Yeah, she did. She admitted it was her at Dieter's that night. She even brought up that we shot her! We didn't mention that. She said it. It was her. Jesus Christ, she even brought up that the guy she ate was a Bulgarian," Marc exclaimed.

"Oh, my God. I can't believe this. We were right," Sarah said, stunned.

Terri sat up, "All right, let's hot wash this thing. Marc, get your notes. Sarah, you follow along while we piece this together and let us know if anything jumps out at you."

When they had finished comparing observations, they had identified three sets of points: those they wanted to explore further, those in which they could possibly exert more pressure, and those they wanted to avoid.

Terri looked over her notes. "She said she spoke Russian as well as other languages. I want to ask her about that next time. What languages does she speak? Is she fluent? I want to explore that a bit."

"Might be useful to know down the road, as well. Worth asking her about," Marc agreed.

Sarah wrote down *language skills and basis.*

"Also, Sarah, let's follow up on that lab name and the village she listed as her birthplace. If we need to, we can run it by OGA Dave."

"Copy that," Sarah said as she made another note. "Why do you think she was so forthright—assuming she was telling you the truth?" Sarah asked.

"Have you ever had those times when you catch a bad guy and they practically thank you? It felt like that," Terri replied.

"Yeah, it's odd, but sometimes they're actually relieved. I had some tell me they were glad it was finally over and they didn't have to look over their shoulders anymore. It's a thing," Marc confirmed.

"Exactly. She's been living with this for—how long?—and she appears to be alone. So yeah, I bet there was some relief at being able to unload some of it more or less safely," Terri observed.

Sarah jotted down *lonely?, talking, release, no judgment.*

"Also, I think she really likes to talk about herself in general. She knows she's smart and–unique," Marc pointed out.

"Agreed. I got the vibe of a narcissist. If we can get her talking about her favorite subject—herself—she may barely take a breath." Sadly, Terri knew the signs of narcissism too well.

Sarah wrote down *narcissistic traits.*

"And what about the thing with Colin Miller? That was the only time I felt like she was on her heels," Terri said.

"Yeah, she clearly had the impression he was a violent man. That was really odd. I'll follow up with Jer and see if there is any way she can double check the tissue samples from Colin for any drug use," Marc offered.

"The most likely source for her impressions of Colin would have been his wife, right? We didn't talk much about Jennifer. Let's think about how we handle that one down the road." Terri wanted to put that in her back pocket for now. If they talked about Jennifer and Alex's relationship too soon, it might cause Alex to shut down.

Sarah wrote *relationship with Jennifer, to be addressed later.*

Marc thought about not bringing up the next topic, but he decided to take a chance anyway. "Did you get the feeling she was probing us? I mean like *mentally* probing?"

Terri looked at him; so he'd felt it as well. "Yes. At the end I wasn't sure what was happening. I thought maybe it was just me feeling fatigue and confusion. That interview was crazy. But you noticed it, too."

"Do you think she has ESP or something?" Sarah asked.

"That thought crossed my mind," Terri said, leaning back in her chair. "I mean, she is certainly very different from anything we've ever met before. If she can 'transform,' as she calls it, then what else can she do?"

"If that's the case, we could be seriously freakin' screwed." Marc wasn't fatalistic by nature, but he said what they were all thinking.

The group fell silent. Terri thought for a bit, replaying parts of the interview in her mind. "It's possible that she is just very intuitive. People make unconscious facial expressions all the time, especially under stress. The conscious mind can't catch these, but the unconscious brain detects them. That's how we can get a creepy feeling about someone without them ever actually doing anything."

"I think the clinical term is having the heebie-jeebies," Sarah said, lightening the mood.

Terri laughed, "Yes, a good case of the willies—that feeling you can't quite figure out when interacting with someone. Maybe she's reading all our facial expressions and nonverbal cues. She does have particularly keen senses."

"Boy, there's an understatement! She's off the charts in the scent department," Marc said with a chuckle. "You might be right though. Sometimes people ask questions knowing they won't get a direct answer, but they're lookin' for a reaction that might tell 'em what they didn't know but suspected. We use that technique in interviews. If she's as perceptive as we think, she might just be reading our faces."

Sarah wrote down *ESP?/ intuitive.*

"Either way, we have to be especially careful around her," Terri pointed out.

"Agreed," said Marc.

CHAPTER 18

KHODYNKA, RUSSIA

The office of Lieutenant General Igor Stepin wasn't opulent, but it conveyed the status of his position as the head of Russian military intelligence, the GRU, nevertheless. The walls of the office were decorated with various military plaques, photos, awards, and other trinkets bestowed upon him during his career. Most notable was a picture of him with Vladimir Putin, smiling and shaking hands at some event. Putin was wearing a business suit, but Stepin was in his formal military uniform, his chest festooned with the somewhat comical display of medals that is customary in the Russian military.

He stepped out from behind his desk as the door opened and Konstantin Kretzky was allowed in. Motioning to a round table with eight chairs, Stepin waited while Kretzky chose a seat. Then he sat down across from him.

"I assume you have heard that Colonel Astov is dead." Stepin was not a man to mince words.

"I have."

"Obviously, that means we will get no information from him. And since we have no other avenues to pursue, we'll have to assume that the beast that escaped from your research facility is still alive."

"Yes. It appears so. Have Drs. Lavroski and Demikhov made any progress going through the records?" Kretzky asked.

Stepin smiled, "You know as well as I do that they have not. Lavroski is giving you almost daily updates." Stepin wanted to let him know that he, too, had people well placed in Kretzky's organization. Kretzky nodded slightly.

Stepin continued, "That is a state of embarrassment that must be corrected. If our lab rat falls into American hands, who knows what she may tell them."

"Lavroski was under the impression that all the subjects, including this one, suffered from psychosis and memory failure," Kretzky countered. "Even if she did fall into their hands, what could she tell them?"

"I do not want to stake my life on the continued amnesia of this person. It would be a tremendous black eye for our nation and do great damage to your personal reputation."

Kretzky knew that this incident, if exposed to the world, would destroy the general's reputation and end his career. Stepin was letting him know that he would not go down alone if that happened.

"I understand, General. I am using all available resources to correct this situation, but operating in the United States is difficult."

General Stepin looked at Kretzky gravely. "Yes, it is. The original matter in the States was an abject failure and needs to be corrected as well."

"Yes, but that wasn't my people's fault." As soon as he said the words, he knew he had made an error.

"Fault?" Stepin leaned forward and very quietly said, "I don't think you want to mention fault, Konstantin. There is plenty to fill all our plates—especially yours."

Kretzky bristled slightly. He wanted to say that the only reason there was a team in the US to begin with was to tie up a loose end caused by the general's greed. But Kretzky bit his tongue, for now. Best to play nice. "The target is very difficult to locate, understandably. If I could request that the General provide some intelligence resources to my group, I will be able to locate the target faster and close this loop for the General."

"What kind of resources do you have in mind? I cannot provide any more human resources. I have covered the tracks of the last failed operation, but one more international incident will be fatal for both of us."

"I am envisioning cellphone records and a mobile cellphone tracking device; one of European origin that can be shipped to the US for use there. I will contract with a group on the ground for the final execution of the plan. There will be no ties to us or the motherland.

"This situation is very important. I need this cleaned up. Don't fail me again," Stepin said pointedly.

CHAPTER 19

"HEY DAVE, YOU GOT a few?" Terri and Sarah popped into Dave's SCIF.

"For you two, most definitely." Dave enjoyed assisting the criminal side of the house. He found the intersection of criminal investigations and intelligence resources to be particularly satisfying. Plus, Terri and Marc, now with Sarah, brought different work. And different could be exciting.

"We have a couple of names of places to run by you. Just wanted to see if your shop could shed any light on their background. They are in Russia." Terri handed him a sheet of paper with the names.

"Yeah, no problem. If there is anything I can share, I will. What's it related to?"

"Possibly K2. We have been interviewing a potential new source, who had some intelligence on these places. We are trying to vet it," Terri said.

Sarah turned to Terri when Dave glanced down to find his pen. "New source?" she mouthed to Terri with a "what the fuck?" face.

Terri shrugged. She knew they had to tell Dave something.

"Give me a day or so. I'll swing by and let you know if I have any hits," Dave said after he wrote the names on his pad. "Also, while I have you here, that intel from your financial source was very interesting."

"Can you share with us?" Sarah asked.

"Yes, but only off the record. Nothing can be used in any court filings or subpoena requests. Standard disclaimer."

"Understood," Terri acknowledged.

"I checked on all the financial schemes—or structures, as your source called them—that you gave me. I focused on the ones that were believed to be European based clients." Dave was not supposed to know the identity of the source. So, Dieter's name was redacted from all documents, and any references were made with gender neutral pronouns or he/she. "I assume there were US-based clients that you are following up on domestically?"

"Yes, we're looking at those and any from south of the border as well—narcos, we believe. Straight criminal stuff," Terri confirmed.

"OK. One of the European ones is something my folks will be very interested in. I'll clue you in for deconfliction purposes and to let you know that this source of yours is pretty damn good, in case you had any doubts."

Terri and Sarah listened intently as Dave described a connection between one of the structures and a certain unnamed Russian general at the GRU who was of great interest to the Agency.

"Now, what are your theories about why a Russian general would use the services of a US-based financial-services provider—AKA a money launderer?"

"I think the most likely scenario is that he is trying to hide his money from what he perceives to be the greatest threat: his fellow thieves in the Russian government," Terri explained.

"Interesting concept," Dave said as he jotted down some notes.

Terri continued, "All these people are trying to hide their wealth from someone—the IRS, law enforcement, whatever poses the gravest threat.

In the case of someone from Russia who stole money from there, they might use a launderer in the US because that person would be outside the reach of the Russian government. The Russians are who he fears grabbing his money the most. Just a thought."

Dave nodded. "That's actually pretty good. Think of him as a thief, not an intelligence player, and this makes more sense."

Terri and Sarah collected their phones from the wall of cubbies and walked back downstairs to the squad area, where there was a palpable buzz of activity.

Terri caught Jim Martin as he was coming out of his office. "What's going on, boss?"

"Child abduction last night in the city. I'm just getting ready to brief the squad on the latest." Raising his voice, he called out, "All right, everybody in the break room!"

Terri and Sarah found Marc and sat next to him.

"OK, everybody, listen up. At approximately 2100 last night, Christian Cortez, four years old, was reported missing by his parents. Christian was last seen in the custody of his uncle, 34-year-old Damien Cortez. Damien was an active target being investigated by our child-exploitation task force. I think we all know what that means." Terri saw Marc visibly tense up. Those were the cops and agents who investigated cases involving the trafficking and sexual exploitation of minors. It was nasty stuff.

"Damien was communicating with an undercover officer about having access to a young boy for videoing. The team was gearing up to arrest him when he must have gotten skittish. He fled the home with Christian between the hours of 1900 and 2100, while Christian's parents were out to dinner and Damien was watching the child."

"This guy is some sort of self-professed survivalist and right-wing militia member. He is believed to be heavily armed and in possession of all types of survival gear."

"His car was found abandoned in Camden early this morning, and an Amber alert was issued. A NJ State Park employee called in and stated that he believed he saw Damien, with the child, driving a late-model brown pickup near Wharton State Forest in Hammonton, New Jersey. Our SWAT team, Newark's SWAT team, and the New Jersey State Police tactical unit are currently searching the woods. The command post is at the Batsto parking lot. Everyone knows that time is of the essence. This character is unstable and likely knows the game is over for him. God willing, they will find this kid in time.

"Our assignment on Squad 1 is to cover any investigative leads that may come in. I need four volunteers, two teams of two to start—"

Every hand in the room shot up.

Terri, Marc, and Sarah were not chosen. As they walked to their desks, Terri pulled the other two aside. "I have an idea. What about Alex?"

"Are you crazy? We barely know her and what we do know is pretty damn frightening," Marc countered.

"Look, this scene is going to play out fast. That forest is huge—thousands of acres. It could take days to find the kid, and who knows what will happen to him in the meantime. Plus, if or when a tactical team gets close to him, then what happens?"

Marc was shaking his head no, but something inside him understood that the urgency of the situation might demand an unconventional approach, to say the least.

Sarah chimed in and whispered, "She did say she targets based on the character of the person. Can you get worse than this guy?"

"Are you really considering putting a child's life in her hands?" Marc asked.

"I think it might be worth talking to her. We know what this kid's uncle is all about. I'd rather take a shot than do nothing here," Terri hissed.

Marc looked at Sarah. She nodded. He was outnumbered. Anyway, he couldn't come up with a better plan.

CHAPTER 20

Terri had told Alex on the phone only that there was an urgent matter that she and Marc needed to discuss with her. They picked her up in front of her house. Marc pulled away from the curb, and Terri turned to talk to Alex in the back seat.

As Terri relayed the situation concerning the child, Marc watched Alex's face in the mirror. Once Terri mentioned that the uncle had taken the boy to the forest, Alex's eyes came alive. Marc could see her pupils dilate to the point where only a thin ring of green remained.

Terri handed Alex a picture of the subject, Damien Cortez. Alex studied it for a moment and handed it back.

"And what do you wish of me, Agent Watson and Detective Peterson?" Alex asked. She knew what they were thinking, but she wanted them to say it.

"We want you to go into the woods, find this guy, and bring the boy out," Marc offered. He glanced back and saw Alex smiling at him in the mirror.

"Is that all?" Alex pressed.

"We do not condone extrajudicial punishment. If you are able to subdue the man in such a way that he can face a criminal trial, do it," Terri said pointedly.

"Yes, of course, you must say that. I understand. If I find the boy alive, what do you want me to do with him?"

"What do you mean 'do' with him? You're not thinking of eating him, are you?" Marc asked in a panic, swerving to avoid the guard rail on the Ben Franklin Bridge.

Alex laughed. "Oh, my dear Detective. I do not prey upon the young and innocent. You should know that. I am asking where I should take him. To you? To someone else?" Alex was practically giddy. She enjoyed the open conversations they had. The fear she smelled on them at the first meeting was almost gone when they talked now.

Marc breathed a sigh of relief.

"A group of officers will be gathered in a parking lot at the edge of the state park. We'll show you on the map when we get there. Take him to them. If he is... if we are too late, don't do anything. The search teams will discover them and recover the bodies. Only intervene if the boy is alive and you can do so in a way that he won't be harmed. Understand?" Terri explained.

"Yes, I believe I do."

As they neared the edge of the state park, Marc had a question. "Alex, when you, you know, transform, can Ter and I watch?"

Terri shot him a look.

"Well, I mean, it's pretty spectacular, I'm guessing. You're curious, too, Ter, I know you are," he teased.

Alex sat stoically in the backseat. "Detective Peterson, I am not a sideshow in a traveling circus."

"I'm sorry. I meant no disrespect."

Alex, for the first time she could recall, felt self-conscious. She thought about this feeling and realized that she feared her new confidants would never look at her the same way if they saw her change into her full form.

They had seen her that night in the rain, but that seemed distant and separate; as if she were two different beings. Watching one become the other could be unsettling, even if they knew basically how it happened. She decided it was ridiculous to feel this way. If they wanted to see her become her other self, they could.

"I understand, Detective. If you wish, you may watch me transform."

Marc really felt like an idiot now.

The sun was setting as the car came to a stop. A sign declared the area adjacent to them to be Wharton State Forest.

"We'll wait for you here," Terri said as Alex stepped out of the car. Terri watched as Alex closed her eyes and breathed in deeply.

Marc turned to Terri and said, "If we have to move away we'll—*whoa!*" He blushed and looked away instinctively as Alex stripped off all her clothes and tossed them in the backseat.

Alex laughed. "You wish to watch me transform, but my naked form unsettles you. You are a funny man, Detective."

"All right, all right. I will pass on the show. Go get 'em," he said, still looking away.

I step into the forest. It is different from the other forest I'd been in recently. The scent of pine here is overpowering. The heat of the day lingers between the trunks of conifer trees and laurel undergrowth. I prefer this rich, humid air to the stale climate provided by air conditioners. This is real and alive. After walking for several dozen meters, I stop and begin the change. As expected, it is exhilarating. I toss my head back and let out a deep, thundering roar. I know the forest is empty of other humans now. The police and FBI have cut off all access to it. I know the teams of searchers have stopped for the night. I am all alone with my prey in these trees. It is as it should be.

Back in the car, Marc and Terri flinched at the sound of Alex's roar. "May Jesus Christ have mercy on his soul…," Marc said, crossing himself as he looked into the blackness of the woods.

Terri finished the thought, "Because she sure as hell won't."

There is a slight breeze. I am not worried about my prey detecting me, I only consider whether the breeze will assist me tonight. I was told that there are two rivers running here, and I can smell water in the distance. I will not search there. The human teams will have combed that area, understanding that water means life and that the prey needs it.

I bound into the trees. They are small and sparse. It is very easy to traverse these woods, and I can see very clearly. I smell a deer nearby. Another night, my friend, and we might have met. Tonight, I have other game in mind.

I cross a small, flowing creek. The cool water is pleasant and refreshing to me. On the other side, I smell food being prepared in the distance. It is faint, but I am sure. There should be no human food so deep in the woods, so this must be my prey. I move steadily in the direction of the scent that the breeze has delivered to me.

I slow my pace to a steady, deliberate walk as the scent grows very strong. I detect mixed nuts with salt and the smell of a stew of some sort. I pause and listen. I can hear a child's weak sniffle and soft sob. There is no conversation. I scan the dark and see a man sitting on the ground, eating, next to a small camouflage tent. The sound of the young one is coming from inside the tent. The blue flame of a camping stove flickers. I am motionless as I stare at the sitting figure, waiting for him to look up so I can see his face. Every muscle in my massive body is taut and ready to explode into motion. At last, the bearded man straightens his back and yawns. It is my prey.

I lunge forward, paws slamming into the ground. The prey hears me and leans over to reach for a rifle propped against a nearby tree. I see him stumble over in his panic, and I am there before he can recover. I stand over him, glowering. I can see the complete terror in his eyes. A steel blade glints as he draws a knife from his belt. My right claw snaps forward and catches him across the face, sending him rolling across the ground. I pounce on him and end him with a snap of his neck. He does not have time to scream.

I look back over my shoulder at the tent entrance and see a small boy staring at me with wide eyes. I run into the darkness and transform back to my human form. I did not like the look of fright I saw on the boy's face. I reemerge from the trees, extinguish the camp stove fire, and put on clothes from his uncle's pack.

"It's OK, young one. You are safe now. Let us find the policemen looking for you and get you home," I tell the boy, as I lead him from the tent.

The trip to the officers takes two hours. I carry the boy on my back and trot most of the way. Even in my human form, he is light, and I do not struggle to move with him. As we near the officers, I can see the bright lights blazing into the darkness and hear the generators hum. Dozens of voices mingle in different conversations, and radios crackle. The smell of cheap coffee mixed with grilled meat and pastries fills the air.

I set the boy on the ground. "You go toward the lights there. They will take care of you now," I tell him and pat him on the head. I watch as he moves off, hesitantly at first, toward the blinding glare of lights. Once I see men running toward him and hear them call out his name, I depart.

I return to the campsite and discard the man's clothes. I transform once more and finish my meal. It is very satisfying.

Alex emerged from the forest as the dawn broke. Terri and Marc were reclined in the seats, half asleep. She rapped on the window, startling them.

She had washed herself in the river before arriving and now put on her original clothes.

Terri looked at Alex in the back seat. "How did it go?"

"The boy is safe," Alex said, smiling as she looked out the window.

"That is great news! Fantastic!" Terri exclaimed.

"And the uncle?" Marc asked.

"He reached for a weapon and I had to act. He will not harm any more children," Alex said coldly, meeting Marc's gaze in the mirror.

Marc nodded. "Good work."

Alex watched calmly as the trees flowed past the window on the drive back to the city. A smile crept across her face. New emotions were swirling inside her. She realized she felt contentment. The prey last night was all that she had been told, utterly evil. His flesh was particularly pleasing. But beyond that, there was something about the boy. Knowing that she had not simply removed a malignant member of society but actually saved an innocent brought her... joy. That was a most rare feeling for her.

She considered Terri and Marc. She felt a great closeness to them at this moment. Though they knew fully who, or more accurately what, she was, they had trusted her. She felt thankful for that as she closed her eyes and relaxed, her mind wandering as she drifted off. Perhaps she was not so different from these creatures after all. Could she really relate to someone after all these years? Either way, the fact that she feels like she could gives it substance.

"OK, one more time please. How did you find your way here, Christian?" the large man with the blue uniform asked again.

Christian swallowed his mouthful of waffle. "There was a huge monster who scared my uncle away. And then a pretty lady showed up. She was naked at first!" Christian said, laughing. "Then she took me here on her back and dropped me off," he said, pointing to the area of the parking lot he had emerged from in the middle of the night. "Can I have another waffle?"

"JERSEY DEVIL SAVES YOUTH?" was the headline. According to the online news article, the family said that "it must have been an angel" who brought their son out of the forest to safety.

I sit in my office and finish reading the story. "Well, which is it, the devil or an angel?" I ask out loud to no one.

The devil or an angel—what an interesting conundrum. I have never thought of myself as either, but maybe I am both. True, I assign a certain priority to my hunting, but isn't a killer who stalks evil men still a killer?

Am I morally superior to the prey I seek? Perhaps not, but last night I saved a life. In the moral hierarchy of the universe, that would justify the killing, right? Devil *and* angel.

That is a matter for debate another day. Today I feel strange.

Something is lurking in the back of my mind: Colin Miller. I did not taste his flesh that night, so I do not have a true read on what kind of man he was. All I know is what I have been told by… Jennifer. The feeling of satisfaction from the events in the pine barrens gives way to unease. I glance at my cellphone and see a missed call from her. I will call her back later. I have work to do today and cannot spend energy or time dwelling on this. I shall put it back into its box and come back to it later.

Classes will resume in a few weeks, and I need to update my lesson plans for the semester. I know the subject, 17th-century Eastern European history, very well. I seem to have an innate knowledge of this period, along with a few others. The task I have is to share what I know in terms that these young, attention-deficit-afflicted Americans can understand and relate to.

I consider that my knowledge of this subject is akin to the languages I have at my disposal, whose origins are Slavic, Germanic, Scandinavian, Romance, Latin, Greek, Aramaic, Egyptian, and Sumerian. There are times when I dream that I can see great mounted armies moving across the steppes or an elaborately painted ancient city made of baked brick sprawling before me. I hear people speaking in lost tongues, but I understand them. I am tied to my distant past but untethered from my own, to use the phrase of Agent Watson.

CHAPTER 21

T HE THREE OF THEM were crowded around Terri's desk, going over the client list from Dieter. They were making good progress identifying and tracking the true owners of the accounts and holding structures. Dieter was a wealth of knowledge. Based on his information, several investigations had been initiated on previously unknown subjects. Terri and Sarah contacted case agents with investigations already open on the individuals he identified. Dieter's information was provided to the case agents, and any questions they had for him were passed along. Needless to say, there were many pleasantly surprised agents across the country.

Terri's phone rang. It was OGA Dave upstairs. "Hey, Dave."

"Glad I caught you. Can you come up? Bring Sarah and Marc, too, if you can."

"Will do. They're here with me now. See you in a few."

Dave closed the heavy door to his drab office and joined them at his small conference table.

"First of all, thanks again for that lead we discussed. I can't tell you what's going on with it because even I don't know, but my people seem very happy." Dave was referring to the information about a certain Russian general that came from Dieter's reporting.

"Anyway, I checked on those locations you gave me, and I can share some interesting stuff with you. The Novaya Zhizn facility was on our radar years ago. It was described as a commercial pharmaceutical testing facility in open reporting. However, there were some rumors that it might have been a front for biological or chemical warfare stuff. This was partly based on contracts it received from the Russian military, which typically isn't interested in cures for acne or eczema. A decade ago, the entire operation seemed to have been shut down. NRO satellite images at the time showed a massive fire after a couple of moving trucks were observed departing the place."

"That is odd, isn't it?" Terri asked.

"Yes, very. Research facilities are expensive. Even if you cease operations there, you typically don't raze it to the ground. Unless—"

"—unless you're afraid that something there will either get out or be found," Marc concluded.

"Exactly. If I had to guess, whatever they were working on spooked them in a big way," Dave continued. "We dug into it a bit at the time, but we got nothing conclusive. If you have someone who might be able to shed some light on that, or on what kind of work they were doing there, my people would be very interested."

Terri looked at Marc, and he shifted uncomfortably in his chair.

"We just started talking to a person, and we're trying to vet some information at this time. It might be premature to set up a meeting right now," Terri said, deflecting. The thought of introducing OGA Dave to Alex made her chuckle silently.

"Gotcha. If you can let me know if the relationship progresses to the point where I can talk to them, I'd appreciate it."

"Will do."

"Now, that village name you gave me is another mystery, and it's possibly tied to the lab. First off, it doesn't exist—at least not anymore. It was listed on maps and other records for years, going back to the Soviet era. We noted that the population was steadily declining—which isn't really surprising, since there isn't much of anything out in that part of Russia, and people tend to leave areas that have no economic future.

What is interesting is that it was only about ten miles from the Novaya Zhizn lab. Days before the lab was razed, the village was obliterated. At the time, it was mostly a ghost town anyway; satellite images showed only about four or five active buildings left. Maybe NRO kept tabs on it due to its proximity to the lab. Anyway, one pass of the big eye in the sky showed everything was normal, status quo. But when it went over the area again 24 hours later, all the buildings were smoldering heaps. All of them. This was no accident; the place was destroyed. Days later, the same fate befell the lab."

"Wow. That is not a coincidence," Sarah said under her breath.

"No, it is not. Something very bad happened there, and somebody went to great lengths to either contain it or cover it," Dave said gravely.

"Who owned that lab?"

"Oh, Jesus, I almost forgot the goddamn cherry on the sundae! It was owned by a holding company tied to Konstantin Kretzky! Here's the name," he said, sliding over a piece of paper. "And remember, this is for lead purposes only, no official documents."

Marc arrived at Terri's door with a square pie from Cucina's Pizza. Most people think of pizza as being round. But square pies are also traditional, and they actually make a good bit of sense from a sharing perspective.

Cucina's was known as one of the best in the city. It barely hit the table before the three of them greedily started to claim their squares.

Terri opened a bottle of Merlot and brought it to the table. This had become their routine when they needed to discuss matters that weren't suited to the office. "Well, Dave sure had some interesting info today."

"Holy crap, was it ever!" Sarah exclaimed. "The time frames match up with Alex's story. I think we know what 'bad thing' happened at that lab."

"Doesn't this put us into a bit of a bind, though?" Marc asked. Terri gave him a quizzical look.

He continued, "We got information from Alex that we can't write up. That information would be interesting to your cousins from Northern Virginia, who want to talk to her. That cannot happen. Additionally, said cousins have given us helpful information that we cannot use officially. The only way to use that information is to determine it independently. In order to do that, we need to rely on Alex's information, that—"

"—that we can't write up. Full loop." Terri nodded slowly as what Marc said, sank in. She had been caught up in the elation of the new intelligence from Dave and hadn't thought it through like that.

"Well, aren't you the Debbie Downer," Sarah joked as she topped off her glass.

"I'm just sayin', this could be very tricky, if not impossible, to pull off."

"What if we really open Alex up as a source?" Terri asked.

Marc almost choked on a piece of pizza. Sarah responded, "Whoa. Hold up a minute here, cowgirl. That is a whole different rodeo." Sarah and Marc clearly thought that this was an insane idea.

"What's going to happen when the supervisor has to meet your girl during one of those annual reviews? 'Hi Alex, I'm Jim Martin, Supervisory Special Agent. Hello Agent Martin, I'm Alex the werewolf. Do you have anybody you want me to eat?'"

"Hear me out," said Terri. "We would obviously have to tell her to rein in any talk of her transformations or propensity to eat bad guys."

"Oh please, do go on." Marc was enjoying this.

"Look, for this to work, she only has to appear totally human for one hour, once a year, for Jim. She is a professor at Penn for Christ's sake; she interacts with people all day. I'm pretty sure she can manage."

Marc sat up. "You got a point. She's only open with us because we made it known that we were on to her. If we explain that he doesn't know about that and would absolutely have a shit fit if he found out, she might be OK."

Sarah started to come around as well. "She does have a myriad of skills that could be useful, like all her languages. Plus, she has knowledge of the Russian lab."

That point made Terri realize another pitfall. "Uh-oh, the lab. If she ever talks to OGA Dave about it, she will have to be very careful. He will want names and details of how she knows what she knows. If she says she was a test subject, all sorts of alarm bells are going to go off with him."

"Maybe she never meets with Dave face to face. Coming from Russia, maybe she doesn't trust the CIA, only us. We filter the Q and A between them." Sarah was really getting onboard now.

"Damn, this might work," Marc said in disbelief.

Terri and Marc sat on the leather sofa in Alex's living room. Terri glanced around as Alex responded to the whistling tea kettle in the kitchen. They had said they didn't want any refreshments, but Alex insisted they try the imported Egyptian tea she had discovered. She told them that pairing it with the honey-laced phyllo pastry she had on hand was life altering. Terri noticed the collection of 19th-century nature paintings arranged on the red wall. She wasn't sure if they were real or prints. There were sculptures as well. Her eye was attracted to a 24-inch Greek or Roman style goddess that sat on a table to her right. The marble woman wore an ornate helmet, propped high on her head, and held a round shield in her left hand, flung wide. Above her head, she wielded a spear. The cold eyes stared at Terri.

Alex returned and set the tray of tea and pastries on the dark coffee table. "I see you like my Athena statue."

"Yes, it is very nice."

"It is a reproduction, of course, but I, too, enjoy it. I like the way she is poised to strike. You can see the strength in her arms and body as she holds the shield and spear. It captures the moment she has fully committed to action, and there is no turning back."

"Yes, she is committed."

Marc tasted the tea. He preferred coffee, but he had to admit, the strong black tea was delicious.

Alex saw the look on his face, "You should now try the pastry. Let the flavors mix. It is exquisite."

"Thank you for the tea, Alex. But we do have something to run by you," Terri said, after taking a sip of the soothing tea.

"Certainly. Please go on."

"First of all, before we go any further, I need to know something, do you have ESP, Alex?" Marc asked.

"Well that is an interesting question, Detective Peterson. And quite to the point," Alex mused.

"I find it's usually the quickest path to the answer," he said, staring at her.

Alex smiled. "No, I do not have ESP. I cannot read your minds. That is what you were asking, wasn't it Detective?"

"Yes, that's what he was asking," Terri answered, glancing at Marc. "But you do exhibit some interesting abilities when talking with us. We want to understand what that is. Perhaps there is a way to utilize those skills."

Alex nodded. She clearly liked talking about herself and obliged them. "You are both very astute in your observations. You see, I can read faces remarkably well, that is true. But I cannot read your minds. Your thoughts are safe, Detective Peterson."

What she failed to mention, partly because she couldn't fully explain it, was that she could 'sense' a person's energy, their aura. She could vaguely see a colored hue surrounding a person. 'Best to keep some details private,' she thought to herself.

"Thank you, Alex," Marc said with a nod. Alex detected a sense of relief flash across his face.

Terri continued, "Ok, now that we have that matter cleared up. I'd like to get to our real reason for seeing you today. We would like to formalize our relationship with you."

"Are you proposing to me, Agent Watson?" Alex asked with a surprised laugh.

"Not quite like that. We want to officially work with you, on investigations. The best way to do that while protecting your identity is to do what we call 'open you as a source'. Nothing will change, you will still work with Marc and me."

"We will obviously not report the more...incredible...aspects of your cooperation," Marc assured her.

"What this will allow us to do is fully utilize the information you give us to investigate the people who hurt you in Russia."

Alex sat silently, drinking her tea.

"Alex, you are an incredible woman with amazing intellect and skills, beyond those involving your... transformations. We would like to humbly ask that you allow us to work with you and use that intellect for the purposes of justice." Terri was appealing to Alex's ego.

"We want you to help us kick some ass. Find bad guys and bring 'em to heel," Marc stated, more bluntly, as he leaned forward.

Finally, Alex smiled. Setting her teacup on the table, she looked at Marc. "Well Detective Peterson, as always, you put things very succinctly. Agent Watson, if this is to be a 'relationship' as you say, what may I expect in return? As we all know, a one-way relationship is doomed to fail."

"We will use our resources to try to find your true identity. The one that was stolen from you in the lab."

Alex raised her eyebrows slightly at that. "Well, that is unexpected and very thoughtful of you." She sat for a moment, looking at the statue of Athena. "I accept."

Terri completed the forms she had brought with her. Alex's name, date of birth, city and country of birth, address, phone number, and so on had already been filled in. She asked Alex a few more questions and wrote the responses down.

For skills, she had listed the languages Alex knew, omitting Latin, Aramaic, and Sumerian. They were pretty esoteric, and given that there was no call for them, they would attract unwanted attention. She also listed "knowledge of Eastern European criminal organizations" as a catch-all for details that would come about the lab.

"You may wish to add 'cyber-threat knowledge' to your list," Alex offered.

Terri and Marc looked up.

Alex shrugged slightly. "I dabble."

One section asked for a description of the source's motivation. Here, Terri wrote *revenge*. It was not uncommon to list this as a motivation, and it was especially true in this case.

There was one final section of the form to be completed. "How do you say wolf in Russian?" Terri asked.

Alex replied, "Volk."

"That'll work." Marc said as Terri wrote the code name: Volk.

CHAPTER 22

Terri carefully crafted the FD-302 of Volk's reporting on the Novaya Zhizn facility. For Terri, Marc, and Sarah, Alex would still be Alex. But to anyone else, she would be referred to as Volk. In the reporting FD-302, however, even the code name wasn't used; she was simply a source. The document therefore had to be written in such a way that the reader couldn't infer the source's position or role from the narrative. Terri included the names of the doctors and other staff that Volk recalled, the layout of the facility, and a general assessment of the work done: unknown biological experimentation on unwilling human test subjects. She omitted any specific references to the testing. With this information officially provided by Alex, they could really start to investigate the ownership and funding of the facility.

When completed, she ran the form by Marc for any edits. "This looks good, Ter. Do you want to add anything about the heavy security presence there? We know they had armed guards."

"Good catch. I'll add that." Terri jotted it down in her notebook to be added when she was back at her computer. "I heard from those agents in San Francisco; they are chomping at the bit to get out here and talk to Dieter."

"Any chance we fly out to California with him?" Marc asked, only half joking.

"Nice try. Uncle Sugar is pretty cheap when it comes to travel. Airfare for two agents from San Francisco versus three travelers from Philadelphia? I'll let you guess which one the Bureau is going to fund," Terri pointed out.

"Yeah, well I had to ask. Never been to San Fran; I hear it's nice."

"If I ever get there, I'll let you know," Terri offered. "Any word back from Jerri on the toxicology tests for Miller?"

"Yes, she called yesterday. She reran the tests on the hair and tissue samples she still had from Colin, and they came up clean. No drugs.

"We might have to talk to Alex about her friend Jennifer soon. But I'm reluctant to go there until we have a longer track record with her." Terri understood that Alex's relationship with Jennifer could be a difficult topic to discuss. All indications showed that the two were close. How close, Terri didn't know. Terri wanted to have a strategy for how to maneuver the conversation to keep Alex onboard with it. She would have to think very carefully about the format and timing.

Sarah stopped over at Marc's desk. "I took the draft 302 you gave me and started running some of the names ahead of time. More corroboration. First off, Dr. Peter Lavroski was listed as the director of the lab in question. He published a paper shortly after the lab opened. It was titled— get this—*Advancements in Tissue Regeneration and Recuperation Through External Stimulation*. In it, he discussed altering human DNA by introducing—wait for it—animal DNA that exhibited increased healing properties. Seems most of the scientific world kinda thought it was quackery and dismissed it."

"Holy shit, this was just sitting out there the whole time, but nobody knew where to look," Marc said, shaking his head.

"There's more. After the lab was shuttered, he went to work at the GRU in an oversight role. I don't think he ever picked up a test tube after that. Also, I think I found D. Astov. There was a LinkedIn page for a Colonel Dimitry Astov that seems inactive. But one of the positions listed was Head of Security for the Novaya Zhizn lab. There was a news story a couple of weeks ago stating that the body of a Colonel Dimitry Astov was found on a small farm in far eastern Russia. Apparent suicide. Gotta think that's the same guy. Seems like our girl is telling you guys the truth so far."

"Any other hits on LinkedIn or any other sites for the lab?" Terri asked.

"No, not a single reference that I could find. They may have been purged. Astov's spelling of the lab name actually had a typo in it. That might explain how it was still there. His profile came up when I searched his name, not the lab."

"Ok, so it looks like she is on the up and up with this stuff. I have an idea I want to bounce off you guys. If we think she is telling us the truth—and, based on Sarah's digging, it increasingly looks that way—I want to try to stimulate her memory. Who knows what else she has in there?"

"What do you mean 'stimulate'—like hypnosis or something?" Marc asked.

"No, not that. But boy, it would be awesome to see the face of the hypnotist if we did do that! No, I'm thinking that if we ask her to speak in the languages she says she knows, it might trigger something."

Sarah nodded, "Definitely worth a shot. I read that speaking, especially in foreign languages, can alter pathways in the brain."

"Exactly."

Alex listened intently as she sat in her large wingback chair. "That is a very interesting idea you have, Agent Watson. Where should I begin?"

"Why not Russian? It is the most recent." It was also the area of Alex's memory that Terri was the most interested in.

"Very well. Is there anything in particular that you want me to talk to you in Russian about?"

"Alex, you can say anything you like. I don't know Russian. Or French, or German, or Italian, or Sumerian, for that matter, either."

Alex laughed and began to describe her favorite US restaurants in Russian. Terri was amazed at how the words flowed with ease. There were no pauses, no *ums* as one would expect when a person switches from one language to another and searches for a particular word. To Terri's ears, Alex sounded like a native speaker.

After about 20 minutes, Terri stopped her. She was curious. "Alex, can you speak to me in Latin?"

Alex immediately switched to what sounded like fluent Latin as she told Terri about wanting to tour Rome and Florence and Venice and how much she enjoyed a fine bottle of wine.

This went on for several minutes. Alex finished talking and smiled. "That was delightful. I think in the future I would like to have a conversation with someone though. No offense Agent Watson, I do enjoy talking to you, but I think it would be beneficial to have someone speak back to me as well."

"No offense taken. I wouldn't venture to any local Russian dance clubs to experiment with that, though. Lots of criminal types frequent those places."

"Oh, Agent Watson, are you concerned for my well-being?" Alex asked, smiling sweetly.

"No, I'm concerned about *their* well-being!" Terri responded with a laugh. "The Bureau has some linguists who have been cleared. I'll try to set up some times for you to converse with them in Russian, German, Italian, and French. You're on your own for Latin, Sumerian, etc. I don't think we have anyone who speaks those languages on hand."

"I don't suppose you do. I'd be happy to talk with any of your linguists, if you can arrange it."

Back in the office, Terri reached out to the language services supervisor, Jody Lin. Terri explained that she had a confidential source who wanted to brush up on their Russian, German, Italian, and French. If any linguists with those skills had some down time, they could contact Terri and she would arrange a telephone call with the source. She stipulated that the conversations were to be topical in nature, nothing about either party's background.

Many conversations later, Jody called Terri.

"I want to talk to you about this source of yours. She isn't just brushing up on her language skills, she is as fluent as a native speaker. My team has been having a blast talking with her. Any chance she wants to come work here? I don't know her history or if she could pass our background checks, but man, would she be a good one to have onboard."

"I'm glad it has worked out, but I'm sorry to say that she won't be filling out an application anytime soon. She is already gainfully employed and there are some issues we are working through."

"OK. Maybe consider a contract linguist spot, part-time? Just a thought."

"Will do. Thanks for the help, Jody."

Terri thought about it for a few minutes after she hung up. Alex working for the FBI—what the hell would that look like? She laughed to herself and got back to her records review.

With the help of Dieter and Dave, she was slowly piecing together the ownership structure of the Novaya Zhizn lab. The biggest delays were getting her hands on the SWIFT banking records.

The company that owned the lab was held by an umbrella corporation that also owned several other pharmaceutical companies and facilities. The banking transactions indicated that Novaya Zhizn was, financially, the largest of the group. This was due to the huge contracts from the Russian military, which amounted to tens of millions of dollars. Dave was right when he suggested that the Russian military was not interested in commercial applications from this lab. Aside from any products developed by the lab possibly being applicable for military use, another reason for the hefty contracts became apparent. Large amounts of money were transferred out of the Novaya Zhizn accounts on a regular basis, totaling about 70% of the Russian military money invested. These transfers were sent to accounts in the names of the other companies and facilities under the umbrella corporation.

Terri had just gotten the latest DVDs for the transactions of these other accounts. She pulled them up, and what she found brought a broad smile to her face. Twenty-four hours after the money hit these accounts, they were wired out again. The recipient accounts of these transfers were set up by Dieter and connected to a certain GRU general whom Dave and company were very interested in. The memo section of the transactions cited "Consulting Fees." Things were coming into focus. It appeared the good general was involved in a massive kickback scheme of Russian military money.

That night, Terri's cellphone rang, jarring her from her sleep. It was Alex.

"What's up, Alex? Everything OK?"

"Yes, I am sorry to wake you, Agent Watson, but I am remembering things, things about the lab. I wanted to let you know." Alex sounded excited.

Terri sat up in bed. "OK, get a pen and write down whatever you have. Marc and I will stop over in the morning."

"I am teaching classes in the morning. Perhaps in the afternoon?"

"Sounds good. See you then, Alex." Terri looked at her phone: 2:30 a.m. She knew she was going to have a hard time going back to sleep. From the foot of her bed, Max gave her a drowsy look before settling back to sleep. *'Oh to be so lucky,'* she thought. Maybe there was an old movie somewhere?

PART 4

CHAPTER 23

Northeast Philadelphia, Pennsylvania

Eberardo Martinez was a hunter. Growing up in the borderlands of Texas, he'd hunted a lot of deer and wild hogs. He knew the importance of understanding prey. One needs to know how the animal thinks: where and when does it sleep, what does it eat, where does it get its water, what trails does it frequent? He found that these same principles applied to humans.

Since he had been hired by the Z cartel, he had become one of their most prolific hunters. His services had been called upon on both sides of the border. His normal targets were drug mules who had gone missing, a courier who came with less than the expected amount of product or cash, a suspected snitch, or even, on occasion, a journalist or *federale* who didn't take the hint to back off. This job was unique in his experience. He was contracted by his organization to a very rich man in Russia—a gangster, he was told. He did not know the client's name and only spoke to some guy by burner phone he had been given to get his instructions.

The target, he was told, was likely to be very hard to locate. He had received a photo of the target and the person's cellphone data. He didn't ask how the client had obtained this data. He assumed it was through payoffs, which were not uncommon where he operated. A low-level employee of a communications company could be corrupted for very little money to provide what seemed like innocuous information but was actually vital to the hunt.

The cellular phone tracker sat on the table. He had picked it up today from an auto repair shop in northeast Philadelphia. The man who gave the box to him didn't ask any questions and didn't want to make eye contact. He likely didn't know what was in the box but knew he shouldn't ask, either.

Eberardo had been here for two days already, getting familiar with the city. He had driven through the area where the cellphone data indicated the most activity. It was upper middle class to affluent, not the barrios he normally worked in. That made it a little easier. People who lived in drug-riddled zones posted lookouts and security; they were necessarily cautious. People in affluent areas tended to be more relaxed and secure in their sense of entitlement.

He took a drag from his cigarette and looked around the hotel room at the four sleeping assassins sprawled on the beds and floor. They had driven straight through from Texas with a cache of weapons, arriving just hours ago. He had worked with them before and had asked for them specifically for this contract.

He snuffed out his cigarette in the full ashtray. Tomorrow he would go out with Luciana and start tracking the target. Luciana was plain, quiet, and petite. Her manner was subtly disarming, neither threatening nor inviting, and she could make herself almost invisible. People, particularly men, let their guard down around her. Unfortunately for them, that was usually the last thing they ever did. She was also ruthless and coldblood-ed.

Terri, Marc, and Sarah made their way to Dave's office. As they walked through the blocks of cubicles in the SCIF, one of the agents leaned out and said, "You guys are up here an awful lot lately. You sure you don't want to transfer squads, come over to the dark side?"

"No thanks, I like getting outside and seeing the sun once in a while," Sarah joked.

The agent started laughing, and then realized he hadn't in fact been outside any day this week except for his daily commute. "Actually, can you guys take me with you when you leave? I think I'm being held hostage."

Terri laughed, "I'll let you know if a desk opens up."

Dave was finishing another meeting in his office when they arrived at his door. As the analysts and agents exited, Terri and crew entered. "Busy day, huh?"

"Yeah, it can get that way. Grab a seat." He closed his door and joined them at the table. "What's cooking?"

"Marc and I met with our source on the Novaya Zhizn lab this afternoon. We'll write it up and route a copy to you if you like."

Dave's people at the CIA were very interested in Alex's reporting. They had wanted to meet with her in person to debrief, but Terri had put the brakes on that, using Sarah's cover story that Alex was uncomfortable with the CIA. Dave had confirmed what Sarah had found on Lavroski and Astov. And he was sure that at one point, someone, somewhere in the Agency had looked at the academic paper Lavroski had written and filed it away. In light of the new reporting coming in, he agreed that the report was extremely relevant.

Dave grabbed some paper and a pen. "OK, what've you got?"

Terri read over her notes. "Source recalls witnessing extensive human testing, which they described as 'torture'. Source stated that the test subjects were exposed to extreme harm in the form of blunt-force trauma, cutting, stabbing, and shooting at various times. Over time, the experiments increased in ferocity and the likelihood of severe injury or death.

"Source recalls seeing at least five human test subjects at different times in the facility but suspects that there were more. Source believes that all the subjects perished as a result of the testing." The last sentence was intentionally inaccurate to protect Alex, but the rest of the report corresponded with what Alex had told them.

Dave finished writing his notes and then looked up. "Jesus. Can I ask how the source was in a position to know these things?"

"You can ask, but we can't divulge that. It would likely compromise the source's identity. The source was well positioned and had firsthand knowledge of this information. We have verified that as best we can."

"Understood. OK, let's step back a few paces and look at this thing with a broad lens. There is a government-sponsored lab in the middle of Nowhereville, Siberia. Dr. Whatever-his-name-is, Lavroski, is listed as the director of the lab and wrote a paper about seeking tissue-regeneration treatments. Your source claims to have witnessed human test subjects there being tortured and killed, ostensibly with the goal of gaining insight into—what? Increased healing properties? Then one day, this lab is shut down and destroyed in a hurry, along with a nearby village."

"That's a pretty good overview," Marc said.

"Something really freaking bad must have happened there," Dave said, shaking his head. "And your source thinks that all the subjects died during the testing?"

"Yes, most likely all died," Terri said, feeling uneasy about not being completely honest with Dave. She reminded herself that she had no choice.

"These test subjects... We don't think they were Russian military conscripts or anything, do we?" Sarah asked.

Dave shook his head. "No. My guess would be criminals, political prisoners, enemies of the state, and possibly other undesirables, such as drug addicts or homeless people who wouldn't be missed if they vanished."

The phrase *enemy of the state* rang in Terri's head. "I think you might be onto something there, Dave. The source mentioned that at least one of the subjects they observed was probably well educated, female, in her early 20s, and possibly involved in computers. Any chance of digging up likely candidates fitting that description in that time period who disappeared?"

Marc looked at Terri with wide eyes as Dave wrote the description.

"I'll see what we have in the archives. It's a long shot, but I'll let you know."

As they left the SCIF area, Marc caught Terri's arm. "What the hell was that?"

"It's not inaccurate. The source has identified a test subject matching that description, right? So why not shoot for the moon here?"

"All right. We'll see what Dave can come up with." Marc was still uncomfortable with providing a description of Alex to the Agency, even couched in "source speak," but he would go along for now.

Sarah checked her phone as they made their way down the stairs. "Looks like the San Francisco agents are cleared for travel. They will be here next week to debrief Dieter on their subject." Their subject was a hedge fund manager who appears to have been operating a Ponzi scheme and hiding his money with the help of one Dieter Schnoll.

CHAPTER 24

DIETER ENDED A CALL to his wife and children in Switzerland. He called them every day at 1 p.m., his time. Today's call was particularly eventful because his wife informed him that she and the children had been contacted by a US State Department representative from the embassy in Bern. They had also met with an FBI legate. They would be coming to the US to join him.

His work for the FBI had paid off. Terri had told him to be patient, and she'd been right. It was finally happening. Terri had explained that the protection program was very stringent and would eventually require a relocation. When asked where he would like to go, he'd immediately said California. But Terri said no, there were clients of his there, and he could not take a chance on running into them. Then he'd said Colorado, and again she'd said no, explaining that he could not go anywhere he was likely to run into someone who knew him. He had forgotten he had an old client in Denver. Finally, she told him that Omaha, Nebraska was very nice; it had good schools, friendly people, and was large enough so that he could blend in easily. He explained that he and his family enjoyed skiing and would rather be near some mountains. He was told to either get used to an eight-hour drive to the Rockies or take up cross-country skiing instead.

Sarah and Marc were coming tomorrow to pick him up for a meeting with some other agents to discuss another client of his. He was looking forward to the meeting. He truly enjoyed talking about the nuances of moving and protecting money. Perhaps he should have been an economics professor, he thought. His life would certainly have been calmer.

⸻

Alex finished teaching her final class of the day. She had lectured on the aristocratic strata of Eastern Europe in the 18th century and described how the widening disconnect between the ruling class and general society had laid the groundwork for their demise. Checking her phone as she walked to her car, she saw a text from Terri, who wanted to come over tomorrow to show her some pictures. *More show and tell. These agents do love this game,* she thought. She was very much looking forward to seeing Terri.

The language sessions that Alex had been doing had sharpened her memories. And not just of her time in the lab but at... other times. Those revelations had led to a theory that Alex very much wanted to talk to Terri about.

CHAPTER 25

E BERARDO HAD FOUND THE general area of the target. The habits of the prey appeared to be random. The target had been seen briefly talking on the phone, but the team was not in a position to act at that time. The area where the prey lived was busy with pedestrians and traffic. It was difficult to set up long-term surveillance on the house.

He opted to leave Luciana strolling casually around the neighborhood; the rest of his team waited in a couple of cars nearby. If the target left the house, Luciana would let them know which direction the target was headed in and offer a detailed description. They would then pursue and complete the contract at an opportune time and location. The man in Russia had stressed that the situation was to be resolved as quickly as possible, which meant that it was going to have to be on the fly. Not optimal, but not impossible.

Terri and Marc met Sarah at her desk to go over the logistics of the day.

Terri started. "There are a lot of moving parts today. Marc, you and Sarah will get Dieter, take him into the basement, and then bring him up for the meeting. Our guests from San Fran got into town last night.

I checked with them, and they are going to walk here from their hotel. They will call Mike when they get here, and he'll get them set up in a conference room if we aren't back yet."

She continued, "I'm going to run over and see Alex for a hot minute and show her a picture array that includes Dr. Lavroski and the late Dimitry Astov for positive identification. Pretty sure we have the right guys, but a positive ID will seal the deal."

Dave popped around the corner just as they were getting ready to head to the garage. "Hey, glad I caught you guys all together. Something just came across my desk." He lowered his voice. "Our friends in Maryland have been keying in on some phone numbers at our request." Dave was referring to the NSA. "They passed along some odd communications between a number tied to an associate of K2 and Kretzky himself. 'Targeting completed. Contract to be fulfilled.' Then there's a call from K2 to a certain Russian general that we are both interested in. The same message was provided to the general. In light of all that is going on, I wanted to give you guys a heads up. I'm providing this information in the interest of officer safety." Dave always made sure to explain why he was able to give what he gave, in case anyone ever questioned it.

"Jesus, Dave, that sounds ominous. No idea who or what the target is?" Marc asked.

"No, sorry, we don't have that. We're not even sure if they are referring to anything in the States or somewhere else. But in an abundance of caution, I'm passing it along."

"Thanks, Dave." Marc turned to Terri. "How about we continue that 'abundance of caution' theme. Why don't you vest up for your meeting with the source? Soft vest, nothing alarming." He was referring to the traditional ballistic vest that is worn underneath one's clothes, not the heavier raid-style ballistic armor that goes on over clothes and has identifying markings.

"Will do," Terri agreed.

"Sarah and I'll do the same. Sarah, you drive. I got a shotgun in my trunk; I'll get that and meet you at your car."

"Do you think that's necessary?" Sarah asked.

"Just want to be on the good side of prepared."

Terri called Alex from the car and asked her to stay indoors until she pulled up outside.

Dave had pointed out a disturbing wrinkle. Under any other circumstances, she wouldn't give it a second thought. But the audacity of the Rostovich-Schnoll affair had changed all that. If they were willing to attempt a murder on US soil, then they were very desperate. And in that situation, she'd been pretty sure who the "they" were, though she and Marc had identified the players only hours before. But if something new was in play now, she was most likely going to be blind to it until it happened. That could mean the difference between life and death.

She stopped in front of Alex's row house, called her, and asked her to come out. As she waited, she scanned her mirrors and the surrounding area for anything odd.

Her passenger door opened, and Alex sat down next to her.

"Did you notice anything, smell anything odd when you came out?

Alex looked at her with a quizzical expression. "No, Agent Watson, I did not." Still, Alex rolled down the window and took a deep breath through her nose.

Luciana called Eberardo on a handheld two-way radio. They had purchased a set of four of them in Texas. The devices had limited range but offered faster communication for the job they had at hand. "The target is out and in a car." She provided the description of the car and direction it was driving.

Eberardo radioed back, "OK, I am around the corner. I will pick you up. Jorge saw the car pull out with the target and is pursuing it."

He thought to himself, *The hunt is on.*

Sarah and Marc stopped in front of the safe house. Dieter trotted to the car and hopped into the back seat. Marc sat in the passenger seat, literally riding shotgun with the large-bore weapon resting against his knee. As they drove off, he kept a close eye on the traffic around them, noting any cars that pulled next to them at a light or drove behind them. Dieter, sitting in the back seat, talked incessantly about something that Marc wasn't paying attention to. Sarah had just turned onto Roosevelt Boulevard when Marc said, "Pull over to the right lane and slow down."

Marc had been watching a car with three men behind them since they pulled away from the safe house, and he wanted to see how the car would react to the move. Sarah pulled to the right and slowed down. The car did too, staying behind them.

"We got a tail. Dieter, do-not-look back," he said.

The blood drained from Dieter's face, and his mouth fell open.

Sarah glanced at the mirror. "You talking about the black car? I can see at least three people in it."

"Yeah, that's the one. I counted at least three too. OK, everyone, stay calm."

"That is not what you tell someone when you want them to stay calm!" Dieter spluttered.

"OK, then try to fake it at least," Marc said quietly. "I'm gonna call for a marked unit to escort us to the federal building. See if we can get another couple of units to pull that car over as well." Marc got on his radio and provided the dispatcher with his identification, what car they were in, where they were, and the plate number and description of the tail. "Request a marked unit to escort us and a vehicle stop of the subject car."

As Marc waited for an acknowledgement from the dispatcher, a second car sped past them on the right, cut in front of them, and immediately slammed on its brakes. Sarah cursed and swerved, taking them over the curb, out of the express lanes and into the local lanes. Horns blared as the car behind them performed the same maneuver. Suddenly, a hail of bullets shattered the back window of Sarah's car and pierced its roof.

The dispatcher came back and requested they proceed to the next light and wait for the escort. "That isn't going to work. We need backup now! We're taking fire. Officer assistance needed immediately!" Marc looked back and saw a man hanging out the passenger window with an assault rifle. "Put your head down, Dieter!"

Dieter was already lying down on the seat.

Marc looked ahead; the second car was coming over the median as well. If they did nothing, they were going to be forced off the road and blocked in by the two cars. He had a pretty good idea what the bad guys' plan would be if that happened: they would rush the car from two directions and kill them all. Better to limit their numbers and take the offense. "Ok Sar, see that little street up there?" he asked calmly.

"Yeah," Sarah said shakily. Her hands were gripping the wheel so hard that her fingernails were digging into her palms.

"You're gonna make a tight turn up that street. When you get around the corner, punch it until I say 'now'—then hit the brakes hard. If they don't ram us, I want you to throw it in reverse and back into them as hard as you can. Got it?"

Sarah looked at him questioningly but took the corner for the side street at the highest speed she could, careening off a parked car but still going. She accelerated, praying that no one would walk out in front of her.

Marc watched as the chase car slammed on its brakes and made the turn. The other car that was trying to get in front of them had missed the turn completely and continued up the main road. The chase car accelerated as well, closing the distance. When it was almost on their bumper and the shooter was leaning out the window, Marc yelled, "Now!"

Sarah hit the brakes hard. The other driver reacted too slowly and slammed into the back of Sarah's car. Immediately, their airbags deployed.

Marc was out the door before the car had come to a complete stop. He racked the shotgun and aimed it at the passenger side of the assassin's car. The assault rifle lay on the street, dislodged by either the impact or the airbags. He heard cursing in Spanish and saw the door open. "Police! Don't move!" Marc yelled. A man emerged with a pistol in his hand. He started to raise it, and Marc fired.

The eight pellets from the 00 buckshot round tore into the man's chest, knocking him to the ground. A large red stain bloomed on his shredded T-shirt.

Marc racked the shotgun again as the driver's door started to open, too, but he couldn't see the driver through the airbags. Sarah had come up by then, pistol drawn, and was giving commands.

The driver pointed a pistol out the open door and started firing wildly. Sarah crouched and returned fire while Marc fired two rounds in rapid succession at the windshield, which shattered into a web of green and gray.

The driver stopped firing and spilled out onto the street.

In a flash, Marc realized that the back passenger door had opened. A third man appeared with yet another assault rifle. Loud explosions rang out in rapid succession. Marc racked the shotgun, but before he could return fire, a round ricocheted off a corner of Sarah's car and struck him in the armpit.

He grunted and fell to the pavement. The burning pain was blinding. He had a sense of bullets striking the pavement around him as he lay in the street, and he heard muffled pops. He saw the shooter double over, clutching his abdomen, and then turn and hobble away. He saw the wounded man get into the second car, which had just caught up with them. It backed up the street and disappeared.

Sarah was suddenly there, looking down at him. She was saying something about staying awake, but he felt so tired. He just wanted to close his eyes. The pain in his chest was easing. Somewhere in his mind, he knew he was bleeding out internally. Faint sirens wailed, getting louder, but still so far away. Sarah clutched his face, imploring him to stay with her. Then—nothing.

CHAPTER 26

W̶HEN TERRI GOT THE call from Jim about the shooting, she dropped Alex at her house and drove frantically to the scene. She felt numb, but her mind was racing. Jim didn't have any word on Marc's condition, only that there had been a shooting, two bad guys were down, a third was wounded, and Marc had been hit. Was Marc going to live? What happened? Who were these guys? The scene was controlled chaos. Police tape blocked the street, and the red lights of a dozen squad cars flashed as crime scene investigators searched for shell casings, putting numbered markers by each one they found. Sadly, this scene was all too familiar in Philadelphia.

Terri saw Sarah sitting on the curb, resting her head on her arms. Jim was at her side. Several other members of the squad stood huddled around them, shielding her from any photographers. As Terri made her way through the crowd, Jim stood up and met her. The pain on Terri's face was palpable.

"How is Sarah?" Terri asked.

"She's OK. Shaken, but OK," he said, looking over his shoulder at Sarah. "I had Jeff and Scott drive Dieter to the office with a police escort. He's safe."

"What about Marc?" she asked.

"Marc—" Jim paused. "Marc is in rough shape. They rushed him to Einstein Trauma in a patrol car."

"Is he going to make it?" Terri realized the futility of asking the question as soon as the words left her mouth.

"I don't know. I heard he's in surgery now. He's tough and young and has the will to live. That counts for a lot."

Terri nodded.

"I need you to take Sarah out of here. Get her home or wherever she wants to go, but stay with her. She's been through a lot." Though Jim certainly wanted to get Sarah away from this as quickly as he could, he knew that he needed to give Terri something to do as well.

"Will do, boss."

During the drive, Sarah looked out the windshield blankly, stunned. "It happened so fast. The impact, the shooting, then Marc—" She turned to Terri. "He saved Dieter and me. I did everything I could." She was on the verge of tears.

"I know you did. Sometimes bad things happen to good people. It's just the way the world works. You can't blame yourself for any of this."

Terri hit a bump and something fell from Sarah's vest onto the floor mat. Sarah looked down and retrieved a large slug that had been embedded in her ballistic vest. She held it up in the light. "Do you have any evidence bags?" she asked absently.

Terri glanced over. "Jesus, where did that come from?"

"It just fell out of my vest. I didn't even realize I had been shot."

"There are some plastic evidence bags back there." She motioned to her shoulder bag in the back seat.

Sarah held up a cigarette butt. "Also, I picked this up off the ground. The driver of the second car tossed it out as he drove away, and I didn't want it to get blown away or lost. I forgot to give it to the evidence guys at the scene."

Terri pulled into the hospital parking lot. Sarah wanted to check on Marc, and that's where Terri wanted to be as well. A half-dozen police cars filled the emergency entrance. Several more were at the main entrance. Terri and Sarah flashed their badges and walked in. Beth was there in the waiting area, looking like a ghost. Terri and Sarah gave her a hug and listened to her sobs. There was nothing else they could do.

"Marc had told me he was working on something dangerous. He told me to get the kids and leave if anything happened to him. Is this what he was talking about?" Beth asked.

Terri held her and replied, "No, I don't think so. You and the kids are all right. He needs you here now to help him pull through. He will need your strength, Beth."

•

Alex knew something was terribly wrong when Terri got the call. She could hear the voice on the phone describe a shooting, and then she heard Marc's name mentioned. Terri wouldn't tell her anything as they sped back to Alex's house, but Alex knew she was distraught.

She found a live broadcast online. The anchor announced the breaking story about a police shootout in which one officer had been gravely injured. Alex knew the name of the injured officer before the newscaster said it. Scenes of police cars at the hospital ER flashed on the screen.

Alex turned off the computer and sat quietly for a few moments. She had only once in her memory felt anything like this. That was when Jennifer had told her that Colin hit her. She had immediately felt anger—no, *rage.* She felt protective of this detective, too. He had treated her with understanding and good humor. He had trusted her and, in doing so, gained her trust. He was a good man. How could this have been inflicted upon him? She had searched long for a group that would accept her and now someone was trying to take that from her.

She paced her living room as she processed her emotions. Soon she sensed another feeling creep into her consciousness, something very foreign to her. Fear. Not of physical danger, but of the possibility that she may never see him again.

Alex left her house and started walking the several dozen blocks up Broad Street to the hospital. She knew she would never be able to get in to see him, but she wanted to be close. Perhaps the walk in the warm afternoon sun would help her sort out the clamoring thoughts in her head.

CHAPTER 27

EBERARDO, LUCIANA, AND THEIR injured man, Antonio, sped away from the scene of the street battle. Luciana had wanted to press the attack and finish the job, but Eberardo had stopped her, grabbing her arm as she tried to get out. He wanted to get away while they still could. He knew they had lost any element of surprise and would have had to shoot and maneuver to close on the target vehicle. The approaching sirens indicated that they did not have the time to do that. Also, how many armed people were in the target vehicle? He had already lost more than half his team. His survival instinct took over.

Antonio lay in the back seat, groaning. He had been shot once in the abdomen and once in the right thigh. Eberardo looked at Luciana; he could tell that they were thinking the same thing. Antonio was now a liability. They couldn't get him medical help for fear of being discovered. But trying to get away with a wounded man would be both difficult and draw unwanted attention. Luciana knew what had to be done. She leaned over the seat and put her pistol to Antonio's forehead. He looked at her, eyes pleading, and started to say something. She pulled the trigger.

Eberardo drove through the neighborhood of vacant lots and shuttered stores covered with graffiti, looking for a place to abandon their car.

He spoke without looking at Luciana. "We are already dead. You know that, right?"

Luciana, staring straight ahead, didn't respond. She knew they were a long way from the border—not that crossing over would offer any real refuge, anyway. If they were captured by the police, they would go to prison, where there was a high probability that they would be killed by inmates on orders from the cartel to prevent them from cooperating. And even if they managed to escape death at the hands of the police, they would likely face death at the hands of their organization at home. They were truly on their own.

Eberardo pulled the car into a weed-covered lot. He placed the small explosive device in the trunk over the gas tank and set the timer for four hours. He then took out a weathered tarp and covered the car. He and Luciana retrieved what they could carry from the car and walked away.

Terri and Sarah were still at the hospital, asleep in a pair of chairs. Other members of the squad and police officers held vigil with them as Marc fought for his life. Jim came by at around 0100. He encouraged his people to go home and get some sleep but asked them to be in the office by 0900 for a meeting. They weren't going to accomplish anything by staying here.

Terri and Sarah gathered their belongings and headed to Terri's car. As they got close, Terri saw Alex standing tall and alert, eyes fixed on the hospital. "Alex! How long have you been here?"

"What time is it? I have been here since 10:30 p.m.," she said without moving. "Will he live?"

"We think so. He was hurt badly. A bullet hit him in the chest, collapsing both lungs and nearly severing a major artery. The doctors gave him several units of blood and repaired the damage in surgery. He is in a medically induced coma right now."

Alex didn't move; she just continued to stare at the building. "I do not pray. I have no faith in things such as a god. But I do know the power of the spirit and the mind. I have been thinking of Marc very intently with a focus on healing." She now turned to Terri and Sarah. "Was that his wife and children I saw leaving earlier, with the phalanx of police officers surrounding them?"

"Yes, it was. Except that is his ex-wife."

Alex nodded.

"Hop in, I'll give you a ride home."

"Thank you, Agent Watson, that is very kind of you. And who is your compatriot?"

Terri had forgotten that Alex and Sarah had never met. "This is Sarah Holmes. She is a fellow agent on my squad."

Sarah was slack-jawed as Alex reached out a hand and said, "A pleasure to meet you Agent Sarah Holmes. My name is Alexandra Stepanova." Alex could tell by the look on Sarah's face that she knew who she was. She smiled warmly.

Sarah absently returned Alex's handshake. She had now met the werewolf in the flesh and was having a hard time wrapping her mind around that.

Alex still wanted to discuss some things with Terri, but now, with Sarah there, she could not. Though the items were important, they were not time sensitive. It would be prudent to wait.

CHAPTER 28

J IM STOOD BEFORE THE squad in the break room. The faces looking back at him were weary from lack of rest and concern. But the energy of a quiet anger simmered just below the surface as well. For the most part, these were men and women of action. Someone had struck at one of their own, and that could not stand. They wanted to be engaged.

Every agent, analyst, and TFO in the office was going to work like hell today to bring the people responsible for this attack to justice. Jim had drawn up assignments toward that end.

"OK, listen up. We are all concerned about Marc, so I want to let you know what I know. Here's the latest. He came out of the second surgery early this morning. He is still in a coma but stable. He lost a lot of blood yesterday, and the doctors aren't sure if there will be any adverse effects on his brain function. I'm sorry to say those words, but that is the situation.

I want to publicly thank Sarah for her actions yesterday," he continued, turning to Sarah, who looked like she wanted to crawl under the carpet. "You exhibited tremendous bravery and tenacity in the face of intense danger. Thank you." Sarah smiled faintly and peered down at her feet. She had never liked to be on center stage.

"Now, here's what we know about this crew," Jim stated. "The IDs are still in the works, but we believe they are part of a Mexican or South American drug cartel. The weapons recovered were all legally purchased in Texas within the past year. ATF is looking into the buyers more closely to understand how the weapons wound up in the hands of cartel members." He hypothesized that they were probably bought by straw purchasers.

"The car recovered at the scene was stolen from a parking lot at the King of Prussia mall several days ago. Our team found two-way radios in the car, the kind someone might use for camping or hiking. Good quality. There was a picture of their target and notes about what had been going on in the neighborhood over several days. It read like a goddamn surveillance log. The final entry was a description of Sarah's car with the license plate number.

Another car was found about three miles away in a vacant lot. The local PD believes it was the second car involved in the incident, but it was burned out, so that's not definite. This assessment was based on the make and model of the car described by Sarah and other eyewitnesses as well as on the items found in the car—including one dead body. Medical examiner's office preliminary results indicated the remains to be that of a man, approximately 25 to 30 years old, who died from a large-caliber gunshot wound to the head. It was also noted that the body still had two 9mm bullets embedded in it." Jim looked at Sarah and nodded. Several heads turned to her and gave her a thumbs up as well. She smiled faintly again and then found something on her shoe to try to rub off.

"From what we've been able to piece together, it appears that two members of the crew remain at large," he continued. "A male and a female, according to eyewitnesses. Police are checking with every hotel in a 30-mile radius for any guests that match the descriptions of our suspects.

The airport and train stations have heavy police presence. Pennsylvania State Police have set up checkpoints outside the city, and the Delaware River Port Authority is checking cars heading to New Jersey.

"This was not random. Not by a fucking mile. This was a professional hit team here to kill the target and anyone else who got in their way." Jim let that sink in for a minute. He wanted his squad to understand what the threat profile looked like.

"Terri, I want you and Sarah, if you feel up to it, to work with your source and see if you can figure out who might be behind this. Also, follow up on his WITSEC application. I, personally, would like to see this guy disappear into anonymity as soon as possible.

"The rest of the squad will be paired up with Philly detectives canvassing hotels, campgrounds, youth hostels, and anything else you can think of where five assholes might sleep. Provide all information, positive or negative, to the command center. Analysts will be working there, coalescing all the data coming in.

"Any questions? No? Good, let's get to work."

When Terri got back to her desk, the first call she made was to Dave.

"Let me just say that I'm so sorry to hear about Marc," he blurted. "I'm praying he pulls through. And thank Jesus Sarah is OK. Sounds like she handled herself quite well, from what I'm hearing up here."

"She did. She's tough as nails," Terri said into the phone as she looked at Sarah, who was now blushing. "I wanted to—"

"I'm on it," Dave interrupted. "I have leads out to my shop and the other organization we talked about yesterday." Dave wouldn't say "NSA" on an unsecure line. "I have asked them to widen their cone and see what they can give us. I'll hit you up on your cell if I get anything hot."

"Thanks, Dave. Much appreciated."

As Terri hung up the phone, Sarah asked, "Do you think it's worth talking to Dieter about this? I think we have a pretty good idea of his client base and who's dangerous."

"I agree. He is sitting with the San Fran guys today in their hotel room. We got him an adjoining room there, so they will babysit him today and tonight. We can stop over and check on him, but I don't see the need to spend the day there. This was supposed to look like a narco hit, but I don't think it was."

The walk to the hotel was only a few blocks. As expected, Dieter was rattled almost to the point of a breakdown. Also as they expected, the meeting proved fruitless. He could offer no new ideas as to who might have been behind the latest attempt on his life. The San Francisco agents would continue to sit with him while the manhunt continued. One of them told Terri as she was leaving that when he started talking about the actual mechanics of his profession, he seemed to calm down. Terri wasn't surprised. That was his comfort zone.

The two women left the hotel, instinctively scrutinizing every person they saw in the lobby. Walking back to the office, they bounced ideas around.

"So, these guys came up from Texas, possibly crossing the border first."

"Most likely. Everything points to that," Sarah confirmed.

"The cars used in the attack yesterday were both obtained locally, right?"

"Yes, stolen from somewhere in the area."

"If these guys had this thing worked out that far in advance, they must have had a plan to get out of here."

Sarah agreed. "They didn't strike me as a suicide squad, so yes, that would make sense. They knew they weren't going to be able to fly out or take any other public transportation. So—"

"Maybe they have a car stashed somewhere here? A car they drove here?"

"That makes as much sense as anything right now. Nobody has found any flights yet. Plus, it would make getting the heavy firepower here easy."

"Exactly. I think they drove. Somewhere, there is a car. The state police and DRPA can't keep checkpoints up indefinitely. They'll just wait it out and try to slip away."

When they got to the office, they ran their theory by Jim. He liked the logic behind it, but the issue was quickly turning into a massive logistical challenge. "The PD is stretched thin. Even with our numbers and all the other federal law enforcement officers augmenting them, it is a herculean task. We simply can't cover every parking lot in the area."

"You OK if we do some digging and try to flesh out a plan to narrow the search?" Sarah asked.

"Absolutely. I'll take any good ideas. Hell, I'll take a half-baked idea at this point."

Sarah put her analytical skills to use. With years of experience as an FBI analyst before becoming an agent, she knew which databases would help. She went to the command post, which was humming with activity. As she walked in, a round of applause broke out, and she immediately turned red. Several people came up to her and congratulated her on the job she had done. They asked how she was doing. She politely thanked them and moved on. *How long will this go on?* she asked herself.

She found a group of analysts in the back of the room at a row of computers. She recognized Samantha and sat next to her. "Do we have access to Philadelphia Parking Authority data?" she asked. The PPA was notorious in the city—in fact, throughout the country—thanks to a reality TV show. The organization was draconian and efficient. There were stories of their tow truck drivers hauling away marked police cars from the street. Sarah had never seen it happen, but she didn't doubt it, either.

"Yes. They haven't given us full access, but we can request searches, and they will run them on a priority basis."

"OK, that's a start. Can you have them check for vehicles with Texas plates towed in the past week? If we get nothing, we'll expand to vehicles with Oklahoma, New Mexico, or Louisiana plates next."

Sam started typing the request. "I like the way you're thinking here," she said.

While Sarah was working on the data, Terri's anger grew. She wanted to see these people taken out. She reasoned that they would not cooperate anyway; but really, she just wanted to see them dead. She shook her head in frustration. This was not productive thinking. She needed to stay busy to keep these thoughts out of her head.

She decided to follow up on the status of Dieter's WITSEC package. Jim was clear that he wanted Dieter out of the division as soon as possible. She guessed that, at this point, Jim would be willing to pay for Dieter's bus ticket with his own money. She suspected that the rest of the squad would chip in as well. Bad luck or not, people around Dieter were dying at an alarming rate. She was told that it would take another week to finalize his new identity and ship him out to some mundane midwestern city. Until then, they would still have to protect him. Not the news she wanted to hear or share with Jim.

Her phone rang. "Sarah here. Breaking news from the CP: they think they found the hotel room these guys were staying in. A dive place in Northeast Philly. Room was rented with cash, fake ID provided upon check-in. No car in the lot. Our guys are with the PD right now, searching the room."

"Good deal! Maybe we'll get some leads," answered Terri. "How are you making out with the tag search?"

"Dry holes so far. No cars towed that fit the bill. We're checking tag scanner data now."

"Copy that. Thanks."

"Oh—they did find one thing in the room right away: an instruction manual and shipping material for a pretty sophisticated cellphone tracker. It was sent to a repair shop in Philly about ten days ago."

"That's very interesting. Was it shipped from Mexico?" Terri asked.

"No, Germany. The guys here are trying to run it all down as we speak."

"When you finish up there, come by my desk. I want to run something by you. I'm thinking of enlisting the services of a force multiplier," Terri said, as she looked at the evidence bag with the cigarette butt.

"Uh, OK. Hold that thought, I'll be up in a few." Sarah thought she might know which force multiplier Terri was considering, and it made her blood run cold.

"I don't like this, Terri," Sarah said bluntly.

Sarah had arrived at the squad area at 5 p.m. Jim was in his office on the phone with his door closed, but the rest of the place felt deserted; everyone was out covering leads with the PD.

"I get it, but hear me out. We are stretched thin. There are too many parking lots to patrol. What if we take Alex out and cruise through some of them, see if she picks up anything? We can look for suspicious tags and she can... do what she does. If she finds something, we run the tags and call it in. All nice-nice."

Sarah thought for a bit. She was sure there was a very good reason that they shouldn't do this, but she couldn't come up with it. "Ok, where do you want to start?"

CHAPTER 29

ALEX WAS GLAD TO hear from Terri. She was not enjoying her thoughts alone. She remembered seeing Marc's family as they were escorted from the hospital. Their faces wore masks of pain, anguish, and worry—just like Colin's brother's had during the funeral and burial. But she'd seen nothing of the kind on Jennifer's face, ever. This troubled her greatly. Combined with the tidal wave of rage she was feeling for the people who caused Marc's injuries, she was on a hair trigger. Was she grateful that Terri had asked for her help or simply relieved to be doing something? Either way, it took her out of her own head and gave her a purpose.

She sat in the back seat of Terri's car, holding the small plastic bag with the cigarette butt in her lap. The acrid odor was unpleasant and distinctive. It was not a common brand of cigarette; at least, she had not registered the odor before. Her anger gave her focus. She desperately wanted to do great harm to the ones they sought. She knew Terri would try to stop her; it was her job. But Alex wanted blood.

All the windows were down in the car as Terri drove slowly through the parking lot. The cool night air felt refreshing. It was their fifth lot so far. Terri and Sarah had reasoned that a long-term parking lot would be their best bet, so they had started with the numerous private lots around Philadelphia International Airport.

Alex was unusually quiet. Maybe having Sarah along changed the dynamic. But Alex did seem to be intently focused on what Terri had asked her to do.

Sarah spotted the car first. It was an older Ford Explorer, very dusty, with Oklahoma plates.

Terri parked several rows away. She wanted to look it over first to see if there was anything suspicious. She also wanted to let Alex use her... senses... around the car to see if she detected anything before they called it in.

Eberardo and Luciana waited nervously in the shadows. Earlier that evening, they had taken a cab to a hotel about a mile away, paying cash. Eberardo had put on a wig and a dress for the trip, and he hoped the cab driver didn't look too closely at him. They then walked to the lot and hid in the marshy area near the river until it was very dark and the lot was quiet. They were almost to the SUV when they saw headlights. Eberardo quickly snuffed out his cigarette. They watched as the car drove slowly along the rows of vehicles.

Their plan was to steal the license plates off another car in the lot and switch them out with the ones on their SUV. They hoped to evade the police long enough to get to Baltimore or DC and find transportation back home. If they could make it, then they'd take their chances with the cartel.

They knew their hotel room had probably been discovered by now. But even if it hadn't been, they couldn't go back to it; the risk was too great. The Explorer, which held cash and fresh identification, was their only lifeline. But now someone was in their way.

Terri turned off the engine. "OK, let's go take a look at this car, see if there's anything in plain sight."

Terri had disabled the overhead dome light so the car would stay dark when the doors opened. The three women got out. Terri turned to ask Alex to look at the SUV as well, but Alex was moving off on her own.

Alex heard Terri hiss, "Hey! Where are you going?"

Alex had smelled it as soon as she got out of the car: the faint odor of a cigarette. Someone else was nearby, unseen.

She motioned for Terri and Sarah to stay quiet as she turned in a small circle, sniffing the air. She paused to try to determine the source of the smell; where was the wind carrying it from? She peered at a reedy area at the edge of the lot and then at the shadows several rows away. Quietly, she slid off her shoes, ducked down, and moved silently over the asphalt.

Terri and Sarah looked at each other, drew their pistols, and stooped low as well. They started moving toward the SUV.

Eberardo watched them from several rows away. One of the women stood tall, turning slowly. Then she stopped and appeared to look directly at him. Before he could get Luciana's attention, the woman had disappeared. The other two were creeping slowly toward the parked Explorer. He could see that they had guns drawn.

He alerted Luciana with hand signals. They drew their pistols and started to move independently, hoping to circle behind the two women with guns. They would get to their car or die trying.

Alex knew they were here. She could smell the odor of cigarettes mixed with sweat. But the breeze swirled around her, making it tough to pinpoint their location. She stared at the shadows. She couldn't be sure, but she thought she saw a glimmer of light. She could have transformed and charged the area, but she decided, for Terri's benefit, to try to help them capture these two alive, if possible. She crouched down and started to maneuver toward the source of the light.

Eberardo was about 20 yards behind the two women. He could see that they were scanning with their pistols as they walked, each covering a different arc to the sides and up ahead. He raised his gun and was taking careful aim when he heard something above and behind him.

Turning toward the sound, he caught a glimpse of a woman with short-cropped hair on a car roof. Moving with incredible speed, she leaped down and attacked him, repeatedly slamming her fist into his face and grabbing his wrist that held the gun. He had been in many fights and been hit many times, but these blows were faster and harder than any he had ever felt. His jawbone cracked and his knees buckled. He fell senseless to the pavement.

Luciana watched from the shadows as Eberardo went down. The woman with short-cropped hair stood over his unmoving body; the other two women with guns were still walking away toward the SUV, unaware of what had just happened. Luciana was overcome with desperate rage. Holding her pistol in her right hand, she drew a knife from the small of her back with her left. Then she rushed toward Eberardo's assailant.

Alex looked down at the would-be killer. The jaw twisted awkwardly to the side, and blood poured from the nose. She was mildly interested to see that he turned out to be a man in a dress rather than a woman. That explained the unusual smell she'd noticed from him. She knew there was another person nearby. But before she could alert Terri and Sarah, she heard footsteps running toward her. She spun to face the sound and saw a small woman charging at her, pistol raised. Alex's reflexes were not as fast as when she was in her other form, but she instinctively swatted away the gun from the small person's hand. It fell to the ground with a loud metallic clunk. Suddenly, hot pain seared her flesh. The woman had thrust a blade into Alex's gut. She snarled and slammed a fist into the chest of her assailant, sending the small body flying backward. She glanced down at her wound. The transformation had started.

Luciana had missed her mark. The knife wound had not been immediately fatal. She gulped for air and tried to regain her feet after the blow to her chest, but her legs were shaky and would not respond.

She looked up and watched in shock as the woman with short-cropped hair pulled the knife from her flesh. She held it up and examined the blade, which had turned a dark crimson color—almost black—in the faint light. Then the woman ran her tongue along the edge with a broad, wicked smile, tasting the blood. Luciana could see that there was something wrong with the woman's face. Her eyes were almost black with a hint of green reflecting in light. It looked like she had fangs. Then there was something wrong with her body, too. It began rippling and expanding, her face contorting into that of a demon. The knife clanged on the pavement when the...thing...dropped it. Luciana crossed herself and said a prayer in Spanish.

The pain of the stabbing had triggered the transformation process instantly, but the change was not yet complete. Alex lifted the small woman up by her shirt and prepared to tear out her throat when she heard Terri and Sarah approaching.

"Alex!" Terri shouted.

Alex turned. She appeared to be in mid transformation. Awestruck, Terri could see the blood lust in her eyes. And though Alex's face was now grotesquely changing, it was still somehow handsome. The muscles of her arms and back were straining the material of her blouse. She easily held the small woman off the ground with her left hand. Her right hand appeared to have large claws and was poised to strike.

Terri knew that she should tell Alex to stop, but she realized that she wanted to watch her tear this assassin to shreds. The blood lust was real. So she just stared.

Sarah screamed, "No, don't do it!" and looked at Terri, who said nothing.

Terri met Alex's stare. She realized that she held this woman's life in her hands at that moment. She knew that if she told Alex to finish her, she would do so instantly. But if she told Alex to stop, she would. After what seemed like minutes, but were only seconds, Terri reluctantly shook her head.

Alex turned back to the woman in her grasp, who was gibbering with fear. Alex opened her hand, and the woman fell to the ground in a heap, still muttering prayers and crossing herself repeatedly.

CHAPTER 30

T ERRI STOOD AFTER HANDCUFFING the two prone figures on the pavement, one unconscious and the other in shock. She looked back at Alex. "You're wounded," she said, pointing to the blood on Alex's shirt.

"I have had much worse."

"Did it hurt?" Terri asked.

"It always hurts," Alex said with a faint smile.

"I thought you were impervious to wounds like this?" Terri asked.

"I am, mostly. The faster an object hits my flesh, the faster it is stopped. Bullets only penetrate a fraction of an inch. Edged weapons that move slowly cut deeper. It is painful. I am not immune to that."

Terri looked down at the bloodstained shirt. There didn't seem to be enough blood for a fresh wound. "May I look? You might need stitches," she said.

"Be my guest, Agent Watson," replied Alex, as she lifted her shirt. Terri was astonished to see that not only had the bleeding stopped, but the gash was closed as well. She touched it gently— Alex's flesh felt hot—and could feel the scar tissue that had already formed.

"Why did you stop me, Agent Watson? I could tell you wanted them dead, just as I did."

Terri mumbled something about it being her job to bring them in alive, that they would get justice through the courts, and perhaps they would provide some evidence that can assist the investigation. The words felt empty.

"Of course, you must say this," Alex said, eyeing Terri closely.

In her heart, Terri knew Alex was right. She had wanted to watch their blood spill out onto the ground. She had wanted to hear them scream with pain and terror. The realization shook her.

Sarah came over to the pair after calling in the arrest on the car radio. "Police will be here in a few minutes. Tell me again, just how are we going to explain this?"

Terri looked around. "OK, we found the car and went to take a closer look when these two popped out of the shadows, surprising us, and we took them down. Simple."

"Perhaps it would be best if I was not here when the police arrived," said Alex. "I will walk to the previous lot we toured and wait for you there?"

Terri nodded. "Sounds good. Thank you, Alex."

"Yes, thank you, Alex. You probably saved our butts tonight," Sarah said with a smile.

"You are most welcome, Agent Sarah Holmes." With that, Alex turned and walked away.

Terri watched Alex disappear into the darkness. "Like I said, a force multiplier."

CHAPTER 31

KONSTANTIN KRETZKY LOOKED AT the text message. It was short and blunt: "Mission failure." He stared at the screen for several moments as he processed the ramifications. He had, of course, planned for this contingency, just as he had planned for success. But the actions he felt he must now take were drastic.

He summoned his personal-protection detail lead and instructed him to call the cars to the loading dock. The SUVs, already loaded with luggage, would take him to his country dacha, where he would be safer to ride out the fallout of the botched assassination attempt on Herr Schnoll.

As he waited for the all-clear signal to move to the freight elevator, he looked out the window of his office at the twinkling lights of Moscow below him. Several police cars and an ambulance came speeding up to his building and stopped near the main entrance. He pressed his head against the glass, but he couldn't see where they went. His heart started pounding for a few seconds before he assured himself that it was a coincidence.

The eight police officers and an ambulance crew towing a wheeled stretcher entered the lobby. The security officer confronted them before they reached the elevators. He was told there was a suicidal man on the ninth floor. When the security officer asked who it was, he was struck by a Taser and pushed aside.

Kretzky heard the ding of the elevator and the clamor of boots in the hallway. He rushed to his office door and bolted it.

He could hear the men approach and watched as the heavy door rattled but held. He retreated to his desk and retrieved a pistol. The weapon shook slightly in his hand; it had been many years since he'd handled a firearm personally. A man in his position has others to do that.

Then he heard the men outside the door move quickly away down the hall. He released the breath he'd been holding. Perhaps his security team had arrived to chase them away.

Suddenly, his door exploded, and he was thrown backwards, landing on the floor. His ears rang as he saw several uniformed police officers rush through the smoke that hung in the air.

As they hoisted him to his feet, he protested groggily. Then, through his muffled hearing, he recognized the sound of rifle fire, and he recoiled. But he soon realized that he had not been shot. Perhaps this was all just to scare him. Maybe they were hoping to extort a payment from him and that was all.

The officers turned him around to face an open window, the glass shattered by bullets. He felt the cool fresh breeze on his face and knew in an instant that this was not a bluff. He was tossed into the night air. Screaming as his arms flailed uselessly, he plunged to the street below.

The men of the Interior Ministry set the spent Kalashnikov rifle on ground near the open window and departed.

Back in his office, General Stepin received the news. Mission completed. He, too, had made contingency plans in the event the operation in the US was not successful.

CHAPTER 32

IN THE TWO WEEKS that followed, Sarah and Terri were both greeted by posters hanging by their desks. Sarah's was of *Crouching Tiger, Hidden Dragon,* where a photo of her face had been cut out and pasted over the Chinese warrior's face. Terri had a picture of Bruce Lee in his yellow jumpsuit, with her face placed over his. She was told it was from the movie *Game of Death.* She had never seen it.

Things were getting back to normal.

Marc was out of the ICU and recovering. When Terri and Sarah went to visit him, Terri told him that this was a helluva way to get out of work. If he needed time off, he could have just asked for it. He replied, "Screw you, too!" and laughed, then winced from a jolt of pain. "Fill me in. I'm goin' outta my mind here. Where does everything stand?"

"Well, Sarah here is probably going to get the Shield of Bravery award from the Bureau. We'll likely both be working for her someday."

"That'll be the sorriest day of your career, if that happens. I know all your tricks," Sarah said with a smile.

"She's right. We'll havta come up with some new ones," Marc added.

"We're putting Dieter and his family on a one-way trip to somewhere other than here. We'll have to work through the WITSEC program guys to set up any interviews with him, but I'm good with that," Terri stated.

Marc laid his head back and closed his eyes. "Thank you, Jesus. Don't get me wrong, I like that guy, but man is he a magnet for trouble. Best if he just quietly disappears."

"Amen to that," Terri confirmed.

"We're pretty sure where this whole thing originated. Dave and his fellow Secret Squirrels got us some good intel. Suffice it to say that Mexico wasn't the source. Looks like it leads back to our friends in Russia," Terri said.

"Why am I not surprised?" Marc said, shaking his head. "I'm really starting to dislike those guys."

Sarah jumped in, "Although, it appears there is one less Russian oligarch on the rolls. K2, it seems, committed suicide. Reports from the Russian news say that he jumped from his office window."

"Whoa. That's very telling. I guess he finally pissed off the wrong person?" Marc concluded.

"It would seem so. Don't worry, we will still have plenty of work to do, so get your butt better and get out of here," Terri said, putting a hand on his shoulder.

"Sure thing, boss."

"I'm not a boss, I still work for a living," Terri pointed out.

"Oh, and I met Alex. Lovely woman," Sarah added.

Marc's eyes went a little wide with that. "Yeah? And how did that go?"

"Well, contrary to the stories of our hand-to-hand heroics in the parking lot, it was Alex that took down the last two cartel assassins. Obviously, that stays between us girls here," Sarah whispered.

"I think she was genuinely worried about you, Marc. She's difficult to read at times, but I think she cares for you," Terri added.

"I'm not so sure if that's a good thing or bad thing," he said with a laugh and another wince.

"Well, I tend to think that if she *didn't* like you, then that would be a *very* bad thing," Sarah pointed out.

"Yeah, I think you're right."

"The night you were shot, we found her in the parking lot here, staring at the hospital," Terri said, motioning toward the window.

"It was almost like she was guarding you or something. That was the vibe I got, anyway," Sarah added, just realizing it when she said it out loud.

"That reminds me, Dave pulled something together." Terri handed a folder to Marc.

He opened it up and gasped, "Holly crap!"

"I know. I'm going to run this over to her tomorrow. She said she had some business to take care of this evening."

That night, Marc dreamed that Alex was standing over his bed, watching him. He tried to speak to her, but words wouldn't form. Alex approached his bed and drew the covers back. Suddenly naked, she straddled him. They rocked together as they made love. He looked up, and her green eyes stared back at him. Suddenly, she was transforming. He tried to pull away, but he was too far gone, and he climaxed as she threw her head back and howled.

He awoke in a sweat. In his post dream haze, he glanced around the room to make sure she was not actually there. He laid his head back on his damp pillow and stared at the ceiling. The dream was strange, as all dreams are, but also incredibly intense. *What had brought that on?* he wondered. He reasoned that it must be the painkillers. He tried to go back to sleep, but fears of what else he might dream about made that difficult.

CHAPTER 33

J ENNIFER WAS HOPING TO be out of town before anyone realized she was gone. She had plans to travel for the next year, starting in Europe. Colin's estate had been settled, and she was the sole recipient of his fortune. His family in England had hired an attorney and tried to contest the will because, originally, his brother was to receive a hefty inheritance as well. But at Jennifer's urging, Colin had changed the document only a month before his fatal fall. The will held, and Jennifer was now sitting on a king's ransom.

Flush with her windfall, Jennifer realized that the Philadelphia area was just too small for her now.

Unfortunately, the news of her resignation at the university had spread faster than she could have imagined. *Those people love to talk, especially about other people,* she thought to herself. Try as she might, she could not get away before soon-to-be-former colleagues reached out to her. One of them was Alex.

Jennifer watched as the blue Volvo wagon pulled into the driveway. Alex's slender form emerged in the fading light, and she walked to the door. She was carrying what looked like an overnight bag. Jennifer would miss their physical liaisons; Alex was a beautiful woman and a passionate lover. Those attributes could be found elsewhere, however. And Alex was also a problem she wanted to get away from.

Jennifer closed the door behind Alex. She wrapped her arms around her and kissed her deeply. Alex returned her kiss briefly, then stepped away. "I am sorry Jennifer, but I am not in the mood at the moment. Tonight is very hard for me."

"No worries. I am just glad you came over for my last night here." Jennifer smiled as she lied.

The house was already empty. The movers had finished earlier in the day. The truck was loaded and destined for a storage facility. Jennifer would decide what to do with everything later. They had left a couple of older chairs, a worn sofa, and a coffee table that Jennifer hadn't bothered to put into storage. Jennifer sat on the sofa, and Alex took a chair across from her. A bottle of 2012 Bordeaux and two glasses were on the table.

"I was rather surprised when I heard that you were moving after you tendered your resignation," Alex said as Jennifer poured them each a glass of wine.

"I'm sorry I didn't tell you directly, love, but this is very hard for me, too. I am really bad at goodbyes. I'm going to travel a bit—Europe, mostly, and maybe the South Pacific," Jennifer explained as she handed a glass to Alex.

"I understand, but I thought we were close. That hurt, Jennifer," Alex said, trying to feel the words she was saying.

"Oh, Alex, I would never intentionally hurt you. We are more than close. I just need to clear my head. I was going to write you a letter explaining all this and have you come to me, wherever I wind up. My life has been spinning since Colin's death. I can't help but blame myself for it. If I hadn't thrown him out, he wouldn't have been in that hotel."

Alex could feel Jennifer trying to get into her mind. "I thought you said he left you?"

"Well, yes, but I didn't protest as vigorously as I should have. I didn't try to make it work. I feel terrible." A fleeting expression crossed Jennifer's face.

"I have some questions, Jennifer," Alex said as she breathed in the wine's aroma, enjoying the fruity notes.

"Oh, love, if they're about us, then as I said, I just couldn't say goodbye to you. I guess I'm like a child in that way. You seem so much stronger than me. Always with the sensible advice when I needed it."

Alex sensed that Jennifer was trying to play to her ego. But as she had told Jennifer earlier, she was not in the mood.

"Colin wasn't using drugs, was he?" Alex already knew this from her conversations with Terri and Marc.

The bluntness of the question caught Jennifer off guard. "What? Of course he was."

"And he wasn't leaving you for some other woman, was he?" Alex asked evenly.

"He was seeing some girl from—" Jennifer continued to babble. Something was different tonight. Her attempts to guide Alex were failing.

Alex now knew what to look for. When she saw the same fleeting expression she'd seen before–the look of deception, she asked, "And he never struck you, did he?"

Jennifer's lips pursed, as she silently sat her glass on the table. There was no use in pretense anymore. "Well, aren't we the inquisitive one tonight? No he never used drugs or hit me, but I think you guessed that by now." Jennifer said coolly. "Now, let me ask you a question: Colin didn't die accidentally, did he?" The change in Jennifer's demeanor was striking. All the warmth of her aura had evaporated and a stone cold hull remained.

"No. He did not. But I suspect you already knew that as well." Alex took a sip of the wine. Despite the unpleasantness of the evening, it was exquisite.

"Yes, my dear, love-blind Alex, I did know that. You are an open book, so I know you killed Colin; I just don't know how you did it. The police thought he'd had an accident in his bathroom. Very well done, my dear. I thought you might shoot him or something, but an accident—that was very nicely done, indeed."

Alex continued to sip her wine. She'd managed to control her rage well up to this point.

"Let me explain something to you, Alex. I have a gift, of sorts. I can read people's minds. I see their emotions and influence them."

"You're a telepath," Alex stated flatly, confirming what she had suspected.

"It's nothing more than a nifty party trick for most of us. Can get me out of a speeding ticket, usually."

"And throw off any suspicion of murder with a police interview, I suppose," Alex suggested.

Jennifer smiled. "Yes, I suppose I can do that as well. Although, I didn't commit the murder, did I?"

She continued, "As a teenager, I learned that I could exert this influence over both boys and girls. Then I found that my teachers were not immune to it, either. In college, my professors were easily swayed, and once I got into academia—well, those people aren't even a challenge. When I realized how to fully utilize my talents, I began to see the potential. All I needed to do was find a man with lots of money, and I was set. Some people have physical or musical talent, others have looks, and still others have drive and ambition. Everyone tries to use their 'gifts' to improve their lot. Mine just happens to be a bit unusual."

"I suppose you're right about that. Is that where I come in? Was I just a tool you used to better your station in life?" Alex asked.

"Some people are... easier to persuade. Those who are desperate for love and companionship, who are searching for another soul to share their life with, are particularly open to persuasion."

"Someone like me? Is that what you saw in me?" Alex asked.

"To be blunt, yes. I found a desperate soul that—"

"—that could be easily manipulated. I see," said Alex. "And when they were no longer needed, they could be discarded."

Jennifer joylessly laughed out loud. "I was trying to be nice, Alex, but yes. I saw what you wanted, and I gave it to you."

"I was right about you Jennifer. You are indeed a very interesting person—just not in the way I thought," Alex said, tilting her head slightly. "I thought you were someone I could get close to. Truly reveal myself to. I thought we might be cut from the same cloth. But I was wrong. You're just like all the rest. Actually, worse than the rest," Alex said with resignation.

"Your trips into my mind should have shown you that I do not like being manipulated or used, Jennifer. I'm guessing that you think the words you've said tonight hurt me, and I will run away crying. But you are wrong, Jennifer. Very wrong," Alex said calmly.

"You're pathetic, just like Colin. He was a fucking lap dog that eventually bored me," Jennifer spat out angrily.

"But divorcing him wouldn't do, would it, Jennifer?"

"And give up half of more than $30 million? Not when I found you, dear Alex. I could feel your blood running hot when we were together. I could feel you were passionate—and violent. That's what I was looking for. You just needed some encouragement to do what I needed done. You passed the test when I talked to you about our financial broker, Schnoll. I knew at that point you were inclined to do whatever I whispered inside your sad little mind." With that, Jennifer reached down into her purse by the sofa and retrieved a small handgun.

Alex glanced at the weapon in Jennifer's hand and shook her head slightly.

Jennifer continued. "I know you are prone to violence Alex, and I suggest you leave. You should forget about us and this whole pitiful affair and go back to your miserable life. Keep searching for that love you so desperately need. After all, you can't go to the police and tell them that I made you kill my husband by putting a thought into your head. I mean, *you* killed him after all, not me."

"You are correct. I have no intention of going to the authorities, Jennifer. And I am, as you say, prone to violence." Alex reached forward to set her glass of wine on the table. Jennifer leaned back instinctively, still pointing the gun at Alex.

Alex slowly sat back into her chair. "Since we are baring our souls to each other tonight, I have a confession for you, as well, Jennifer. I am not what I appear to be." Alex stared unblinkingly.

"Let's do an exercise, shall we? I will fully open my mind to you, Jennifer, and I want you to tell me what your telepathic powers show you. OK?" With that, Alex dropped all of the barriers that shielded her inner self. The rage she had been containing was now fully ablaze.

Their eyes met as Jennifer focused. Suddenly, Jennifer recoiled in shock and gasped, "My god, what are you?"

Alex stood. "Don't you recognize me, dear Jennifer? I am rather disappointed. But I suspect it has been many years since you have considered a being like me. Let me help you. I am what you always feared was lurking in the dark as a child," Alex said as she rolled her head, audibly cracking her neck.

"When you were a little girl, going to bed at night, I am what you prayed to God to protect you from," Alex continued, now unbuttoning her blouse.

"I am what you continue to fear, dear Jennifer, even as an adult." Alex removed her blouse and dropped it on the floor.

Jennifer's face was frozen in terror as she watched Alex begin to transform.

Alex's pupils dilated, her face contorted, as her body grew into its alternative form. Her head now almost touched the nine-foot ceiling.

Jennifer stared, mouth agape, at the creature looming before her. The windows rattled and the walls shook as Alex threw her head back and roared. Trembling, Jennifer let the gun slip from her hand and fall to the floor.

"I am vengeance!" Alex hissed in Sumerian, taking a stride toward Jennifer.

Jennifer didn't understand the language Alex was speaking. She was paralyzed. She suddenly became aware of her pulse pounding in her head. Their eyes met.

"EGO SUM MORS!" Alex roared through fanged teeth, massive arms flung wide.

Somewhere in the back of her mind, Jennifer realized that Alex was speaking Latin and understood the phrase to mean "I Am Death." It was the last thought she had.

Alex tidied up. She changed into the fresh clothes she had brought with her. Then she went to her car and retrieved the cleaning supplies she had packed. After washing the hardwood floors, she sat alone and wept.

CHAPTER 34

T HE NEXT AFTERNOON, TERRI relaxed on Alex's sofa and sipped the obligatory cup of tea. This one was Turkish and very strong but delicious.

"Tell me, how is Detective Peterson?" Alex asked.

"He is doing OK. They think he will make a full recovery. Thanks for asking."

"I am happy to hear that. He is very strong. I do enjoy his company and hope to see him again soon."

"Yes, we will all be happy to have him back on his feet. He is a good man," Terri agreed. She had a question to ask Alex before she got to the real reason for her visit. "Alex, I wanted to ask you, why were you trying to attack Dieter Schnoll?"

Alex set her cup on the table. "That was an odd circumstance. I was led to believe that he was helping someone who was hurting a friend. Once I did some... research, I found that he was not a good man. I made the decision to remove him. It was the classic 'two birds with one stone'. As you well know, I do prefer the bad boys," Alex said, deadpan.

"Yes, he was certainly that. This research, was that in the form of a Trojan horse virus sent in an email? Terri asked.

Alex smiled. "You are very astute, Agent Watson. I must say, I am genuinely impressed with your skills."

"We try. And the friend that you mentioned, was that Jennifer Miller?" Terri asked.

Jennifer's name hit Alex like a hammer blow. The smile disappeared, and she glanced blankly at a painting on her wall. "Yes," she replied.

"And Colin Miller?" Terri pressed.

"Yes, that was the most unfortunate incident. I was led to believe that Colin was abusing drugs and physically hurting his wife. I most regret his killing. I know now that I was being used by his wife to accomplish a very unsavory task."

"I hear Jennifer has left the university," Terri mentioned offhandedly.

Alex stared back at Terri. "Yes, I hear she was planning to leave the country."

"Too bad. I would have liked to have tried to make a case on her. Not sure how I would have done that, but I hate to see someone slip the noose of justice," Terri said with a tinge of regret.

"I wouldn't say she escaped justice, Agent Watson. She has merely avoided the courts," Alex said coolly.

Terri's brow furrowed as she thought about what Alex said. She considered asking a follow-up question about Jennifer's whereabouts but decided against it. Some questions are best unasked.

She decided to change the subject. "Thank you for your candor, Alex. The real reason for my visit today is that I have something for you." Terri slid a folder across the table.

Alex seemed surprised. After last night, her opinion of humans had dropped to a new low. She opened the folder and stared, wide-eyed, at a photo of herself smiling and looking relaxed with a glass of wine. In the picture, she seemed to be younger, but she could not remember the setting. She looked at Terri, confused. "What is this?"

"It is some of your past. We believe your true name is Catherine Garin," Terri said.

Dazed, Alex looked at Terri with deep gratitude. Terri didn't know it, but this was exactly what Alex needed most at this moment, a gesture of kindness. Her heart raced. "Thank you, Special Agent Terri Watson."

"I try to keep my promises," Terri replied. She nodded toward the folder. "There's some background information on your previous life in there as well. It appears you were a 'white hat' hacktivist, part of a group accused of trying to access and divulge Russian state secrets. Your group was arrested. You were sent to a prison; the name of the facility is in there somewhere. The Russian government said that you died of an unnamed illness while in custody. That photo was the last photo you posted online—two days before you were arrested."

Alex hurriedly flipped through the documents, commenting, "There is so much I wish to learn, Agent Watson. I do not know what to say to this revelation."

"I understand. You have a lot to process." Terri rose to leave. "I imagine you can do some digging on this, if you like. I don't have information on any family. Hopefully you can find some closure there. I hope this helps you, Alex—or should I call you Catherine?"

"I think, for now, Alex is better. Catherine is a beautiful name, but it feels foreign to me."

"Very well, Alex it is. If you want to change that, just let me know." Terri was standing and ready to move to the door.

"There is a matter that I wish to discuss with you Agent Watson, unrelated to this information. If you will indulge me for a few minutes, please sit."

Terri resumed her spot on the couch.

"If you would, can you tell me about your mother?"

"My mother? Why? What does she have to do with anything?" Terri immediately became cautious and stared at Alex hard. She was not in the habit of talking about her mother to anyone—least of all a source. Terri reminded herself that Alex was incredibly intelligent, narcissistic, and charming, as most true narcissists can be when they want. Who knew what else was lurking in that beautiful head of hers? Was this some sort of game or attempt at manipulation?

"Let me explain. I have been having success retrieving some of my memories, or at least memories from others before me. The language therapy has helped, I suspect. In any case, I've experienced some revelations of my own and, on that basis, I have developed a theory."

"Ok, I'm listening," Terri said warily.

"It seems that all those before me who have borne the burden of the wolf were women. I do not think that is a coincidence. I believe there is a genetic predisposition to the wolf trait in some women, at least in the line I come from. It is, of course, possible that in other lineages, if they exist, there could be a male."

"And how does that relate to my mother?" Terri asked, now fearful of the answer.

"I believe you have that predisposition—that 'gene', for lack of a better term."

"What? Are you saying I'm a werewolf and I don't know it?"

"No, I am saying that somewhere in your family history, there was a female shapeshifter. I believe the gene is passed along the maternal lines, and I believe that you, Agent Watson, have this gene." Alex paused. "I saw the desire for blood in your eyes that night in the parking lot. You wanted to kill those assassins as much as I did."

"But I didn't! I stopped!" Terri was defensive now.

Alex persisted. "I can smell the difference in you, Special Agent Watson. There is a scent and something in your aura that is distantly familiar. A wolf knows her own."

"You really think I might have this gene, and that I could become a werewolf?"

"I do. I believe you have the, let's call it a latent gene. I believe it will stay dormant unless..."

"Unless what?"

"Unless you are exposed to something to activate it."

"Like what?"

"I believe, from my memories and research, that that would be an exposure to genetic material from one of my kind. A catalytic event. Historically, this was a bite of some type."

"So, that means that somewhere in your ancestry, there was a wolf incident as well? And you were exposed to something in that lab, something derived from a werewolf that activated the gene?"

"Yes, that is my theory. I must have the gene, and it was turned on in the lab. That is why I survived. Pure luck—whether good or bad."

Terri sat back on the sofa. Could this be true? What Alex was telling her was incredible. Six months ago, she would have written this whole thing off to some type of psychosis. But today, sitting in this woman's house, she knew it was based on truth. She had seen too much to be skeptical of anything that Alex told her.

Terri's scientific mind started racing. "Where does this trait come from? Who was the first one? Where did she originate?"

"I don't know the first, but I can tell you that I have memories from as far back as Mesopotamia, Ancient Greece, Ancient Egypt, Rome, and so on. The memories are vague and unclear, making it difficult to create a timeline. I have memories of my kind being worshiped as gods at some ancient times and feared and hunted at other times," Alex explained, closing her eyes, as if trying to will the memories to make more sense. Without opening her eyes, Alex asked, "Your mother, what was she like? Where did her family line come from?"

Because of her background, Terri had always been very circumspect with the details of her life. Marc was the only person she made an exception for. He was as close to a true friend as she had ever had. Maybe that was why she had flown into the rage the night he was attacked and not, as Alex surmised, because of some darker side of her being.

Finally, Terri spoke, "I'm having a little trouble taking all this in, but I can tell you I never saw my mother howl at the moon, if that's what you're asking me."

"No, I don't suppose you ever did Agent Watson, but the trait may have been there nonetheless. I understand you must be very confused right now. You have provided me with startling information on my life, and I thank you. I, in turn, have provided you with what may be even more startling information."

Alex sensed Terri's unease and hesitation. "I do not want to pry into your life; I certainly do not like it when someone tries to pry into mine. As you can tell, I don't keep many people close to me. Perhaps I do so to protect them as much as to protect me. But you already know my secrets, and I am happy to be able to share myself with you. I don't ask you about your history, and particularly about your mother, for reciprocity, but because I know you are different, and I want to help you understand that."

Was this the narcissist's charm, telling Terri she was special? Terri didn't think so. She detected a depth of authenticity to Alex at this moment that she hadn't seen before. She could see that Alex was troubled by what she was remembering. Sometimes, not knowing your true origins is better. You can then make up a more appealing history.

Terri had blocked thoughts of her mother from the forefront of her memory for most of her life. Now those memories broke free and flooded her mind. She felt like a child again, scared and unsure.

Terri was on the verge of tears as she finally answered the question. "She was very beautiful and smart. Everyone who met her was enamored with her and strived to be the focus of her attention, even for the briefest of moments." Terri paused, remembering. "Unfortunately, she loved herself more than anyone else, including my father and me. My parents divorced when I was young, and I never saw her again."

Alex recognized the anguish on Terri's face. "I see. I am sorry to ask you such a personally painful question. What was her genealogy? What part of the world did she come from?"

"She was Swedish. I remember her as tall with blonde hair and blue eyes," Terri added, looking past Alex, back to her childhood.

"Like you are today, Agent Watson."

"Yes, I suppose."

Alex thought for a moment, closing her eyes. "Have you heard of the Norse berserkers, Agent Watson?"

"Yes, of course. They were vicious warriors who wore bearskins into combat or something," Terri replied absently.

"Yes, that is the conventional archeological explanation. The name comes from the Norse words for 'bear shirt'. Some of these warriors, at least one I recall directly, was female. Her name was Bodil. She was a shapeshifter and a revered warrior."

Terri felt the room starting to spin and needed fresh air. Was Alex describing one of her ancestors? Was she really a descendant of a shapeshifter? She suddenly wanted to leave. "I have to get back to the office, I have some—"

"It's OK, Agent Watson," Alex interrupted. "You have much to think about. I am here if you wish to discuss this further. Remember, just having this knowledge doesn't change who you are. Unlike me, you may choose whether or not to walk this path." Alex reached over and took Terri's hand as she stood. "But if you choose it, there is no going back."

Terri felt the warmth of Alex's hand, and when she looked into Alex's eyes, she saw understanding and concern. Things that she had never seen in her before.

As Terri walked to her car, she realized that she was no longer stunned by Alex's revelation.

Somewhere, deep inside, she felt a profound serenity. The quiet part had finally been said out loud. She knew Alex was right. Now she needed to consider what to do with this information.

EPILOGUE
ONE YEAR LATER

AFTER ELIMINATING KONSTANTIN KRETZKY, Lieutenant General Igor Stepin had enjoyed a week in the Mediterranean on his private yacht with his mistress, Petra. They were seated in a bar in the Fiumicino Airport waiting for their flight home when two Italian customs officers approached. They asked Petra to come with them to explain something discovered in her checked luggage. They assured Stepin that it was likely a misunderstanding and would be cleared up quickly. He watched nervously as they led her away. Immediately, two nondescript men dressed in casual business attire approached and sat, uninvited, with him in the booth. Before he could protest, one spoke to him in perfect Russian.

"Dear General. We are here to give you a proposition. We are aware of your theft of Russian government funds connected to the Novaya Zhizn lab contracts. We know you did not share this money with your superiors."

Stepin stared at them stonefaced.

The man continued. "We know how and where you hid these funds. We know that you authorized two separate murder attempts on US soil to conceal them. And we know you acted without notifying your government of the true purpose for the first attempt or even of the attempt at all in the second instance."

Stepin sat silently, but a trickle of sweat ran down his right temple.

"You have a choice. You can keep your yacht and your accounts, continue in your position, and enjoy your lifestyle. All you have to do is work with us. If you refuse our offer or attempt to move your assets, we will freeze your funds and let this information reach your superiors. We both know that the consequences of that disclosure would be extremely detrimental to your career, to say the least." Igor knew that such a revelation, regardless of whether it was traced back to a hostile intelligence service, would mean his untimely death.

The man continued. "Here is a phone number and an Italian SIM card. You will call this number within 48 hours. If you do not, we will assume that you have made your decision, and the details of your thefts and extraterritorial exploits will be made known to your superiors."

The other man slid a business card with a SIM card taped to the back across the table. Igor stared at the men for a moment and then, without speaking, took the card and put it in his wallet. Despite his best efforts, his hand was shaking.

"Very good, General. We look forward to hearing from you soon." The man looked up, "Ah, I believe the matter with the Guardia di Finanza has been cleared up, and Petra will be returning soon. Good day, General."

With that, the two CIA agents rose and walked into the terminal, disappearing into the crowd of travelers.

Luciana Sanchez pleaded guilty to her role in the attempted murder of Dieter Schnoll, Detective Marc Peterson, and Special Agent Sarah Holmes. She admitted killing her fellow assassin and other American and Mexican citizens over several years. She claimed she needed to atone for her crimes because she had seen *el diablo* and feared for her eternal soul. She is serving a life sentence in a witness protection unit at an undisclosed prison.

Faced with Luciana's potential testimony and the mountain of evidence against him, Eberardo Martinez pleaded guilty with no cooperation agreement. He was stabbed and killed in prison before sentencing.

Special Agent Sarah Holmes did receive the Shield of Bravery from the FBI. She continues to work with Detective Marc Peterson and Agent Terri Watson on organized-crime investigations, as well as on some "special" investigations.

Detective Marc Peterson recovered and returned to duty. He was decorated by his department for valor and awarded a citation by the FBI for his actions as a task force officer. When he returned to his desk at the FBI, a framed document was waiting for him in his cubicle. It read:

Top 5 Lessons for Marc:

5. If the PD asks if you want to go to the FBI as a TFO, say no.

4. If Terri asks for help on a "routine" surveillance, be busy.

3. If Terri asks for help with a source, be busy.

2. If Sarah asks for help transporting a source, be busy.

1. If you have ignored points 5 through 2, then at least learn how to duck.

———

Authorities searched Konstantin Kretzky's home after his death. In his basement, a massive mummified wolf, preserved in a clear freezer, was discovered. His staff said he referred to the wolf as Anna.

When word of the frozen wolf reached Drs. Peter Lavroski and Vladimir Demikhov, they immediately petitioned for the remains to be remanded to them for further study.

Shortly thereafter, Lavroski enjoyed a resurgence in his career. It seems that there was renewed interest in his prior work at the Novaya Zhizn lab. He is planning to attend a genetics conference in Vienna in the spring.

His sudden rise in prominence was not lost on Alex. She started following his career very closely and, through some online sleuthing, found his plan to attend the conference. She noted it on a little piece of paper that she slid under her desk blotter.

She had not been to Vienna in a very long time. Perhaps a trip there in the spring, to meet an old friend, could be in the cards.

———

Honorable Louis DePalma had become a second tier celebrity of the far right. Earlier in the day he had given a speech to a moderately attended forum in Washington DC on the dangers of the liberal media and the Me Too movement. He had just polished off his second gin and tonic in the hotel bar when an attractive woman with short dark hair approached him. They talked for a while and had a drink together. He was last seen leaving with her and then disappeared without a trace. Upon questioning from the police several days later, the bartender stated he paid very little attention to the pair while serving them but he did recall one piece of conversation. He said the woman asked the Judge "If he was a bad boy. She had an insatiable hunger for bad boys."

Terri Watson scanned the headlines over coffee in her condo. Max the cat lay on the table, casually pawing at her keyboard to get her attention. A story caught her eye: "Another Killing in Arizona. Possibly the Work of the 'Pima Predator'. The bodies of a young couple were discovered by hikers in the Coconino National Forest, north of Phoenix. Law enforcement officers described the bodies as looking like they'd been scavenged by a large predator or predators. This marks the sixth murder with the same MO this year across the state, the first being a homeless man in Tucson." Terri read the story hurriedly and discovered that the victims appeared to have been chosen at random, had all been dismembered, and bore the marks of large animal predation. There was no discussion of any criminal activities tied to any of them. Her heart sank. It appeared that Alex wasn't alone in this world. She sent a text to Marc, Sarah, and Jerri to see if they were available for pizza at her place that night. This was something they needed to discuss.

The shrill whistle of the kettle rose in intensity. Alex carefully poured the steaming water into her delicately decorated cup. It was an early 20th century bone china cup and saucer she found at an antique store. As the black tea leaves steeped and turned the water a dark hue, she realized she felt–content. Terri, Marc, and Sarah: what a wonderful pack they made.

GLOSSARY

Novaya Zhizn: Russian for "new life"

TFO: Task force officer; personnel from other agencies or departments assigned to FBI squads

SOG: Special operations group. In the field division of the FBI, this represents covert surveillance teams

FISUR: Physical surveillance

ELSUR: Electronic surveillance

TIII: Title III, court-authorized ELSUR activities, usually carried out on a telephone line

SCIF: Sensitive compartmented information facility. A space that is specifically designed to grant access only to those with proper clearance and to protect the information and conversations taking place therein from eavesdropping or other collection methods. Home of the Secret Squirrels

Secret Squirrels: Nickname given to agents who work on counterintelligence and counterterrorism matters

OGA: Other government agency. Acronym applied to agencies other than the FBI—such as the CIA or the NSA—to avoid disclosing their parent organization

The Farm: CIA training facility

UNSUB: Unknown subject

NRO: National Reconnaissance Office. Responsible for satellite image collection used for intelligence purposes

CONTACT

Follow me on Facebook: @D. Werkmeister - Author

www.thestorywerks.com

dwerkmeisterauthor@gmail.com